A Pelican Original
The People's Land

Hugh Brody was born in 1943, read P.P.E. at
Trinity College, Oxford, and, from 1967 to 1968,
taught Social Philosophy at the Queen's University,
Belfast. He was for three years a research officer
with the Canadian Department of Indian Affairs and
Northern Development, during which time he lived
and travelled in the Arctic, and learned two Eskimo
dialects. His publications include *Indians on Skid
Row* (1970), a study of drinking and drunkenness
among Canadian migrants, and *Inishkillane:
Change and Decline in the West of Ireland* (Allen
Lane 1973, Penguin 1974).

Hugh Brody

The People's Land

Eskimos and Whites in the
Eastern Arctic

Penguin Books

Penguin Books Ltd,
Harmondsworth, Middlesex, England
Penguin Books Australia Ltd,
Ringwood, Victoria, Australia
Penguin Books Canada Ltd,
41 Steelcase Road West, Markham, Ontario, Canada
Penguin Books (N.Z.) Ltd,
182–190 Wairau Road, Auckland 10, New Zealand

First published 1975

Copyright © Hugh Brody, 1975

Made and printed in Great Britain by
Hazell Watson & Viney Ltd, Aylesbury, Bucks
Set in Linotype Times

For Moose Kerr

Contents

But you, who are wise, must know that different
Nations have different Conceptions of things and
you will therefore not take it amiss, if our Ideas of
this kind of Education happen not to be the same as
yours. We have had some Experience of it.
Several of our young People were formerly brought
up at the Colleges of the Northern Provinces:
they were instructed in all your Sciences; but, when
they came back to us, they were bad Runners,
ignorant of every means of living in the woods ...
neither fit for Hunters, Warriors, nor Counsellors,
they were totally good for nothing.

We are, however, not the less oblig'd by your kind
Offer, tho' we decline accepting it; and, to show
our grateful Sense of it, if the Gentlemen of
Virginia will send us a Dozen of their Sons, we will
take Care of their Education, instruct them in all
we know, and make Men of them.

– Response of the Indians of the Six Nations
to a suggestion that they send boys to an
American college, Pennsylvania, 1744

Acknowledgements

The author and publishers wish to thank the following for their permission to use illustrations: Janine Wiedel for plates 8 and 11; Mrs Kay Gimpel for photographs taken by Charles Gimpel, plates 7, 9, 10, 12 and 13; Mrs D. B. Marsh for photographs taken by Donald Marsh, plates 4, 5, and 6; and the Scott Polar Research Institute, Cambridge, for plates 1 and 2. Every effort has been made to communicate with the copyright-holders of photographs included in this book, but in some cases this has not proved possible. Nevertheless, the publishers wish also to express their thanks to the copyright-holders of those photographs which are included without explicit acknowledgement.

Foreword

The summer of 1971 was unusually poor in northern Canada. Days of fog and drizzle followed each other, days that were inimical to flying: even the intrepid bush pilots of Atlas Aviation were often obliged to postpone or cancel their regular flights into small settlements of the Eastern Arctic. It was therefore something of a surprise one afternoon to hear the drone of a light aircraft passing back and forth overhead, flying low but still hidden by fog. After a succession of passes, a small seaplane emerged from the murk, low over the sea, and, despite appalling conditions, it appeared ready to land just offshore.

The arrival of an aircraft is always an important event for a small northern settlement; no sooner is the drone of engines heard in the sky than a buzz of rumour and speculation begins on the ground: everyone guesses at the identity of the plane and the purposes of its passengers. Often, of course, the Whites in the settlement know in advance something of an expected arrival, but the Eskimos are not usually so well-informed, and must rely on the blend of hearsay and observation that serves them so well in many aspects of their life. On this occasion, no one in the Eskimo community had heard or observed anything that could explain the mystery of why this plane should now be dropping out of the sky.

As it settled on the rough sea, a large group of people hurried to the beach to watch. I had arrived among the laggards, and found myself standing among some of the older Eskimo men towards the back of the crowd. At the very front stood the Whites; the settlement manager and his clerk were getting a canoe and outboard motor ready to help the aircraft and its crew to the beach. The old men urged me to find out who these visitors might be, so I made my way to the Anglican missionary, who was standing a little to one side of the main group of Eskimos. He was usually as well-informed as anyone about the comings and goings of aircraft, but all he could report in this case was hearing that the plane had come from Yellowknife. I passed on this slender piece of information to the old men, and left the missionary to discover more exact details.

The visitors, nine of them in all, soon climbed out of the plane. As they came ashore, someone called out to the missionary to ask who this group might be; the missionary asked a teacher, who in turn asked the settlement manager's clerk. The answer came back: 'Fish.' One of the old men remarked to me that they looked more like Whites from the south than like fish, but added that no doubt these men had come to do some fishing. The clerk then led the visitors to the village hotel, and the crowd dispersed, its curiosity partially satisfied. Later that afternoon it emerged that the party was on a fact-finding tour: they sought information about Arctic char, wanted to know where the Eskimos of that community fished for them and how many they usually caught. The members of the group were reported to be authorities on, or keenly interested in, Arctic fish resources. We also learned that they had intended to spend only a few hours here, and were dismayed at the prospect of spending the night. As the fog thickened on the hills and inlets around the village, that prospect became a certainty. At least this once, there was going to be plenty of time for the experts to make their inquiries.

I visited the fish men in the hotel. They were all sitting around a coffee-table, lamenting the vagaries of Arctic weather. For one half of the hour I spent with them, they quizzed me about how the Eskimos fished for Arctic char near the settlement. I reminisced about a few fishing trips but my knowledge of the subject was scanty. I repeatedly suggested that they talk to some of the local hunters who were at home because of the bad weather. A meeting with the best informants could easily be arranged, and I assured them that these hunters would be very interested to hear what they had to say about char fisheries in other places. No, they said, their time was too short. But, I pointed out, their time here had been extended by the weather, a misfortune that could be turned to real advantage. In the High Arctic, summer evenings last all night, no one feels bound to go to bed at any particular time, and they could talk as long as they liked. No, they said, they had been invited to visit the home of one of the Whites in the settlement; that night they would not have time for any prolonged discussion.

The party did indeed visit one of the Whites that evening, a local official who later told me that he had found it rather strange to be asked so much about fishing in the surrounding territory. The visitors seemed reluctant to leave, but lingered long into the night, despite his inability to supply much information about fishing. Like me, he could do little more than describe occasional outings with local fishermen. However, he did mention that only two miles along the coast there was a stream at the mouth of which the Hudson's Bay Company clerk often caught small Arctic char with rod and line, and that near by there were some house remains of the Thule culture. Over cocktails, they agreed that if the weather kept them next day, they would walk over to look at the stream and the old houses. The party left the settlement the next afternoon with one of the local Whites and examined the Thule site. Soon after their return, the weather cleared briefly, and they flew off, leaving the villagers to carry on fishing as before.

At no time did these experts on fish and fishing discuss with the local people their reasons for visiting the settlement: they did not so much as suggest that a meeting might be arranged with a few of the hunters best informed on the subject of their researches. The people criticized their failure even to *appear* to obtain local information, which was, after all, the formal reason for their visit, but neither did the people try to communicate with the experts. Rather, Whites and Eskimos alike accepted that these visitors, being White, would naturally spend their time with the White community. Whereas to some Eskimos the behaviour of the party of fish experts seemed merely ludicrous, to others it was just another example of the disregard that Whites so often show for the Eskimos and their knowledge. I found one of the experts more interested and sympathetic than the others, and I talked to him at some length. I asked if, in the ten other settlements they had visited in the course of their fact-finding tour, they had anywhere found occasion to meet the local people. No, he said, this visit was much like their other visits, and now their tour was over.

He was not happy with the way things had gone, and he was aware of the irony of visiting ruins of Thule houses instead of talking to the Eskimos of today. But he could not control the attitude of his superiors, even if he did not like it. At each settlement they visited, White officials had met them, entertained them, and had given them – in the course of entertainment – such snippets of information as they had gleaned. The generosity of Whites, he remarked, was more lavish than the information they had to offer.

This incident took place after I had been in the north for only six months. My work in the Canadian Eastern Arctic was for those months, and a subsequent fourteen months, financed by the Federal Department of Indian Affairs and Northern Development in Ottawa. Originally I had thought that a study should be made of problems that Eskimo hunters and trappers experience when they try to adjust to contemporary life in the settlement, notably to wage-labour employment. With that specific objective in mind, I began to learn the Eskimo language. I learned in the most informal and casual way and, as time passed, my lessons grew into simple and friendly conversations. My teachers did not try to restrict conversation to any set topics, and our exchanges let me glimpse the issues that preoccupied them. Their conversation, I began to notice, returned again and again to White–Eskimo interaction – to questions raised by episodes such as that of the fish men. That kind of episode recurred so often during my time in the Arctic that it came to define for me the subject of my study. The nature and consequences of White–Eskimo interaction are at the heart of this book.

I am aware that this restriction of the book's scope will dismay or offend many White northerners. Some, perhaps many, will feel they have been criticized or belittled. And it will seem to them ungracious, if not arrogant and unjust, that someone who received hospitality and cooperation from them should now proceed to write what may be read here. I can only hope that most of the White northerners who have known me will see that I have tried to separate them as persons from the roles they play in the contemporary northern scene. My effort to preserve the anonymity of both persons and places reflects my appreciation of the importance of this separation.

In fact I owe a great debt of gratitude to many, in and out of the north, who have helped this book get written. Simon Annaviappik was a patient and wonderfully encouraging teacher of Eskimo and took endless pains to help me shed at least some of the foolish preconceptions with which my own society had armed me. Elizabeth and Peter Karlik, Isaac Amituq, Charlie Crow and the Aragutainaq family all helped me far more than they can know.

Inuk and Inooya made me a home in their home, and never ceased to encourage me to overcome the awkwardness I so often felt in being an intruder. Paulussi Inukuluk, Seatee Inuk, Enoogoo, Arnaujumajuq and Peter Kattuk all were kind enough to take me travelling and hunting with them. In Ottawa, Moose Kerr, and Graham Rowley, and the staff of the Northern Science Research Group made the logistics of the entire project possible. In England, the Scott Polar Research Institute provided excellent facilities that made the writing of the book possible. Supplementary data and fresh insights provided by Arnold Cragg and Christine Moore, both of whom spent time in Arctic settlements, were of great help.

Drafts of my manuscript were prepared with the help of Jackie Denton, Jessie Miller and Lisa Hunt. Edward Horne made penetrating and valuable criticisms of the penultimate draft. And I must acknowledge an enormous debt to Alan Cooke for his painstaking care in editing the final draft, as well as for encouraging me to keep on writing when writing seemed to me the most useless and least pleasant activity in the world.

The predicament of the contemporary Canadian Eskimo is

deeply troubling. It embodies – within its very short history – the destructive processes and social deformations that colonialism everywhere entails. Despite this book's anthropological biases, it is not concerned with traditional Eskimo society as it may have been before its transformation by southerners. Nor does it dwell on the Eskimo people's initial responses to that intrusion. Rather, it is based on the conviction that it is the present situation of both Eskimos and Whites in the north that deserves attention. That conviction explains the structure of the book: it is a way of expressing my solidarity with the Eskimo people who have so tirelessly tried to help me understand what is happening to them now and what they fear may happen to them in the future.

1 • An Introductory Story

A few years ago there was a crisis in one of the small settlements of the Canadian Eastern Arctic. It is a crisis that survives still in the memories of persons there who were only marginally involved, and one that remained until recently among the most savoured subjects of local gossip. It was not long after my arrival in that settlement that I was treated to its details – details, that is to say, as they had been filtered by time and by intensity of feeling, and that were provided, in the first instance, by the settlement's Whites.

There had been a difficult time, I was told, with a young teacher whose sexual interests had brought him into a most terrible conflict with the Eskimo people. Preceded by a reputation for homosexual tendencies, the new teacher had from the outset been the object of White suspicions and rumours. For a year or so, no great difficulties arose: it was said that the school principal disliked him but also that he was exemplary in the classroom. The crisis was eventually precipitated by the school principal's Eskimo wife, who is said to have reported to her husband stories circulating among the Eskimos. There was, apparently, much to be told.

Alerted to such scandalous possibilities, the school principal and the settlement manager began their own investigations. They interviewed one of the boys thought to be involved, and from him assembled a list of other boys and some account of their activities with the young teacher. It appeared that sexual irregularities between the teacher and young boys had been frequent. The school principal interviewed each of the boys in turn. It was claimed that they were happy to give full and detailed accounts of these activities. It was also claimed that these activities included financial arrangements that were little – if at all – short of prostitution. Although the principal assembled his evidence over some days, apparently he did not tell the teacher about the inquiries, but left him to agonize over the developments that were obviously taking place in the settlement. Indeed, according to gossip, boys were called from the teacher's classroom during lessons, one by one, to interviews with the principal. I was told that the investigators showed a ferocious rage against the offender, and that they pursued their inquiry in a way that would aggravate his growing fears.

Eventually, of course, the teacher himself was summoned to an interview and was presented with details of his wrongdoings. No one could describe just what took place in that encounter but one of the gossips told me that the culprit was by then acutely distressed, and that the proceedings were tape-recorded. The teacher's confession was extracted, official indignation expressed and the parents of some of the boys involved were called in to give their view of the matter. Only after this private inquiry had run its course were the Royal Canadian Mounted Police, who maintain a permanent detachment in the settlement, called to the school. The young teacher was formally charged, confined to his house in lieu of detention, and eventually 'taken out in handcuffs' to Yellowknife.

These were the broad facts of the matter as White residents in the settlement outlined them to me, but there was one other aspect of their reminiscences: the Eskimo view of the events. One of the local investigators of the affair described to me in vivid detail the Eskimos' indignation. He characterized the house arrest, for example, as having been the only way of protecting the young teacher's life, because Eskimos – particularly the fathers of the boys concerned – were 'after him with a gun'. Indeed, he asserted, local outrage reached such a height just prior to the investigation that it was fortunate for everyone that the crisis had broken when it did: had the matter continued, the Eskimos would probably have dealt with the teacher in more summary fashion. Other Whites, who had not participated directly, were also convinced that Eskimo feeling against the teacher was strong, growing, and likely to become dangerous. It was generally maintained that the fathers, summoned to the interviews just before the police laid charges, had expressed fierce indignation against the White man who had drawn their sons into homosexual practices. I soon came to believe that the subject was one to be avoided and that the community would nurse for all time an undying grudge against the disruptive immorality of southerners. After all, I was told, these boys had been exposed to moral corruption, and their parents would not forget the anger they had expressed to the investigators who had made it their business to clean up local morals.

Some of the Whites who talked to me of those bad times did not approve of the attitudes the school principal and settlement manager had shown, nor did they approve of the extraordinary anger some other Whites had so readily expressed. One teacher found such virulence as distasteful as the activities of the offender, adding that one government employee had hoped that the death sentence would be imposed and had even chosen a site for the gallows. Another teacher speculated on the possibly ambiguous sexual feelings of the school principal, and thought he saw signs of a troubled personality in such extreme hostility towards homosexuals. The White missionary criticized the manner in which the inquiries had been pursued and suggested that the teacher might have been offered help. Help was certainly not given by the cloak-and-dagger investigation, moral outrage and punitive measures that constituted official response to the scandal.

Divided though the Whites were in their judgement of the way in which a difficult situation had been handled, they were nonetheless in agreement on the depth of Eskimo indignation. All of the Whites who spoke of the crisis felt that the course of events at least reflected the local view of the crime; the law had, after all, apprehended the criminal and taken him away for punishment.

As I came to know the settlement better, and gradually learnt more of the Eskimo community, I began to participate in conversations with Eskimos about the past. At first, I let the subject and range of these conversations be established and contained by the Eskimos. Faltering and nervous, afraid of saying the wrong thing or of saying things wrongly, I avoided taking conversational initiatives. During these conversations I never heard anything of homosexual Whites, although there was a great deal of talk about school and teachers. Eventually, I felt able to begin a series of discussions, focused on local problems as seen by the Eskimos themselves. The discussions were somewhat systematic and formal in so far as I attempted to follow a series of topics, and were informal to the extent that I conducted them only in households that had invited me to pay a visit. I listened to complaints against institutions and against individual Whites; I heard much about the ways in which life in general had improved and ways in which it had deteriorated. All of these points of view were conveyed in the form of reminiscences, anecdotes and specific requests for information. It soon became clear that many persons in the settlement were ready to express substantial criticisms and anxieties. Indeed, my general impression was of doubt, confusion and occasionally indignation. But nobody raised the matter of the teacher who had been taken away to jail.

One day, when conversation with a young couple was running especially easily, and I felt their willingness to talk freely and openly, I asked if there had been any difficulty with schoolteachers. Oh yes, they told me, there had been difficulties: there had once been a very good principal, but he had left, and now the principal was not so good; the people often wished that the other man would come back again. We talked for a while about what made one principal better than another, what kind of teachers got on best with children, and what teachers should be doing in the settlement apart from teaching.

Eventually I took courage and asked the fateful question: 'I have heard that there was once a teacher here who had to leave because he liked to make love with the young boys. Is that what happened?' Yes, came the answer, that was a very bad thing. The husband to whom I was speaking had heard before that teacher came to the settlement that White men sometimes liked to make love with other men, but he had never really understood why. Maybe such men were lonely. But it had been a bad thing, the way it had happened here. The bad thing was the way the teacher had left – suddenly taken away by the police. The Whites had been terrible in the way they had behaved. After all, he had been making love with Eskimo boys, not with White boys. So it was a matter for the Eskimos. I asked what should have been done about it and the man said: 'He should not have been sent away at all. Instead, he should have had a meeting with the Eskimos, and we would have told him, "We like you very much and we think that you are a good teacher for our children but we do not like you making love with them. So, please stop doing that." He should have been warned by the people, and then he would have understood what we wanted, and he would probably have stopped doing that, and then he could have stayed working in the school. But instead the Whites decided everything, talked to him, did not ask what the Eskimos thought, and then just took him away.' The people of the settlement had been angry about that. Certainly it had been 'a very bad thing to see Whites doing those things to that teacher without asking Eskimos what *they* wanted'.

I was of course astonished, not only by the answer, but by this man's readiness to discuss the matter. I therefore asked others about the episode, and always asked what should have been done, and what they felt about what had in fact been done. Then, gradually, without specifically intending to do so, I assembled a picture of the teacher as he had come to be seen by the Eskimos. All the versions I heard were akin to the first. Most significantly, I found later that I had talked of the matter in great detail with three fathers of boys who had been involved, two of whom had participated in the settlement manager's investigation. One of the two was the first man with whom I had raised the subject. The other, Attak, spoke of it frequently and in many contexts during the next eighteen months.

That teacher, Attak told me, was unlike other Whites. He was more like Whites who had come to the settlement years before, when southerners had wanted to learn the language and get to know the people. That teacher used to visit families in the settlement, and even visit some families often. In that way, the people were able to get to know him, and he came to understand many of their ways.

In particular, he made a great effort to learn the language, and, although he did not find it easy, he managed after a time, after many visits, to carry on simple conversations. So he talked with people and became friendly with them. Attak himself was one of the men he most often visited, and Attak took special pleasure in teaching the teacher. Also, the children liked him; Attak had heard from many of the pupils how popular that teacher was. In all these ways, he compared very favourably both with other teachers and with settlement Whites in general.

Yet for some time it had been rumoured among the Eskimos that the teacher showed sexual interest in some of the boys. It seemed, from Attak's accounts, that this was not a serious matter, not a cause for real anger against such a likeable man. But then the Whites had heard these rumours, and they had become angry about it all. Of course, if it were all true, it should not continue. But Attak felt that it was for him and other older men of the settlement to discuss these rumours with the teacher, and to tell him how the Eskimos wanted him to behave with the young people of the community. Attak was indignant at the way the school principal and other officials had taken the matter entirely into their own hands, and he was firm in his feeling that the RCMP should never have been involved. The police had far more important things to do than to interfere with a teacher whose activities were the Eskimos' concern. If the Eskimos had needed the RCMP's help, then they would have asked for it. But they were never given a chance to say what *they* thought should be done. The police were more usefully employed in keeping an eye on parties where people were drinking, to make sure that no one collapsed in the snow and froze to death. Their intervention in the business of the teacher and the boys was neither called for nor useful, and it meant that a good teacher was taken away to prison, never to return. Thus, through police interference, the Eskimos had lost a White who had shown interest in their life and was able to learn about it.

Almost two years after I met Attak, he invited me to look at his old photographs, and spend several hours sorting through scraps of paper and faded pictures he had kept in boxes. After we looked at the pictures in the boxes he asked me if I knew everyone in the pictures he kept pinned on his walls. Some I had never looked at closely, so he took me on a tour of them. Eventually we came to one on his bedroom wall; it was small and out of focus. Did I know who that was? I did not know. 'That is a man who used to be a teacher here; he was a really good man, one of the best men ever sent here to work with the people.' Attak mentioned the man's name, and I realized that it was indeed the young teacher. Attak then asked if I knew where he was now, or what he was doing. It appeared that he knew more than I, and he had also heard that the teacher was now married and had some children. 'Perhaps,' reflected Attak, 'he will come back to the settlement one day, and at least visit us again. There are so few Whites whom one can talk with and become friendly with.'

2 • New Kinds of Northerner

> 'A colonial situation is created, so to speak, the
> very instant a white man . . . appears in the midst of
> a tribe . . . so long as he is thought to be rich and
> powerful . . . [and has] in his most secret self a
> feeling of his own superiority'
>
> — Octavio Mannoni, *Prospero and Caliban*

Remarkably few Whites have ever gone among the Eskimos simply to live. Early traders, the first missionaries, even some whalers, did live among or near them to trade, to evangelize or to hunt, and some of them stayed so long, or returned so many years, that they might well be called resident. These men occasionally took Eskimo wives and had children, and no doubt some of them gradually came to feel that they were almost Eskimos. But most did no such thing. They lived at the edge of Eskimo society, distanced from it by their purposes, by their life-style and by their central interest in transforming rather than adapting to the peoples they encountered.

In the Canadian Eastern Arctic, such men were numerous during the late nineteenth century, when the whaling industry prospered, and they continued to ply their various trades until the 1940s. These men were willing to live in a cold climate and in relative isolation; many of them were great travellers, sledging thousands of miles from camp to camp; some were avaricious and most of them had a taste for adventure. Morris Zaslow, in his scholarly book *The Opening of the Canadian North* (1971), gives as an example a brief summary of the Whites who have lived in one area:

The region north east of Great Bear Lake, explored by Cabell and Camsell in 1900 and by Hanbury in 1902, for example, was occupied almost continuously from 1908 by a succession of white men who represented a veritable cross-section of motives and personalities. There were J. C. Melville, the wealthy hunter and traveller; Jack Hornby, the romantic, ill-starred misfit; Stefansson, the ambi-

tious, head-line hunting anthropologist, and Anderson, the natural-
ist, popping in and out; the Douglas party ... and the geologist
August Sandberg came to see the celebrated copper occurrence ...;
d'Arcy Arden, the hunter and trapper who settled down and made
the area his own; and the Oblate priests, the agreeable father J. B.
Rouviere and the zealous father G. LeRoux.

These pioneers into remote regions of the Arctic are today regarded as heroes for the privations they suffered, the distances
they covered and the isolation they endured.

   When the whaling industry collapsed soon after the turn of
the century, there were many fewer Whites in the Eastern
Arctic. Whereas whaling crews wintered in groups, traders and
missionaries were usually alone. But there was a paradox to
their solitary lives: behind them stood institutions vaster in
scale and much more committed to the transformation of life
in the north than whalers had been. These institutions – the
churches, the Hudson's Bay Company, and the Government of
Canada itself – were determined to exercise an hegemony over
the minds and lands of the Eskimo. The representatives, the
advance guard, of these institutions were the solitary men
of whom I now write. They lived and travelled without the
daily support of other southerners and with a bare minimum of
material comfort.[1]

   Because of the solitary and often dangerous lives these men
led, they have since become the subject of romance and legend.
Their deeds are taken as examples of the mystique and lure of
the north, and the attitudes they formed towards the land and
its people continue as an established tradition of the life of
Whites in the north. Ray Price's book, *The Howling Arctic*

<hr />

1. Most of the early free-traders (in this context, free-traders means
anyone not connected with the Hudson's Bay Company) arrived in the
Eastern Arctic as whalers. When whaling ceased a few whalers were
either left in the Arctic or decided to stay there and live by small trading
in furs. But none of them survived the extension of the Hudson's Bay
Company posts into the remote settlements of the Eastern Arctic in the
1920s. Some of the free-traders felt they were imprisoned in a geographical
and spiritual wilderness; their minds were troubled and hopes centred on
return to the south. This restlessness is recorded in books of this period
and it is equally the subject of older Eskimos' reminiscences today.

(1970), uncritical and inaccurate as it is, succeeds brilliantly in evoking this aspect of romance and legend: to him, the early traders, missionaries and policemen are, by definition, heroes. Many of the principal characters in his book made long journeys in hard conditions, endured privations – some even starved – and some were killed by Eskimos. In much the same manner and with much the same view of northern life, the early missionaries are celebrated in *Eskimo*, a magazine published by the Oblates, a Roman Catholic missionary order; and traders find their praises sung in *The Beaver*, the organ of the Hudson's Bay Company. The following passage from Price's book is illustrative of the whole literary genre:

> Jack Turner was a big man. Although not a tall man there was a bigness about him that was inescapable. He was big in character, personality and spirit. The Eskimos called him the 'real man'. There was a no-nonsense determination about Turner that made itself felt. In a way rarely achieved by white men he won the Eskimos completely. They loved him ... Jack Turner was an Englishman, a member of the Bible Churchman's Missionary Society and a dedicated Evangelist; a single-minded man who knew what he believed and why he believed; a man who knew he was right.[2]

There are two important reasons for lamenting this idealization of the Whites who first represented powerful southern institutions in the north. In the first place, it obscures the negative attitude that many of these men had towards the Eskimos and their land. Because they went north with commercial or ideological motives, they were intent on radical changes in Eskimo life. Many features of Eskimo culture and personality were inevitably the objects of their criticism and distaste, although of course they varied individually in the intensity of their hostile reaction. To the extent that they were committed to effecting transformations, they were committed also to the abolition or modification of very many well-established local customs. Missionaries, policemen and traders all expressed strongly negative attitudes towards Eskimos in general and discovered in individuals or in families manifestations of deviance from or ignorance of the principles or practices they had come to teach.

2. Price (1970), p. 67.

The descriptions of these southerners as men of distinguished personal strength and integrity generally ignore the fact that their attitudes and roles inevitably made them hostile to much Eskimo life. And these Whites were self-selective, that is, only a few individuals from a limited range of personality types were chosen to become missionaries, policemen or traders, and these roles themselves encouraged further development of the self-righteousness and authoritarianism for which they had initially been chosen. *Beaver*, the magazine of the Hudson's Bay Company, commented in 1924: 'The service we have rendered warrants us in holding the position we have today. It has been a case of *the survival of the fittest*. When we survey the animal world, we see the stronger preying upon the weaker.' And in 1945 Father Mouchard, Oblate missionary to the Eskimos of the Kazan River, prayed for guidance in the following terms: 'Good Lord help me to instruct these poor people, to tear from their hearts and souls the pagan beliefs which have a tendency to return and bother them.'

The second reason for lamenting the idealization of southerner pioneers in the north is more theoretical. By concentrating on the adventures of individuals, historians and old-timers alike seem to be almost entirely unaware of the overall nature of the involvement of northern institutions with those of the south. Northern history can be – and has been – written as the saga of a few heroic individuals; it *should* be written around the combined operations and purposes of a small number of institutions. The traders, police and missionaries constituted a joined – if not joint – endeavour: the incorporation of the Eskimos into the mainstream of southern life. Although the field-work was carried out by rugged individuals, who may well have had curious ideas of their own about what they were doing and who may have even believed that the purposes of the three institutions were separate and irreconcilable, their purposes and methods neatly dovetailed. Such a combination is familiar enough in the history of colonialism, but rarely in that history can the alliance have been so complete. Price touches on the social aspect of the alliance in writing of the policeman Jack Doyle:

The isolation appealed to him. The close camaraderie he was able to enjoy with the other White men in the small settlements appealed to him. The police, Hudson's Bay Company employees and the Roman Catholic missionaries spent quite a lot of time in each other's company and invariably had a get-together on Friday evenings. Quite often the RCMP would do the entertaining and when they did there was always a good spread. Lobster sandwiches and the like were the order of the day.[3]

Such easy sociability among the Whites of a settlement was not, however, invariable. Tensions and jealousies between individuals and the agencies they represented have always been common. Yet, whether or not these Whites enjoyed easy sociability, they were broadly united in working towards the establishment of southern influence in the remotest corners of the High Arctic. If, at first, it was perhaps unclear whether it was England, Canada, or merely Euro-American civilization whose agents aimed at incorporating the Arctic, it eventually became clear about the turn of the century that Canada intended to establish beyond any doubt, internationally, nationally, and in the minds of northern indigenous peoples themselves, that the whole of the land area between the Alaska boundary to the west, Newfoundland and Labrador to the east, and the highest Arctic islands to the north, formed part of the national territory.

Thus it came about that Canadian interest in the eastern Arctic had a typically colonial aspect: land and people were incorporated into a growing political entity without regard to the people's own wishes. Eskimos would indeed have found it hard to express wishes in the matter, for they had heard little of the institutions and less of the nation that was carrying out the process.

Certainly most of the Whites interested in northern Canada at this period were convinced that incorporation would be the best thing for Eskimos. They probably believed that, were Eskimos able to express views on the subject, they would themselves join enthusiastically in realizing the objectives of the colonizers. But the Eskimos were ignorant of all that, and some missionaries were of the opinion that Eskimos were not in fact

3. Price (1970), p. 177.

rational. Separately sure of their purposes and jointly convinced of their rightness, the three southern institutions began in the early 1920s to draw the Canadian Eastern Arctic into their compass. Generally speaking, missionaries, policemen and traders never 'discovered' Eskimos; by 1920, there were none left to discover. What they did, rather, was discover Eskimos who were 'in need' – of Christianity, trading posts and enforcement of Canadian law.

One splendid example of collaboration between the three institutions is *The Eskimo Book of Knowledge*, a work published in 1931 by the Hudson's Bay Company, and written by George Binney, at that time an employee of the Company. It was translated into the Labrador Eskimo dialect by two Moravian missionaries, W. Perret and S. Hutton. The author, in his foreword, and in capitals, poses the contemporary problem and a set of 'difficult' questions:

YES INDEED IT SEEMS THAT THE TIMES ARE CHANGING AND THAT OUR PEOPLE ARE LIKEWISE CHANGING WITH THEM. WHY HAVE THINGS CHANGED WITH US? BY WHAT MEANS CAN WE RETAIN IN OUR CAMPS THE FORMER HEALTH AND HAPPINESS OF OUR FATHERS? AND FULLY ENJOY THE PROSPERITY WHICH COMES FROM OUR TRADING WITH THE COMPANY?

The book proceeds to answer these questions by laying down rule after rule by which Eskimos should order their lives. The rules are those of trader, missionary and policeman, and they are collected under the umbrella of Empire. A great potentate lurks behind every passage: 'Not only is King George a man of great prudence and a hard worker, he is also a great hunter ... He is likewise a great sailor, which is a fitting thing for a man who lives on an island.' There is a history of the British Empire, which in the most selfless fashion has brought the advantage of civilization to every land. The Hudson's Bay Company represents these advantages of commerce and industry. And with Empire comes law, another good. The Eskimos are told that if they try to enforce their own laws among themselves, they may be 'also guilty of crime, and ... likely also to be punished for breaking the Law'.[4] Rather, 'It is your duty to report to the policeman, or, if there is no policeman, then to the Company's Trader or to the Man of God any serious crime which one of your people may have committed.'[5] The policemen are 'the officers appointed by the King to uphold the Laws and are wise men after the heart of King Solomon ...' and here the book tells the story of Solomon judging the two mothers' competing claims to a child.

After a résumé of the Laws, which includes a section on 'Laws relating to Sex' that are 'common to all civilized countries', there is a chapter on 'The Men of God', whom the Eskimos are enjoined to respect and to follow. The text avoids sectarianism: *all* Men of God are to be revered. Moreover, the Eskimos are warned against a materialistic attitude towards belief:

This much you should know. In some parts of the country the Men of God complain that because you attend their services and profess yourselves to be Christians, some of you expect to receive gifts of food from the Men of God who are not rich in possessions. This is a disgraceful thing, unworthy of the Christian belief which you profess.[6]

The book has a biblical ring throughout, and its evangelical tone evokes that Methodist spirit which sits so easily with entrepreneurial endeavour. The message intended for Eskimo trappers is never less than clear:

You know that if you give your dogs too much walrus meat, they grow fat and slack and that you frequently have to use the whip on them ... It is the same thing in trade among people of all countries: if the Traders are easy-going, then the people become easy-going.[7]

In his rousing conclusion, the author warns of things to come:

4. Binney *et al*. (1931), p. 60.
5. ibid., pp. 61–2.
6. ibid., p. 80.
7. ibid., p. 84.

Take heed, Innuit, for the future will bring even greater changes than have taken place in your country in the past twenty years. There will be White trappers who will trap the foxes out of your country; strange ships will visit your harbours and strange traders will come among you seeking only your furs. Many White men will explore your lands in search of precious rocks and minerals. These traders and these trappers and these wanderers are like the drift-ice; today they come with the wind, tomorrow they are gone with the wind. Of these strangers some will be fairer than others, as is the nature of men; but whosoever they be, they cannot at heart possess that deep understanding of your lives through which our Traders have learned to bestow the care of a father upon you and upon your children.[8]

If it is difficult to know today what the Eskimos thought of *The Eskimo Book of Knowledge*, it is easy to see what the Hudson's Bay Company thought of the Eskimos – and of itself.

Dependence upon the Hudson's Bay Company and other traders was not, of course, the beginning of Eskimo dependence on Whites' society. In many parts of the Eastern Arctic, the whaling industry had already transformed many features of traditional life. Before the advent of whalers, the Igloolik Eskimo, for example, often spent the months between break-up and freeze-up walking inland, hunting and fishing. The arrival of whaling ships in early summer, however, encouraged many families to remain on the coast, for the whalers offered material and social benefits, including firearms. Moreover, material culture from the south advanced ahead of southerners. In the Belcher Islands, for example, no one can remember a time when there were no guns there, although people can remember Robert Flaherty's 'discovery' of the islands in 1914, when he became the first White to visit and map them.

The permanent trading posts created different degrees of dependence. The traders systematically encouraged Eskimos to spend more time hunting the animals with skins most highly prized in the southern market and to spend less time hunting animals that merely offered a supply of food. This shift in hunting sometimes left the Eskimos hungry, and it created a

8. ibid., p. 234.

need for new equipment with which to trap. The imbalances that accompanied this shift were in some measure rectified by exchange: the hunters-become-trappers traded skins for food and new equipment, and thereby their dependence upon trading posts rapidly became acute.

Between 1925 and around 1935, the relationship between trappers and traders was relatively easy; prices for furs, especially fox skins, were high, and well-equipped trappers were able to feed their families and large dog-teams. The quality of the trappers' life was enhanced by reliable supplies of tea, tobacco and other luxuries, as well as material necessities. During those years, Eskimo life in almost every part of the eastern Arctic shifted from a traditional subsistence economy to one based on trade. It was in some degree possible for a hunter to adjust to the new life at his own pace: so long as guns were available and game was plentiful, he had no compelling need for the trader's new goods. By far the majority of families continued to live in camps and to follow their traditional cycle of seasonal movement, but the trader's central interest lay in persuading all of the better hunters to become trappers and to enter into a relation of dependence on trading posts and southern goods. In this object, the trader was, at first, greatly assisted by the missionary, and only after the collapse of fox-fur prices in the 1930s could he exert real pressure directly on the hunters. By the late 1930s and throughout the war years, the economic plight of the Eskimo trappers was serious. Kleivan, in a study of White–Eskimo relations in Labrador, concludes: 'All in all, it is no exaggeration to suggest that the economic dependency of the Eskimos upon the [Hudson's Bay] Company increased in step with the poverty in the 1930s and onwards', and he quotes another writer's description of the 'economic serfdom' that characterized the relation of the Eskimos to the Hudson's Bay Company.[9] Once the people living in hunting camps were short of basic foodstuffs, a trader could effectively dictate his will to individual families by extending or refusing credit at the store. The 'reliable' or 'good' hunter would of course receive emergency rations; those hunters who were not 'good', who had

9. Kleivan (1966), p. 7.

resisted the pressure to shift from subsistence to exchange, would be left without rations. In regions where game was not abundant or in a bad season, this practice might lead to starvation.

I have never heard that during this period the hunters of north Baffin or Igloolik actually starved, for marine mammals are usually available in those waters. But in the 1940s there was starvation among the Caribou Eskimos west of Hudson's Bay, an event that was at least partially due to their enforced dependence on trade goods that were not made available to them. Some Belcher Island Eskimos described to me the appalling conditions, with several deaths from starvation, which prevailed there during the early 1940s. There is no doubt but that this comprehensive attempt to incorporate Eskimos into the southern economic community created an unstable situation, which, once disturbed, quickly produced hardship.[10]

During the same period, missionaries were engaged in an analogous endeavour. If the Hudson's Bay Company may be said to have established an economic serfdom, then the missionaries sought to establish a moral serfdom. Kleivan's description of the Moravian missionaries' work in Labrador shows how spiritual leaders in the Eskimo tradition became the object of remorseless criticism in an attempt to undermine their influence. Customary social practice, from sexual life down to the minutiae of games, was attacked. Conversion was encouraged by trade, medical benefits, threats and tireless exhortation. Conversion tended to involve a move from camp life (under the influence of traditional social authority) to settlement (under the influence of the new church). The Moravians' own writings, which are voluminous and rich in detail, show their preoccupation with the overall quality of Eskimo life: godliness, cleanliness and an abundance of other-world virtues were seen as a package deal offered to the heathen through conversion. The

10. Diamond Jenness made this point at its most general: 'The new barter economy – furs in exchange for the goods of civilization – made life harder instead of easier, more complicated instead of more simple. The commercial world of the white man had caught the Eskimo in its mesh, destroyed their self-sufficiency and independence, and made them economically its slaves' (Jenness, 1959).

Moravians did not distinguish between the sacred and the secular in their view of Eskimo life, but regarded their flock as primitive because heathen: they linked the material condition they saw with a mental condition they imagined. Many other missionaries have expressed this view of Eskimo life. Father Jean Philippe, an Oblate missionary working in the eastern Arctic, wrote in 1947 on 'Eskimo Psychology' and came to the plain conclusion that 'he (an Eskimo) does not think' and added that

intellectual exchange can scarcely be carried on with an Eskimo. He is not accustomed to analyse and coordinate his thoughts ... In his mind, far from being close together, the ideas laboriously follow one another, one giving place to the other ... More than once I asked an Eskimo an explanation of his way of acting, of a rule in grammar, etc. ... an explanation calling for an intellectual effort on his part.

The first reply is evidently: 'Amiashook' (I do not know).

I insist ...

The Eskimo looks at me for an instant and ends by saying: 'Why? because we do it thus ... because it is like that.' Certainly it is not a rational answer ... These people, with so little intellect, are always happy. They soon forget their past miseries and ignore the plans and cares for the future. They live from day to day without worry ... He has no trouble falling asleep even when he knows he has no food for the morrow, and famine lies in wait for him and his family.[11]

Yet the Eskimos of the Eastern Arctic readily became at least token Christians and, by the 1950s, the large majority of Eskimo camps had accepted Christian teachings, and most families observed the principal Christian rites. One important reason for the Eskimos' acceptance of the ministrations of missionaries and the attention of other White colonial agents during this critical period was their poor physical health. During the 1930s and 1940s, in the regions commonly visited by tuberculosis and other infections, diseases were widespread. In the Eastern Arctic, however, especially in northern Baffin Island, the Eskimo was still

11. *Eskimo*, June 1947, pp. 5–7. Compare the comment of a low-church missionary: 'The Eskimos, like the Jews of old, are under a spiritual death sentence' (Ledyard, 1958, p. 176).

relatively isolated, and many settlements were visited only annually by ship. The Eskimo population itself was scattered and the
incidence of epidemic infections does not appear to have been
high prior to 1950. Around 1950, however, when the price of fur
had been depressed for some time, the medical situation took a
sharp turn for the worse.[12] During 1948–9, an epidemic of poliomyelitis broke out among Eskimos living inland on west Hudson
Bay: eighteen adults died and sixty were paralysed (representing
just under 8 per cent of the infected population). In some communities the incidence of infection was close to 100 per cent.[13]
In early 1952, southern Baffin Island saw a serious measles epidemic (the first recorded incidence of measles in the area), during which the mortality rate in three communities rose to 22 per
cent. During that measles epidemic, there was a concurrent out-
break of Influenza B, and the epidemic was followed by the
spread of both scarlet fever and mumps. No Eskimos died of
the latter infections, but the cumulative effect was severe, and
the high incidence of infection intensified feelings of vulnerability and dependence upon White agencies.[14]

In the early 1960s, anxiety in southern Canada mounted at the
high incidence of tuberculosis among Canadian Eskimos. It was
discovered that 55 per cent of all households in Baker Lake had
at least one case of tuberculosis, and that one half of the children
in that community were infected.[15] This confirmed medical find-

12. The following episode shows how Greenland Eskimos suffered a
century earlier: 'A boy and a girl, the only survivors of the six Green-
landers who had been carried to Denmark in 1731, were sent back to their
native country, in a sickly state of health, by this year's vessel [1733]. The
girl died at sea; the boy reached his home, apparently safe and well: soon
after, however, a cutaneous disorder broke out ... It soon became evident
that the disorder was the small pox ... Those who had caught the infection fled as long as their strength permitted, and since their countrymen
persisted in the custom of denying no guests, the distemper gained ground
every day' (Crantz, 1820, Vol. 2, pp. 12–13).

13. See Adamson et al. (1949), pp. 339–48.

14. See Peart and Nagler (1952); and for details of 'flu at Pangnirtung
in 1963, see Simpson (1953).

15. See Moore (1964); and compare this with an account of the same
region, written only thirty years before: 'Fortunately, hardly any disease
has yet spread so widely among the Caribou Eskimos that it may be said

ings in the 1950s that the tuberculosis rate among Indians and Eskimos in Canada was between fifteen and twenty times higher than among Whites and, although the birth rate among northern natives was double that of Whites, the infant mortality rate stood at three times the southern figure.[16]

It is hard to know exactly when the deterioration of health among Eskimos living in the camps made their economic and social dependence on trader and missionary acute, but by 1950 that dependence was virtually total. In the three decades before that date, the RCMP had begun to establish posts throughout the Eastern Arctic, and in many places they had arrested Eskimos on criminal charges. All the White agents saw much of traditional Eskimo practice as immoral or criminal, and they must bear some responsibility for exaggerated accounts of Eskimo customs of infanticide and parricide. Rasmussen, in his report on the Fifth Thule Expedition, laments the tendency to judge Eskimo customs (which Rasmussen thought of as rational and necessary) by southern legal standards, thereby discovering criminality where in fact there existed only the normal operations of a well-ordered society.[17]

An early example of police intervention in Eskimo affairs occurred in the Pond Inlet area during 1923, when three Eskimos were tried for the murder of a free-trader, Robert Janes. Local hunters had shot Janes because they regarded him as a dangerous man, who had threatened to shoot their dogs. Staff Sergeant Joy investigated the case, and his investigations were followed by the arrival of a magistrate, with all the other personnel required for a full court procedure. The jury was taken from the crew of the ship bringing magistrate and lawyers. One of those charged was eventually found guilty of manslaughter, another was aquitted, and a third was convicted of aiding and abetting. The sentences passed were two years' close

---

to be of social importance. This is true both of venereal diseases and tuberculosis ... As a whole the Caribou Eskimos give the impression of being healthy' (Rasmussen, 1930, Vol. 5, p. 299).

16. See Moore (1954).

17. Rasmussen (1931), Vol. 8, pp. 17–21.

confinement in Pond Inlet for the lesser charge, and ten years in a southern prison for the manslaughter.

Van den Steenhoven, in a study of leadership and law among the Eskimos of the Keewatin district, describes an occasion on which the RCMP considered that Eskimos had, according to the Canadian legal code, acted in a criminal manner:

Eerkiyoot, 21, son of the woman Nukashook, was found guilty by a six-man jury made up of RCAF and Department of Transport personnel, who attached a recommendation for clemency to their verdict. He was sentenced to one year's imprisonment by Stipendiary Magistrate A. H. Gibson, who presided over the trials ...

Nukashook, who was in an advanced state of tuberculosis and in pain, had last summer asked her son Eerkiyoot to help her die, according to the facts alleged against the two accused. Eerkiyoot asked his friend Ishakak to help him. They went to the woman's tent, where Eerkiyoot tied both ends of a sealskin rope to the ridge-pole so that the loop hung to within about two feet from the floor. Eerkiyoot helped Nukashook to dress and then Eerkiyoot and Ishakak helped her over to a sitting position beside the rope, and Nukashook placed her head through the loop, exhorting her son to hurry the procedure. Eerkiyoot pressed down the back of Nuka-shook's head until the woman was dead ...

Both accused were shown to be intelligent types. They are able to read and write Eskimo syllabics and seemed to grasp the essential factors involved in the trials. It is hoped that the trials will have the desired effect of bringing home to Eskimos that assisted suicides are forbidden. The comparatively light sentence given Eerkiyoot avoided, however, any unnecessary harshness towards an individual whose sense of filial duty and adherence to Eskimo custom led him to contravene the Criminal Code.[18]

The members of the jury in this case were troubled by the evident lack of criminality, as they saw it, of the accused, and they sought advice from the magistrate. In summing up, the magistrate made the position clear:

18. Van den Steenhoven (1962), pp. 174–6 for discussion of this case and some of the problems it raised for law. He comments *inter alia* on the question of jury selection, remarking that if 'an Eskimo jury is felt unable to realize what is expected from them, then how can the Eskimo accused himself realize what the Criminal Code expects from him?'

There may be a different standard of observance in areas occupied by primitive people. I find it very difficult to express this; perhaps I should put it this way: we could not accept for one part of the country a lower or different view of duty from the one that was meant to apply throughout the country.[19]

Despite this explicit statement, the jury still returned with a special question: was it by local custom that the case should finally be judged? The magistrate replied: 'The answer is that you are to govern yourselves by Canadian Law, that is the law that I have stated is the law that you will apply to the case.'[20]

There was, of course, some difference between the Canadian legal code and its interpretation or application by the individual policemen who manned detachments in the high Arctic. These policemen were not there merely to enforce the law; rather, they occupied a curious congeries of roles, visiting camps that were thought might be short of food, making sure that information about Eskimos was gathered accurately and reached the central governmental departments concerned with northern affairs, and seeing to it that Canadian law ran throughout the land. From the Eskimos' point of view, the police were seen to have enormous power that they could direct against any one they chose, a fact amply demonstrated in the court cases that occurred and the sentences that were passed. Moreover, the police were obviously in alliance with the other Whites: juries were selected from the local and migrant Whites, even for cases in which every word had to be interpreted from Eskimo. The evident influence and power of the three separate institutions merged because the Eskimos saw southern society as a single thing, and they had no reason to doubt that the purposes of Whites were assimilated to one another. Of course, the police did emphasize their most important role, that of enforcing Canadian law, and they did arrest, try and imprison Eskimos who did things which, for reasons obscure to the Eskimos, they regarded as wrong. The police added fear to the many other reasons for accepting the southerners' wishes and acquiescing in their demands. Rasmussen gives an example of how effective they were:

19. ibid., pp. 147–8.   20. ibid., p. 150.

The man I killed was married, and according to the customs of my country I could marry his wife, but I did not . . .

Now if there had been no white men in our country the dead man's relatives would take vengeance upon me, and I would not be afraid of that; but now I was told that white men would come up from Chesterfield and take me away to punish me in the white man's way. White men were masters in our country and they would take me home to their own land, where everything would be wild and strange to me. So I grew afraid and came back to my own country and now I live in the mountain regions where no white man has ever been before.[21]

On the local level, the police put an official seal on the other Whites' determination to change Eskimo life; on a higher level, they represented the fact that one nation was determined to include the vast Arctic hinterland, not only within its geographical frontiers, but within its moral and legal boundaries as well. The missionaries may have been French or English, the traders may have been Scots; but the police, whatever their origins, were deeply Canadian.[22]

The days when missionary, trader and policeman alone held authority in the Arctic are now regarded as the 'old days' – not because there are no longer missionaries, traders and policemen, but because today other and more powerful agencies are everywhere present in the north. The old days are lamented by the old-timers; wistfully they recall that time when 'individuals could make decisions', when there was no continuous communication with and interference from the south, when a man could live and travel 'along with the Eskimos'. Old-timers rightly feel that their influence has been curtailed or eclipsed by more recent changes that are, in their terms, mainly for the worse. They say that before 'the great change' the Whites in the north 'knew the people', and it was possible then to live in the north in freedom, a freedom compounded of unique environmental conditions, special duties, clear purposes, and distance – above all, distance. This freedom is in striking contrast with their modern-day

21. Igsivalitaq, a Netsilik Eskimo, quoted in Rasmussen (1931), Vol. 8, p. 21.

22. See Freeman (1971) for a history of the police in Grise Fjord and for evidence of how they established influence in that isolated community.

subordination to a bureaucratic administration based in Ottawa. Laments of old-timers are loud and clear.

Some social scientists echo their laments. One author introduces his study of an Arctic Quebec community with a sense of new beginnings:

In 1959, the people of George River went through an intensive period of social change ... the impetus for change came from the Government of Canada's program of social and economic development and had two main objectives: first, to gather the scattered Eskimo people together in settlements for administrative efficiency and complement the social services already existing in the rest of Canada, and second, to improve and organize the economy based upon the formation of Eskimo cooperatives. George River, in 1959, became the first of these communities.[23]

The main force of the change was to concentrate the Eskimo population into settlements. The settlements themselves had existed long before this concentration began; most of them had been missions or trading posts. With the concentration of the Eskimos came the building of new housing, schools, medical facilities and a full-time local administration. These new social services were partly caused by a growing awareness in southern Canada that the northern natives were severely deprived and lacked the medical, educational and other facilities seen to be the necessary conditions for equality, freedom and a competitive place in the nation's life. The Second World War also significantly altered the nature of southern concern with the north, creating strategic and new nationalistic dimensions. In the international climate of the cold war, all land was seen to have a place in the balance of forces and hypothetical logistics, while national integrity assumed a vigorous new importance. Thus the Eskimos' future was involved in forces as remote from their

23. Arbess (1966, p. 1) and Balikci and Cohen (1963, pp. 33–47) discuss briefly the consequences of commercial soapstone carving, introduced as part of the government emphasis on local economic development, while a spate of *Area Economic Surveys* reflects the Canadian concern with reforming or at least vitalizing (or perhaps conventionalizing) Eskimo communities throughout the country. The *Area Economic Surveys* were published by the Canadian Federal Government, beginning in 1958.

own lives as national security at a time of international tension. The post-war situation revived Canada's colonialist activity and the expanding economy of the times provided the means for it. A growing humanitarian concern, represented internationally by the United Nations, encouraged governments to use national wealth to improve the lot of their less advantaged citizens. New political ideologies everywhere created a willingness to express dissatisfaction with the sort of free enterprise that had left to traders the determination of the fortunes of northern peoples. These several causes brought more Whites to the north, giving the Eskimos more contacts of all kinds with the south, while the provision of new services for the Eskimos encouraged them in turn to adopt a more settled and materially more elaborate lifestyle.

The earliest administrative endeavour (and that endeavour is still in its early stages) may thus lead us to expect significant changes in Eskimo–White relationships; it would perhaps appear that exploitative agencies were displaced by supportive ones. But there is a fundamental continuity between what can be termed the pre- and post-administrative periods. Whites in the north have always been intent on causing change; in realizing these changes, they have dominated the Eskimos, and they continue to do so.

The pattern of domination is common to all the agencies: Eskimos have come to depend upon (or become convinced that they depend upon) things which only Whites can dispense. This applies equally to the beneficence of a Christian God, to an antiviral vaccination or to office in a local political organization. The basic relation between Whites and Eskimos has therefore remained the same. The material conditions of life have changed, among Eskimos as well as Whites, just as their vulnerability to national and international considerations has increased. But these changes have remained in the hands of southerners: it is *they* who decide what Eskimos need or should need, and it is they who decide how those needs are to be met.

There has been a continuity in the nature of the changes the Eskimos have undergone, a continuity best explained in terms of incorporation: whereas missionaries and traders desired moral and economic incorporation, the newer institutions aim at incorporation that is broadly ideological (through education), national (through law and medicine), and finally political (through local government). Whites who live in northern settlements today are, most of them, agents of the incorporating agencies.

Gradually even the Canadian Eastern Arctic, which for a long time was regarded as the last preserve of Eskimo life in anything like its traditional form, is in danger of becoming yet another empty suburb of the North American metropolis. Although the following chapters concentrate on the details of life in this small society, these details are shaped by the largest social forces. The social conditions in these communities represent the latest phase in the colonial history of North America.

3 • The Whites: Some Hard Facts

'When we came to the village the women crowded
out of the houses, and the mischievous men
shouted aloud about the remarkable find they had
made – travellers who seemed to be neither traders
nor policemen'

—Knud Rasmussen, *Intellectual Culture of the Copper Eskimos*

'Canadian awareness of the indigenous people in
the North developed rapidly during [1939–45] and
the government has attempted to draw these
people into the overall Canadian society by
embarking upon massive and ambitious
programmes of education, housing and health'

– D. K. Thomas and C. T. Thompson, *Eskimo Housing as
Planned Culture Change*

When old-timers in the north recall the glorious freedom of the
past, they do so with tales of their own adventures. Those tales,
like any other body of myth, serve a direct purpose and are
instructive. They concentrate on simple themes, on the land and
living on the land, on difficulties encountered and, through per-
severance, overcome. They lament the passing of a life of
nature and its replacement by a life of culture. I shall return to
this point in a later chapter, but, by way of introduction here,
something should be said about the shift from nature to culture
in its simplest and most material aspects. Old-timers cheerfully
describe the considerable difficulties of their earlier lives, their
crude accommodations and the poverty of material and intellectual resources among which they lived. This harshness was
romantic – the price, as they saw it, of their freedom. Their
stories emphasize travelling and they are embellished with the
details of dog-teams, native companions, the hardships of the
journeys, and, put more simply, of their personal exposure to
the *place*. They lived with few comforts, they were dependent
on 'the natives' and they had to adjust to the ways of these

people who lived, by southern standards, in conditions of elemental simplicity.

The White community of the present, the old-timers declare, is pampered with ease and luxury. And the old-timers are right. Today, every government employee is provided with a furnished and well-equipped house that is heated and serviced. They have showers and washing-machines, curtains and carpets, electricity and, in most settlements, they have telephones. Water is delivered and garbage removed. Such houses are comfortable even by the high standards of southern Canada, although there are often drawbacks. In some settlements there is no running water and therefore no flush toilets, and the notorious 'honey bag' is ubiquitous. But these sewage containers are usually removed and replaced daily as part of the local service.

Of course the Whites themselves complain about their houses and concentrate especially on defects of equipment and services: there is a broken chair, a set of cutlery is missing, the vacuum-cleaner doesn't work or the water supply has been low for eight days. This concentration on detail suggests that living conditions generally are regarded as adequate. It is indeed a demanding southerner who thinks that his accommodation in the north is really unsatisfactory.

Northern housing is not uniform in quality. Government officials and teachers are provided with two- or three-bedroom single-storey houses. The settlement manager usually has a double basement house, built on two levels, with a generous ground floor that may be used as an additional bedroom, for storage, or as a workshop.[1] Nurses live in stations that are equipped with stereophonic gramophone, electric sewing-machine, video-tape TV set, washing-machine, refrigerator and deep freeze. The Hudson's Bay Company store managers have houses that compare favourably with those of government employees. Missionaries have more modest homes that often lack modern electric stoves, but are equipped with paraffin heating and cooking units. Their houses are usually older and show

1. Lack of uniformity is to some extent a measure of hierarchy within the White community. More senior officials have been provided with slightly better homes.

signs of wear. But the missionaries' houses might be said to gain more by way of character than they lose by discomfort.

Just as the living conditions of the Whites are those of the southern middle classes, so they eat almost exclusively southern foods. Each family orders its supplies annually and buys supplementary foods from the Hudson's Bay Company store, which caters to southern tastes at higher than southern prices, or orders them by air-freight from elsewhere. There is, for example, no significant difference between the diets of the school-teachers in Arctic Bay and school-teachers in Ottawa. For dinner there would be meat, potatoes, green vegetables, with cake or ice cream, coffee and cream. There might be an aperitif or cocktail before the meal and a liqueur after it. Medium-priced imported wine is drunk at northern tables almost as often as in the south.

The high material standard of life among the Whites of these small northern settlements is the consequence of federal policy: in the early 1950s it was decided that sufficient numbers of properly qualified personnel could be attracted to the north only if financial rewards were large and the conditions of life there no worse than elsewhere in the country. The assumption was that young teachers, administrators and nurses would choose between the north and any other place of employment primarily on the basis of relative material advantages. The attraction of more money would, on that view, be the means of offsetting the disadvantages of the place itself. This policy emphasized uniformity as a goal and minimized idealism as a means. The north was intended to become more like the south, and to have increasingly conventional White residents as government employees. Once the material conditions were defined and given, the social life of northern Whites was inevitably transformed. It became possible, even necessary, for northern employees to bring their families with them and to lead 'normal lives' – that is, the same sort of lives they would have led elsewhere in Canada.

Now that the majority of Whites, even those in the smallest and most isolated settlements, live in comfortable houses, they spend a large amount of their time at home. There is no need to travel for food or recreation. Their contact with the snow or the wind or the land itself is likely to be limited to a stroll in good weather from home to the store, from the store to a friend's, from there back home again. Of course, some of the White community like to walk a little farther, and some even enjoy a day or two out hunting now and then. There are small boating expeditions away from the settlement in summer to fish or picnic, and some teachers use their spring holiday to go camping at the floe-edge. Such adventurers, however, are few, and they do not go for the sealing – virtually no Whites eat seal meat. In the winter, some of the younger White men like to hunt caribou, the meat of which is a useful and welcome supplement to southern food. But even if the new northerners wished to travel, they would find it hard to get away from home and the settlement. Among them, only teachers have a holiday long enough to wait on the uncertainties of Arctic weather; other Whites have only weekends for adventure. And the teachers go south for their long vacation. Almost to a man they leave the settlements the day after the school year ends, and return the day it begins again in the fall. In the High Arctic, this means that they leave before ice breaks up and they return about freeze-up. Moreover, the northern climate is harsh and few southerners are willing or able to undertake even brief journeys. Most of them have small children, and none of them are accustomed to outdoor living. Very few Whites have winter clothing that is adequate for any journey longer than a walk through the settlement.

And, of course the Whites' inexperience of northern conditions makes them even more nervous of going beyond the safety of the settlement or experimenting with unfamiliar foods. It takes time to learn how to live and travel in the north, it takes time to learn to wear Eskimo clothing and to look after it properly, and it takes time for the body and mind to adjust to the climate – but the jobs and the life-styles of the present generation of northern Whites do not allow time or the opportunity for learning, experiencing and adjusting to these new things. There are many reasons why Whites are reluctant to leave the safety and comfort of home, including apathy, personal discomforts in work and social life, as well as acute awkwardness in approaching Eskimos for help. They are, moreover, intimately connected with the south by aeroplane and radio, by culture, by all the details of daily life: furnishings, mealtimes, clothes. In fact, they cannot move outside their enclaves for more than a brief and occasional foray. Perhaps the stories of the old-timers about their hardships with dog-teams, struggling, starving and battered, from camp to camp, may intensify the newcomers' feelings of unease and their fear of moving outside their material and cultural fortress. Added to the very visible and sensible impressions the environment makes on a stranger, the knowledge that these extremes of climate and geography have taken the lives even of Eskimos is likely to create nervous awe of the land itself. On the other hand, many Whites enjoy the idea of living in such a fierce climate and take great pride in having been especially far north. There is endless preoccupation with statistics about the weather, which reflects the idea that living in the north is an exotic adventure. Very few Whites in the north realize how little degrees of latitude or temperature, each taken by itself, can influence living conditions. They tend towards a purely intellectual or narrowly arithmetical appreciation of the environment, not linked with being in it. To a sedentary person, it is naturally more interesting and important that on Tuesday the thermometer stood at $-45°F.$, whereas to an Eskimo, that temperature was of no importance whatever. What mattered to him was that on the same day the wind, snow, and ice conditions made travel dangerous and seal-hunting impossible.

By comparison with the new Whites in the north, those of thirty or forty years ago were hardy, able men who lived close to the environment. Most of them were single, and most of them learned some Eskimo. Indeed, they would have been disappointed if life in the north had been without privation and challenge. Missionaries, perhaps, did not regard privation or adventure as intrinsically worthwhile, but it is not too much to say that many missionaries found that hardship and self-denial made important contributions to their self-image. A trader too, could not be unaware of the long tradition, almost the culture, of solitary pioneering and adventure beyond the edges of civilization that he shared with generations of Hudson's Bay Company servants. And at some level he was gratified by the influence he had in being the lone White man among savages to whom he was slowly bringing the advantages of commerce. The RCMP constable who went north and did *not* travel by dog-team with Eskimos, did *not* experience the recurrent malevolence of the climate, would surely have failed to realize his dreams of going north. Nor should it ever be forgotten that such solitude was a corollary of vast influence and a sense of real power. And what person, travelling alone, in a position to influence the thoughts, minds and actions of the Eskimo, could fail to sense something grand and heroic in the opposition of his will to the great loneliness of a vast and almost empty land?

The clearest testimony to the worst aspects of old-timer attitudes to the north is to be found in the pages of Duncan Pryde's book *Nunaga: My Land, My People*, the autobiography of a Scottish junior employee with the Hudson's Bay Company. The book dwells on the violence, dirtiness and sexual availability of the natives, and suggests that, thanks to the aggressive behaviour of the book's author, they were improved. Perhaps the most distasteful piece of writing to come from northern colonialists, it does give a great deal of insight into some of the arrogance and self-righteousness that often typified their manner. Pryde also dwells, of course, on how rugged his own life-style was: after all, he was at times the lone civilizer among the uncivilized, eating *their* food, sleeping with *their* women, and in a host of other ways enduring the privations that his job entailed.

There is no reason to think that any of these old-timers ever really lived like an Eskimo. Rather, they lived on the edge of the camps, at the edge of the people's lives; they followed and experienced to only a limited extent the Eskimos' ways. Today the situation is exactly reversed: it is the Eskimos who live at the edge of southern life. It is striking how many of the old-timers despair at the new dispensation. In 1954 Frank Vallee noted the irony in the missionary's lament at the passing of Eskimo traditions.[2] Behind the irony, however, is a real sense of loss – the

2. See Vallee (1967), pp. 153–4.

missionary's sense of his own loss. Those for whom northern life was the people, their language, their life, must lament the emergence of a conventional middle-class White community, for it denies many of the reasons for having come north and destroys their pleasure in the experience.

Today southern institutions stand at the political centre of northern settlements. Indeed, they are basic to their very existence, and were the spurs that hastened the people in from the camps. The heart of the settlement is its school, store, nursing station and government office. The people who manage these institutions are central and powerful, the social and political heirs of the old-timers, urging changes and reforms on their Eskimo friends. They have brought with them new power and influence, and now the Eskimos depend on them. Yet these Whites are in but not of the north; they have created in small pockets the conditions of the south and have established a mode of life that is as middle-class as it is White.

This change, this emergence of a middle-class life-style, is of considerable importance. It throws much light on the interaction of Whites and Eskimos and on their mutual distrust. It also sheds light on the way the White community conducts its own affairs and how it reacts to newcomers and outsiders. Only through a proper understanding of the White community, its social style and its class orientations can a parallel understanding of the Eskimos' predicament be made possible. It is a change that, in the Eastern Arctic at least, can be dated with some accuracy, and is not so much a process or a trend as a particular reconstitution of things. However, although the decisions in Ottawa that precipitated the change can be dated, we are still dealing with a community and with a continuity of personnel. There was no displacement of an older group by a sudden rush of newcomers, but for a time two styles overlapped. The settlement grew, the camps contracted and disappeared, new offices were created and new men arrived to fill them. To that extent it was undeniably a process. Furthermore, no one institution was alone involved, and no one decision-making body controlled all the Whites in any community. The Federal Government may have changed direction and therefore changed its personnel – but it did not, of course, attempt to manipulate directly the activities of the missionary or trader.

Shortly after the Second World War, the Federal Government decided that control over the northern part of the country should be extended. This new direction in northern policy was supported by two quite different considerations: the hope that the north might become a major supplier of new resources, and the appalling consequences of the collapse of the fur trade. Since the fur trade no longer provided a living to Eskimos and Indians, and since an education given by missionaries and their helpers could not be adequate to both present and future needs of a segment of the Canadian population, the Government's non-interventionist attitude to the north underwent a radical change. In the broadest terms it can be said that a welfare attitude displaced acceptance of *laissez-faire*. And for the first time since the depression Canada was prepared to spend money on the north, while the war had resulted in vastly improved northern transportation systems. It had become possible for the Canadian parliament to vote to spend farmers' taxes on the north.[3]

However, the Government's acceptance of the fact that welfare and education were needed was not accompanied by Government intervention in northern economics. The trader's position and activities had never been subjected to federal scrutiny or control, a fact obliquely indicated by Diamond Jenness in 1966:

Since the early post-war years Ottawa has spared neither money nor effort to expand her northern health or education programmes, and to discover ways and means of making them more efficient. She has flooded the Arctic with white administrators, school-teachers, doctors, nurses and welfare officers, all committed to raise the Eskimo cultural level and improve their standard of living.[4]

3. During the inter-war period there had been concern with the north, notably in the old Department of the Interior, but the depression rendered any extensive activity impossible. For very similar reasons, the Soviet north also experienced a great revival of interest and expenditure during the 1950s and 60s.

4. See Jenness (1955). The passage continues: 'but progress has been disturbingly slow, and nearly twenty years of effort have aggravated her

Jenness makes no mention of any plan aimed at reconstituting or even reconsolidating the economic situation of the Eskimos. Rather, his acceptance of one form of southern exploitation gave way to faith in another: the fur trade was to be replaced by extractive industries as the mainstay of Eskimo economic life. It need hardly be said that employment in any extractive industry requires skills radically different from those of a trapper. The federal education programme came to be seen as the road to these skills, and Jenness observed that 'Canada must greatly improve both the formal education and the vocational training of her Eskimos before they can enter her skilled labour market, and become integrated into her national life'.[5]

The Government's new preoccupation with the north was the direct cause of new White communities engaged in the extension of more services to Eskimos in the remotest parts of the Arctic. A policy was devised to recruit Whites to go to these remote parts. Policy-makers in Ottawa must themselves have been steeped in a vision of a savage north that was scarcely fit for human habitation. Certainly they were convinced that enough Whites could be found to go north only if the financial and material incentives were great enough. From this attitude it followed quite naturally that large salaries, superior accommodation, good transportation and communications all had to be established immediately. With the adoption and implementation of this policy, the era of the short-term northerner began.

It is the blend of affluence and family life that most typically characterizes middle-class life-styles. Material goods afforded protection against the environment and made family life possible for non-Eskimos; and, of course, family life reinforced the need for material goods. A visitor to an Arctic settlement, newly

_____

problems rather than solved them'. It should not be forgotten that Jenness was strongly inclined to the view that the real solution to the Eskimo problem lay in encouraging many of them to leave the north for wage-labour and integration in the south – though that particular miscalculation never became official policy.

5. ibid., p. 26.

arrived from, let us say, a middle-class suburb in Ottawa, might be struck at first by some superficial differences between his home and the home of his northern hosts. He would notice, for example, Eskimo carvings and locally sewn *appliqué* wall-hangings, with which many Whites adorn their houses. But he would soon see that the main pattern of northern life was not, after all, very different from his own: the northern home would appear prosperous and its occupants deeply committed to a specific form of family life, almost all the furnishings and decorations of the house would reveal plainly enough the status of his hosts in relation to mainstream southern society.

Most of the Whites living in a northern settlement are occupied in one or another of a few key institutions. Here, for example, is the profile of a typical White sub-community. Out of a total population of 430, there are thirty-four Whites. Of those thirty-four, eighteen have permanent positions in various federal agencies and there are seven spouses and nine children. The range of institutions that employ them is typical of the Eastern Arctic:

Administration:	2
Education:	7
Nursing:	2
Hudson's Bay Company:	2
RCMP:	1
Missions:	2
Social Welfare:	1
Local Cooperative:	1

During 1972, these eighteen persons earned a total annual income of $201,190, an average of $11,177 each. Their salaries ranged from $4,000 to almost $18,000. The least well paid were the missionaries and Hudson's Bay Company clerks, and the best paid were the most experienced school-teachers. At the time of this calculation, the average age of these Whites was 31.9 years. By January 1973, only two of the Whites had been there for more than five years; two had been there for more than a year, but less than five years; and fourteen of them had been there for less than one year. Nine of the Whites were working for the first time in the north; five others had had between one and five years' experience in the north before taking their present jobs.

These employees were young, well paid and, for the most part, new or comparatively new to the environment in which they were working. High pay combined with unfamiliarity with the north in general, and with the Eskimo community in particular, meant that the distance between them and the native community was likely to be great. With such brief experience of the north, it was virtually impossible that any of them could have acquired any fluency in Eskimo; with such large salaries, it is unlikely that they would choose to lead a life that bore any resemblance to the life of the people among whom they lived and worked. Seven of the Whites were married, but it might have been expected that the single men and women would have fuller and easier communications with the Eskimo community. In fact only three of the Whites had sexual attachments among local people and one of these – a Hudson's Bay Company employee – was encouraged to leave the settlement when his liaisons came to the attention of a more senior employee. There was, in fact, only one White who, with his wife, regularly visited Eskimo homes, and they did so nervously and confessed that the language problem made it all but impossible to communicate with any of the older persons unless they took an interpreter with them. Eskimos regularly visited only four of the White homes, two of which were the homes of missionaries with whom the local people felt they had a special, if limited, relationship.

The facts for this one settlement need to be compared with those of other settlements in the region to indicate to what extent the pattern is common. Obviously, in so small a sample, the figures can be distorted by a few atypical instances. The time spent in a settlement by agency Whites may be, in a given community, the consequence of unusual circumstances and may not offer any basis for generalization. Since generalizations about these Whites is central to this study, we must look at a larger sample, although it is difficult to collect data of the required kind, and the facts and figures given below are limited –

but they are still broad enough and comprehensive enough to give a firm basis for some general remarks.

In the case of government personnel (for example teachers, administrators, nurses), the figures are complete for the north Baffin administrative region. They are incomplete in the case of non-government agencies (for example traders and missionaries). There were sixty teachers in the region in 1972 and they constituted by far the largest group and offered the most valuable information.

	Regional district	One settlement
Average age	30·5	29·5
Unmarried or separated	40 per cent	42·86 per cent
Women	61·66 per cent	42·86 per cent
Salary	$12,590	$13,500
Average number of years in present settlement	1·75	1·14
Average number of years in north	2·5	1·29
Non-Canadians	21·66 per cent	28·55 per cent
Average number of years teaching experience	6·32	4·12
Five or more years in the north	18·33 per cent	14·28 per cent
One year or less in north	41·66 per cent	71·44 per cent

Administrative personnel tend to be older and more widely experienced in northern life than teachers. Here are the facts for ten settlement managers in the same administrative region:

Average age	35·7
Unmarried or separated	10 per cent
Women	10 per cent
Average salary	$14,036
Average number of years in settlement	1·64
Average number of years in north	7
Non-Canadians	30 per cent

Five of the ten settlement managers began their careers working for the Hudson's Bay Company as clerks and assistants in northern stores. Only one out of the ten went directly into administration; the remaining four had first been school-teachers and had moved into full-time administration only after several years. (Some of them had been both teachers and administrators in settlements where there were no full-time administrators.) One settlement manager had moved into administration from teaching and had worked as a northern service officer before local administration became the responsibility of the Territorial Civil Service based in Yellowknife. He was, therefore, one of the more experienced – and more successful – of northern employees. In contrast, the settlement manager whose difficulties are at the heart of Chapter 6 came directly into administration after a career in the armed services.[6] This man had had no experience of the north, and he was bedevilled, as the account of his fortunes will illustrate, by a blend of naïvety and inexperience that exacerbated the difficulties with which he had to deal in his settlement.

The store clerks of the Hudson's Bay Company are young and often from the United Kingdom (there remains a tradition of recruiting clerks in Scotland). Some arrive in an Arctic settlement with only a vague idea of what to expect, and having seen virtually nothing of southern Canada. But they are often more ready than the members of any other group to be drawn into friendly relations with young local people; indeed they are often criticized for giving alcohol to young Eskimos and themselves to young Eskimo women. Because the junior Hudson's Bay Company employees are young and independent of government agencies, and are at the very bottom of the White social hierarchy, they are at a clear advantage in Eskimo society. The Hudson's Bay Company has evolved a number of policies that seem to be related to a clerk's independence of the prevalent local sanctions and restraints. A clerk who marries must leave

6. He was, in fact, in a different administrative region from the one being described here, a region that appeared distinctive in its readiness to fill administrative positions with men who had had long careers in the armed services.

his job (sometimes on the grounds that accommodation cannot be provided for the wife and family of a junior, even though the fellow may wish to live with his wife's family), and a clerk whose activities cause too much local disapproval is soon moved to another settlement.

Hudson's Bay Store managers, on the other hand, are invariably men with years of northern experience – indeed, they can become manager only after having spent time as a clerk in a northern store. These men rise to managership through the exercise of commercial and social virtues: the wild young clerks who fail to learn a nice blend of commercial and social skills are weeded out (or, more likely, weed themselves out). Although it is unusual today for a Hudson's Bay Company manager to gain the social esteem achieved by teachers or administrators, the selection process guarantees that the Company's residence is occupied by a man conscious of his respectability. The managers have suffered a marked decline in influence and importance in relation to the Eskimo community and to the northern White community itself. In the past the Hudson's Bay Company's officers were the spearhead of northern development and arbiters of northern society. Their exercise of judgement and power used directly to affect the welfare of hundreds, perhaps many hundreds, of families. But now the mighty have fallen to the status of supermarket storekeepers who carry on a small sideline in the purchase of furs and local crafts. If the reminiscences of old-timers and the back issues of the Hudson's Bay Company's magazine *The Beaver* accurately represent the past, then the Company's managers were members of a remarkable group that cultivated personal idiosyncrasy and were as committed to long-established traditions of service as to the north itself. Today, however, they are of secondary importance in a strikingly conventional, not to say stolid, community; they participate cheerfully in a small closed society that values the niceties of a suburban cocktail party above any individual's eccentricities or assertiveness. In the settlements of the contemporary north, the developing hinterland of an industrialized metropolis, the shopkeeper finds and keeps his customary place.

The nurses are neatly integrated into the larger White community in a similar manner. The single White men are, of course, much preoccupied with the single White women of any settlement. The keenness of their concern with physical attractions and the availability of women appears to be greater than elsewhere, perhaps owing to the tendency, widespread in the north, to be both vocal and blunt. Many northern Whites like to play the frontiersman – and like to claim that going north is, after all, a going away from the constraints and inhibiting social forces that restrict self-expression 'at home'. So it is that young nurses are regarded as a social resource, well suited to young men who – in their southern lives – would very likely be too inhibited to approach them openly. Nurses are therefore strongly encouraged to participate actively in the everyday social life of White communities. Refusal, or even a slight disinclination, to participate can easily generate hostility, whereas a too-ready friendliness may be seen as disgraceful promiscuity. A particularly distasteful episode illustrates the first of those reactions.

One nurse, young and attractive, was quite frank in wishing to restrict her circle of friends among the Whites in the settlement. She had built up some close friends among the teachers. With others she was affable, professionally competent, but – by northern standards – a little remote. She did not go to parties that did not include her friends – she did not, that is, attend parties merely for amusement or to show solidarity. She was quite straightforward in rejecting the advances of young men with whom she felt she had nothing in common. There was some bad feeling caused by her behaviour and finally one of the disappointed single men precipitated a small scandal.

Drunk and somewhat resentful, the man telephoned the nurse late one night and scolded her for paying no attention to him nor to other suitors' attentions: obviously, he told her, she was homosexual. He named one of her friends as the lover in a supposed affair, and asserted that he was not alone in his view of the matter.

The nurse was of course shocked and angry at this accusation and deeply troubled by the suggestion that he spoke for others. She told her friends what had happened, and the subject was, for a time, the centre of gossip and discussion, and opinion in the settlement was polarized. Some people besides the late-night caller felt unfriendly towards the nurse and, although they hastened to dissociate themselves from the specific charge, they revealed in their remarks that they had also been made unhappy by her firm discriminations. This matter, like most other disturbances in local social life, soon subsided, a process hastened by the man's decision to move back to the south.

To return to colder facts, the average age of the sixteen nurses in the administrative district in which the incident described above occurred was 32·7 years. Ten of them were 30 or under; all of them were single. Their average length of experience in the Eastern Arctic was a little over two years, although three of them had been for varying lengths of time in other administrative districts in the Western Arctic. A high proportion of the nurses, six out of sixteen, had British qualifications.[7] The average earnings of the sixteen nurses was $7,492 per annum, in addition to which they received an annual supplementary income of approximately $1,500.

Because the majority of men and women working for southern agencies are young, and because the incentives aimed at attracting southerners to the north are themselves the result of young policies, it is impossible to predict how long and in what manner the Whites presently living in the north will stay there. The incentives may bring people to an Arctic settlement, but they do not keep them there. Of the sixteen nurses described, only one had been in her present job for more than three years; ten of them were transferred to their jobs within the previous six months; and three of them were seeking transfers to other regions. By comparison with teachers, however, the nurses are more inclined to stay in their jobs. Of the sixty teachers for whom figures have already been given, only thirty-one wished to remain in their jobs; twelve were hoping to be transferred to other settlements in the north; and seventeen were resigning from the Northern School Service altogether.

7. Some preference may have been given to British nurses because their basic training includes midwifery, a skill important in an isolated settlement, and not one that is necessarily part of American or Canadian nurses' qualifications.

Let us again look at the situation in one settlement in which, between 1971 and 1973, the entire teaching staff of seven changed. Of those who came to the village in 1972, one transferred to another region and three resigned at the end of the school year in 1973. During the same period, there have been four Hudson's Bay Company clerks, whose periods of work never overlapped; the police detachment had two changes in staff; the Anglican missionary changed; a Social Development Officer arrived; there were three different settlement mechanics, each of whom stayed only a few months; there were altogther five nurses to fill the two positions; there were two settlement managers. Of the Whites working there at the end of 1971, only one was still there in 1973; of those working there during the summer of 1972, only seven were there at the end of 1973. Only one of these many changes was a result of institutional re-arrangements.

Obviously there is a difference between moving from the north to a southern job and remaining in the north but moving from one Arctic settlement to another. Of the eighteen employees who left this one settlement between 1971 and 1973, nine moved to other northern positions and nine left the north altogether. It is possible, however, that the period of very short-term northern employment is ending, and that in the future it will be looked back on as an awkward transitional phase between those long-term old-timers and new long-term northerners. Three factors are at present urging events in that direction. There is a growing number of Whites married to Eskimo girls who are often deeply reluctant to move south. These men tend to be in, or to move into, administrative positions, although often they met their wives while working as a Hudson's Bay Company clerk, a role that encourages contact with local people, and they have made careers in the north that have led to monetary and class advancement. As more Eskimos grow up within the new social milieu, so marriage between them and the Whites in middle-class roles becomes more likely. This is already shown by the increasing number of young teachers who have married Eskimo girls. Secondly, the present employment situation in the south has led an increasing number of candidates to apply for jobs in the north, a trend that is likely to continue, at least in the near future. Thirdly, everyone sees the need for a pool of labour that is familiar with specifically northern problems. There is a growing emphasis in the Eastern Arctic on the use of the Eskimo language, and federal employees are encouraged to learn it. Special skills as well as length and variety of northern experience will no doubt attach more and more Whites to their positions in the north.

But there is no reason to think that the northern bird of passage will altogether disappear. Whereas old-timers suffered restrictions from poor communications and infrequent supply services, and were simply not able to spend much less than a year in the north, northerners today can leave at any time they feel they must. No one who goes north today need fear becoming trapped by an environment that he finds – albeit quite unexpectedly – insufferable; he can, thanks to his large salary and to good communications, easily make his escape back to home in the south. And the figures do show a sizable number of Whites who, after a few months in a northern settlement, feel oppressed and homesick. There will no doubt continue for many years to come to be a complement of those who want to take advantage of the short-term gain in money and personal prestige that the north extends to them, as well as those who merely want to have a brief try at its comfortable adventure.

Southerners and northerners sometimes ask: Why do Whites go north? Behind that question is often concealed an assumption that gives the question its apparent importance. The assumption is that no ordinarily motivated, well-balanced, happy person would want to go north. The question hints at some mental or moral aberration and implies that northern settlements are full of refugees who sought in the north some escape from disturbances in themselves or in their backgrounds. It implies that such persons carry their disturbances with them and it is these disturbances that lead to the difficulties recurrent in settlement life. The assumption is, in plain words, that Whites in the north are crazy and may do harm. If they are not crazy, why are they there? The point deserves consideration. It might, after all, be true.

A White may talk about why he came north, but much more often he is eager to explain why one or other of his colleagues came north. Probably the most frequent attributions of motive are related to money – someone who wants a fast buck goes and finds himself a northern job. Such allegations may be justified to the extent that northern positions are well paid. Although pay levels for many occupations, such as teachers, policemen or nurses, are the same in the north and south, federal and territorial appointments often carry special payments and income supplements. Nurses get their $1,500 additional payment a year; teachers receive a similar yearly addition of between $2,000 and $2,500; administrators receive a 'settlement allowance' of $1,300 a year. Some teachers work additional hours in the adult education programme, which has a permanent but overworked staff in many settlements, and they earned (in 1973–4) about $9.50 per hour on an overtime rate. In some instances teachers may also benefit from the employment of both husband and wife, a practice encouraged because it reduces pressure on limited staff accommodation in the smaller villages.

But the real financial incentive for employment in the north lies in the high rate of savings. Rents are not much lower than elsewhere, but furnishings are provided, and the paucity of retailers and entertainments sharply reduces a family's expenses. Most Whites complain that northern life is expensive, but this must be regarded as a version of a common and widespread phenomenon – the middle-class pretence of poverty. Northern Whites are in a situation that permits them to save, and no doubt most of them save far more than they would or could working and living in the south. But even if this motive is not the first cause of a person's going north (probably most do not realize the scale of the savings that are possible), it is likely to be a reason among those who stay on from year to year. The middle-class Whites do not often speak of their own financial circumstances, nor do they often place money high among the advantages they say they find in the north – but there is a ring of truth to their gossiping attribution of financial greed to their colleagues.

That ring is not very loud, however, and it is muted by other considerations. The White community I am describing is made up mainly of professional people in relatively high-status positions; they are the representatives of southern culture, and embody its intentions and purposes. They are by definition concerned with development in its social, economic or religious aspects, a sort of development that has assimilation as its guiding principle and long-term aim. For the most significant sector of the White population, therefore, to go north is to play a definite part in changing a people – a people, moreover, who live in a remote place. There is a doubly exotic quality to many northerners' lives: the remoteness of the place and the strangeness of the people.

Most Whites enjoy the idea at least of living among Eskimos. Only very few are unqualifiedly idealistic or optimistic about the part they can play in the future of the north, but most feel some deep attraction to the special features of the place and people. There is a romance woven around northern life, a romance nourished by the old-timers' myths and legends as well as by their own knowledge and experience of the present. Aspects of this idealization of life and work feature large in conversations and it provides exhortative and enriching qualities to being in the north. Such romance gives an aura of idealism to the doings of those who enjoy and perpetrate it. It is idealism in the sense that it rests on ideas which yield enthusiasm and even purpose. This may be contradicted or constrained by other aspects of northern life but it does introduce factors beyond and above the mere matter of savings. High salaries and comfortable accommodation may be the necessary conditions for going north, and equally necessary for staying north, but enthusiasm for, and an emotional involvement with, the north, its land and its people, is also important to many people and, more than any other cause, keeps them there.

The complexity of this involvement includes – almost amounts to – the attraction and gratification of being important. Not only do many settlement Whites live a good life materially, they also have a degree of power to which they were never likely to have had a chance to become accustomed had they remained in the south. In the north they may be big fishes in small ponds, or – more appositely – they are big fishes in a pond of small fishes. Again, this advantage may not have been part of the package of attractions that brought a man north in the first place, but it may keep him there. The material aspects of middle-class life are thereby enhanced by access to and participation in a group that is, very self-consciously, a ruling group.

The strengthening of middle-class views among northern Whites has a multitude of ramifications. Based on material goods, family life, socially reinforced identity and active influence, their role is formed of a complex of elements – both for the individual and for the White group as a collective. Their own perception of their role is worth looking at more closely, for it will reveal both their attitudes to the north and a possible objection to the argument thus far.

The objection lies in the fact that the individuals who carry out in the hinterland the purposes of their colonizing nation often themselves have highly developed ideals of service to humanity generally and to the colonized peoples in particular. They often feel charged with personal responsibility for the fate of peoples whom they administer, teach, evangelize or bring within the web of trade. They have been idealistic, that is to say, in bringing to primitive peoples southern-style souls, minds and goods. Although such idealism may at last be discredited in the minds of some, it is still an important element in the attitudes of others towards their roles in the Arctic.

During the summer of 1971, however, a study was made in Frobisher Bay of the attitudes of Whites to their roles and to the future of the north. The findings were striking and revealed a high degree of unease and despondency. The interviewer carrying out this project asked Whites to talk about their role in the north, and 'to offer generalizations about the directions and success of various government programmes'.[8] The general com-

8. This and subsequent quotations in this chapter are from the unpublished report written by Arnold Cragg in fulfilment of a contract with the Northern Science Research Group, Department of Indian Affairs and Northern Development, Ottawa. 1971.

ment the author makes on the basis of more than 100 interviews is particularly striking:

The majority of Whites interviewed ... were gloomy about the present situation and future prospects of the native peoples. Roughly 75 per cent of them believed that native people in general had serious problems of adjustment which they seemed to be making little or no progress towards solving. Less than 25 per cent expressed confidence that the enormous government effort in the north is effectively helping them towards solutions. A significant minority, perhaps 20 per cent, believed that government activity as a whole was exacerbating rather than improving the situation.

A focal problem of the report was 'an examination of why so many Whites are as gloomy as they are'. It was concluded that many of the Whites living in administrative centres such as Frobisher Bay found their principal satisfactions in the social life of such a town: they enjoyed the benefits deriving from its smallness, from easy conviviality, and from their freedom from many of the oppressive features of much southern life. Their roles, therefore, were not valued for features related to bringing the benefits of civilization. In general the Whites of Frobisher Bay did not feel that they were bringing a *good* civilization to the Eskimos, but that they were instead part of a tradition – now well established – of destroying or disrupting Eskimo livelihood and well-being.

It is dangerous to generalize on the basis of fieldwork carried out in an administrative centre. Frobisher Bay bears a relationship to the remoter communities of Baffin Island that a capital city often bears to its hinterland, and in the minds of those living in the remoter communities, it is associated with high and rough living, with drinking, and with novelty of all kinds; it is viewed with disapproval and disgust and invested with qualities which are systematically opposed to the qualities of home life in the small villages. And those views are not altogether wrong. Frobisher Bay is notorious for its high population of social deviants, and many Whites who live and work there are preoccupied with and influenced by the social pathology that surrounds them. They are depressed by what they see and inclined to question the usefulness of their own

roles, especially when they see those roles in the wider frame-
work of modernizing a traditional people. The widespread
pessimism of this kind is well encapsulated by remarks by two
Frobisher Bay resident Whites:

> Maybe we should go right now ... all we're doing is getting them
> keyed up to our rotten way of living ... the idea behind it is one
> great happy family – different cultures all living side by side. Maybe
> it's unattainable. Maybe it is just a crock of horseshit. I don't know.
> Maybe they'd be happier if we just left them alone.

> This may be a doomed culture but we're not replacing it with
> anything worthwhile ... the development of the north has been
> disastrous. They've made every mistake made in the British colonies
> and then some ... If we reappraised the whole thing and said to our-
> selves – let's dip in the bucket and see what we can offer them – if
> we asked ourselves that honestly I can't believe we wouldn't get up
> and leave.

Such cynical views are less often heard from Whites in the remoter, more northerly settlements. They are indeed unhappy
about the prospects of success in the long term, but most of
them feel that some good *could* come of their work if their
sponsoring agency reformed its operations. But there is cynicism
enough to establish that for most people the satisfactions of
living in the far north do not derive from bringing anything
that might be labelled 'the treasures of civilization'. Settlement
Whites of today live in material comfort, enjoy high standards
of living and are men of influence. They enjoy the romance of
being in the north – a romance enhanced by their mobility.
These values are basic to the White community, and they are the
very things that secure the community in its middle-class fortress, barricaded – whether they like it or not – by abundance
of goods, privacy of family, and influence. The next three chapters will look at this distinctive group in its social, attitudinal
and political dimensions. A number of themes will recur
throughout, but the recurrence should help elucidate the remarkable degree to which the Whites are split off from the
people they live among.

4 • The Whites: A Sub-Community

'They have power, comparative luxury, feel superior
in their technological knowledge and, if all else
fails, they are "White men" who by self-definition
are always right. Behaviour towards ethnic
persons is prompted no doubt by attempts to appear
friendly but it is often only recognizable as
facetiousness and favouritism'

– R. W. Dunning, 'Ethnic relations and the marginal man in Canada'

Whites in the smaller settlements are inclined to exaggerate the rigours and hardships of the life they live. Distance from civilization, limitations of diet and the absence of various amenities are forever emphasized. They suggest that life is hard for them, and only because of an almost heroic blend of self-sacrifice, discipline and devotion to the far north are they able to endure at all. Indeed, it is said that many do not endure and that under the stress of such a difficult and impoverished existence, they begin to develop peculiar attitudes and behaviour. There is thus a standard for the society and an aetiology of the pathological conditions that such a society can engender. Members of the permanent White community are alert to deviance and like to explain it by reference to the intrinsic hardships of the life they all claim they are forced to lead. The pathological condition which precipitates deviance has a name: anyone who fails to endure the difficulties of environment and life-style is said to be 'bushed'.

In the most general terms, quietness and withdrawal of any kind are taken as symptoms of a morbid emotional conscience. In the Western Arctic, when the fur trade was prosperous in the 1920s there were many White trappers who lived far out in the bush, well beyond the reach of settlement life. These men, who lived in very real geographical and cultural isolation, were often said to be 'bushed'. Unmotivated and unconstrained by conventional social demands, they 'let themselves go', became dirty and profoundly antisocial, and grew so absorbed in their isolation as to repudiate company even when they encountered it. They no doubt did assume a reserved and withdrawn attitude towards other Whites, and no doubt also evolved idiosyncracies. In the Eastern Arctic today the term 'bushed' has been transferred from its true context to a more definitely social context. A White is bushed when he lives in the settlement but not actively within the White community. In this way that community draws a tight circle round itself. There is a fixed pattern of behaviour in isolated northern settlements, and the deviant who does not respond to its pressures and conform to its standards is systematically excluded.

It is evident that deviance is thus explained and discounted by a device which bears a remarkable similarity to devices prevalent in Euro-Canadian society as a whole. In essence it is on the model of psychological explanations in which antisocial or asocial behaviour is seen as an indication of personal disarray. That is to say, antisocial behaviour is explained in terms of parasocial or nonsocial factors. For a simple example, the school-child who exhibits aggressive attitudes towards his teachers or his school work can be said to be developing a syndrome based on the way in which he has been treated as an infant. In that manner, the burden of explanation is shifted from the actual context of his behaviour to some other sphere, and no part of the explanation concerns the extent to which his teachers and his school work may be systematically eliciting aggression. In the same way, Euro-Canadian society as a whole has tended to see any nonconformity as evidence for personality derangement rather than as a product of socially induced stress. At this level of argument, the common attitude tends to discount the opinions of those who oppose or resist social standards and to allege an irrationality that is taken as evidence for emotional disturbance. Similarly, northern Whites dismiss nonconformists of many kinds as bushed, implicitly attributing nonconformity to rigours of northern life which have become too much for the individual concerned. This dismissal proceeds by exaggerating the rigours of climate and geography as well as by underestimating the tight control which the White community seeks to exert over each of its members, irrespective of what a particular member may himself wish to achieve from his life in the north. A man is bushed who does not live up to the expectations of his fellow Whites.

Examination of the term's usage therefore shows us something of the prevailing idea of normality and reveals the kind of society northern Whites expect to maintain and the sort of behaviour that can and cannot be tolerated. To call someone 'bushed' is to express hostility, but it is also to discount. A person who is bushed cannot be taken seriously, he is no longer held fully responsible for his actions, he is thought to have partially lost his reason. Thus his acts of protest and his antisocial dispositions are as irrelevant as the irrationalities of the mentally disturbed. The White community protects itself against the possible critic from within by collectively insisting on the irrationality of those who do not conform to customary proprieties, and in this way it also asserts its standards.

The Whites expect solidarity. Each member of the community is expected to show goodwill and friendliness towards others. Any failure to get along with others breaches an informal social code. A man who expresses hostility openly or allows his resentment of others to influence his everyday social life is categorized as bushed. In one settlement, for example, relations among the teachers degenerated. By mid-winter, the school principal was so hostile to one of his colleagues that he felt unable to have any social dealing with him. He would not speak to him when they passed in the street and in school he communicated by written messages. Other teachers sided against the principal, saying that he must be bushed. A year later they still spoke of the time when the school principal had been bushed; they did not reflect on the causes of his anger nor did they seem willing (in the course of ordinary conversation) to consider the possibility of his being justified. Rather, they considered that no amount of justification should lead to the *expression* of anger – that is, the principal's anger was one thing, but his refusal to keep a social face was another, and it was this breach of convention that put him beyond any possible justification. He was bushed because he had allowed his anger to intrude into everyday life, not because he was angry. He had failed to maintain the degree of self-repression which facilitated the maintenance of easy social relations within the White community as a whole. Even the principal's closest friend, when recalling the situation, simply commented that 'poor old X had been a bit bushed that winter'. It was much the same as explaining some social indiscretion by drunkenness. The abnormality of the behaviour was, in its way, the excuse. By being bushed, the offender was beyond the range of normal judgement, and the criticism meant that forgiving and forgetting would be easy and quick.

Another example helps to illustrate the point. A young teacher arrived in a settlement to take up his first job. Arrangements had miscarried and he found his house was not ready and his possessions had not arrived. Consequently he was obliged to stay with another official. Very quickly relations between them became strained, and the newcomer was subjected to a series of social snubs. On one occasion he was conspicuously not invited to a dinner party, even though it took place in the house where he was living, and included all the other Whites in the settlement. He made no secret of his anger, and certainly did not conceal his hostility towards his host. Subsequently he was treated with disdain by two other Whites in the community, and once again he reacted openly and vocally, asking them to say why they were behaving in such a disagreeable manner. When he found that they were unwilling to discuss the matter with any honesty, he avoided them and often made a point of not attending social gatherings at which they were likely to be present. Since most of the social gatherings in that settlement included all the Whites living there, it followed that he was conspicuously absent from almost all parties and festivities. As the disputes between this newcomer and other Whites in the settlement became intense, sympathies were expressed for one or another's attitude. But the newcomer ultimately found no sympathy and was repeatedly dismissed as having been 'bushed before he got here'. Of course it was freely admitted that he was quite right to be indignant at the way he had been treated, but that in effect was no part of the final judgement. He was bushed because he had caused confrontations. However, a few months later, when the newcomer was better settled, a strong friendship grew between him and the official who had pre-cipitated hostilities and who had been most vocal in deprecating his temporary lodger as bushed.

In similar fashion, any White who is thought to be turning his back on the White community as a whole is held to be bushed. Sometimes a person can no longer endure the round of parties and dinners that occupy a central place in the community's social life. It may not be easy to refuse the invitations, but it is harder still to make a show of having a good time. The result often enough is a token appearance, a subdued manner, and evident withdrawal from others. Such withdrawal is not readily tolerated. The quiet guest is quizzed, teased, tempted in every possible way to a fuller participation in the event. Should he maintain his distance and remain quiet, he is quickly stig-matized as one who is on the verge of breakdown. Other Whites become urgently anxious about his condition, anticipate dis-aster, and suggest that perhaps it is about time for him to 'get out of the north'. Because he has repudiated the White com-munity, he is obviously bushed.

This repudiation of the Whites is, of course, often combined with involvement with Eskimos. Northern Whites' inclination to discourage too much fraternization with local people has been well documented,[1] and participation in Eskimo life is seen as a threat to the purposes of the White presence in the north. Such an attitude is a likely correlate of White concern with re-forming Eskimo customs, a by-product of that missionary zeal which saw in native eating and living habits a threat to health and a source of immorality. It was, after all, the supposed im-purity of Eskimo life that had brought many Whites north to introduce southern institutions and services. Essentially, the White community is conscious of its distance from the Eskimos; it follows that a too-intimate association between Whites and Eskimos is a threat. Of course few of the Whites do spend very

1. See, for example, Dunning (1959), Vallee (1967), Parsons (1970) and Smith (1971).

much time in association with Eskimos, but there are some Whites engaged in research of various kinds who have chosen to, or feel that they must, mingle freely with local people. Such men are sometimes said to be bushed, and often tend to be excluded from the White community by virtue of their occupation.

There are two contexts – alcohol and sex – in which Whites are most often criticized for their contact with Eskimos. Drinking and drunkenness are an important part of northern social life. White newcomers are expected to drink; any shortage of liquor invariably gives rise to much lamentation, and a lack of it reveals the Whites' deep sense of isolation and disadvantage. Only with abundant alcohol can the Whites entertain each other. Yet, as in most societies, there are clear and exacting conventions surrounding drinking and drunkenness. The community maintains limits beyond which liquor should not spread. A man who drinks heavily during the week or is drunk at work becomes the object of disapproval. And the drunk who grows morose or aggressive is frowned on at first, and should such behaviour recur, he is eventually dismissed as bushed. But the most important delimitation is between Whites and Eskimos. The White community as a whole strongly discourages inter-racial drinking. Any White who drinks with Eskimo friends or invites Eskimos to drink with him is suspect. Should he drink with Eskimos indiscriminately, that is with any Eskimo who visits him, rather than only with those who may be more acceptable to other Whites, he is abhorred.

Jim arrived in the settlement during the winter. From his first week, he was under suspicion, for he arrived with a case of hard liquor and proceeded to drink it in a style that showed no regard for local White convention. He was drunk some week-day mornings, and he shared his liquor with anyone who chose to visit him. The longer he stayed, the more flagrant was his disregard for the local drinking customs. Jim was a spree drinker and, like all spree drinkers, he enjoyed the liquor while it was there, sharing generously and abandoning everything for the sake of a party. Sometimes he was away from work for two or three days. Gradually the other Whites developed a keen dislike for him. He was pointedly not asked to parties and was treated with polite disdain by the majority of the White community. Disdain and dislike turned into bitter hostility when it became apparent that Jim had no intention of curbing his wish to share liquor freely with all comers, including Eskimos. One White official tried to persuade Jim that he should change his ways, arguing that he was a dangerous influence on the Eskimos with whom he habitually got drunk. When criticized in this way, Jim readily acknowledged his fault and swore he would mend his ways. But the next case of liquor to arrive seemed to blur his memory of such assurances, and the attraction of another all-comers' party was not easy to resist: a spree was quickly under way. As it became evident to all that Jim's ways were not amenable to social pressure, he was isolated more completely. Attempts were made to have him transferred to another settlement, although throughout his stay some said that he would be better off out of the north altogether, since he was so conspicuously bushed.

Far beyond the perimeters of acceptable White behaviour are most sexual relationships with Eskimos. A man who discreetly woos a local girl is tolerated, and a man who selects a pretty and acculturated girl for his wife may be encouraged to introduce her into the White community. But anyone who gives himself to an Eskimo girl on *her* terms, who allows that relationship to lead him away from the society of other Whites and into the Eskimo world, is said to be bushed. More particularly, any White who decides to leave his job but remains in the north with his Eskimo wife or girlfriend outside the White community, without an acknowledged role in one or another of the White institutions, is seen to be in dire trouble. Such repudiation of social values can easily result in withdrawal of all the White enclave's support and services. One man who married an Eskimo and decided to live in his wife's village, with his wife's family, in the hope of earning a living there, perhaps as a trapper, could find out nothing about local movements of aeroplanes. Many Whites seemed to take malicious pleasure in his difficulties in trying to arrange travel and told one another that no White agencies would give him a job; after all, he was thoroughly bushed.

In his study of Baker Lake, Frank Vallee comments on the strong pressures the White community exerts on newcomers. They are expected to conform to an exacting code of behaviour, while failure to conform 'touches off immediate reactions, such as gossip, scolding, ridicule'. Vallee does not discuss the notion of a person's being bushed, but he emphasizes the relationship between demands for conformity and that deviance which is feared essentially because Whites feel it will 'make them look bad in the eyes of the Eskimo'. He links this to the Whites' role in socialization, as 'exemplars' for the Eskimos. Having defined 'socialization' as the operation of a sanctions system on a people who are held to be socially inadequate and evolutionarily inferior, he writes:

We can say that nearly all Kabloona [Whites] in the Baker Lake region assume the role of socializer *vis-à-vis* the Eskimo there. With the exception of a few individuals who are not directly involved in Eskimo affairs, every Kabloona encountered feels impelled to change at least some features of Eskimo behaviour and bring them into line with his or her conception of the desirable person ... We refer here to the missionaries, teachers, nurse, NSO [Northern Service Officer, i.e. the administrator], and RCMP. However, other Kabloona, such as the spouses of these persons, some DOT [Department of Transport] and HBC personnel, also feel impelled to adopt a teaching and protective attitude with the Eskimos, young and old.[2]

Vallee's research was carried out in Keewater District between 1959 and 1961. My findings suggest that Whites in small northern settlements of today have in common, and so gain solidarity by sharing, many of the attitudes towards their roles that Vallee describes. It is that solidarity and sense of role which in many respects determines their resistance towards any member of the community who appears, on these criteria, to be deviant.

In a small community interaction among the Whites is neces-

2. Vallee (1967), p. 129.

sarily multifarious. They constantly meet one another as they go about their daily routine: much mutual aid and cooperation are needed despite the technological elaboration of White northern life-styles. Whenever Whites meet each other they tend to stop and talk. In similarly convivial manner, one family or household is usually quick to look to others for aid or provisions. Also, there is much casual visiting. It is indeed surprising, therefore, to find that a large sector of the Whites' social life is self-consciously organized and that parties are very important. They reveal the divisiveness of the community, which needs to be overcome so that the community may express the solidarity that is felt to be so necessary.

Newcomers to the north are likely to be surprised by parties that are explicitly for the Whites and which deliberately include all members of the White *bloc*. The exclusion of a particular member from such a party can only be seen as an insult, the expression of collective disapproval. Often these parties are occasioned by visits from senior officials, or by the departure of a member of the community, or by a seasonal event (Christmas or the end of the school year). In contrast to such collective occasions, there are also parties that are limited to circles of friends or colleagues. Thus the teachers might have a party, or two families may get together for a dinner. This kind of festivity is very common, and occupies many evenings of each month. Often these restricted parties follow closely on the delivery by air of liquor to the settlement, and heavy drinking is more common during them than in the case of the inclusive occasions. Both inclusive and exclusive parties are limited almost solely to Whites. Only rarely did I see local Eskimos at these events, and Whites and Eskimos alike felt their presence to be exceptional and uneasy.

In sociological terms, parties are often the occasion for some relaxation of established convention. Or, if not so much for that, then they can be seen as occasions for displacement of a restraining by a releasing conventionality. Given the dominant role played by alcohol on such occasions, a party provides an opportunity to contravene those inhibiting restraints which order everyday life. Drunken behaviour is itself orderly, of course, but its orderliness is different, and there are often clear opportunities for behaviour which in everyday terms (or in sober terms) would be characterized as profoundly uninhibited. A drunken party is thus the escape – though it is as much an escape *into* as *from*. It might be expected, therefore, that such parties would be characterized by deviation from the conventionalities of everyday settlement life. For example, it might be expected that parties would allow some greater conviviality between Whites and Eskimos and would effect some reversal in the everyday White dominance. Instead, parties are the clearest and most forceful affirmation of southern ways. At parties the Whites are on show to one another, and accordingly are anxious to affirm their good qualities – the willingness to have a good time, exchange jokes and make amusing conversation. But, more significantly, they also include ability to drink heavily without becoming too drunk, be drunk without becoming anti-social (i.e. violent, morose or aggressively sexual); and for a host or hostess they provide the opportunity for abundant and impressive generosity. Eskimos have no place at such functions.

Parties are heavily middle class in style. If they are centred on a dinner, the dinner will usually be elaborate and somewhat formal. The table is laid 'tastefully'; there may even be candles and French wine. The food is good and the cooking subtle. ('We landed at Fort Chimo at 7.30 and five minutes later we were sitting . . . eating baked ham, croissants and apple pie.')[3] Shortages in one element or another often make the meal incomplete by the southern standards of middle-class *haute cuisine*, but such gaps in the ritual are not overlooked: possible social failure or omission is obviated by dropping a comment on the rigours of northern life which reveal to guests that the host is 'failing' because of circumstances rather than ignorance. If the party is centred on drinking, the participants usually exhibit a restrained and orderly drunkenness. In one settlement, the Whites usually danced as they drank, but even when the dancers were quite drunk, they scrupulously refrained from either overt sexual or physical aggression. Emphasis was always on the order typical of middle-class or petit-bourgeois southern life-

3. Iglauer (1966), p. 2.

styles, and because these communities have such a low tolerance for deviance, that order is exacting indeed. A Hudson's Bay Company employee once remarked to me that he found the restraining and inhibiting atmosphere unendurable during parties where people were drinking and dancing. He developed a habit of going to sleep at them.

Whites generally are anxious to give an impression of solid middle-classness, an easier task for some than others, and one that introduces a special tension into much casual social life. The community is beset with gossip, and everyone knows that the conversation among any group of Whites is usually taken up with criticism of other Whites. Gossip and criticism being so widespread, everyone attempts to maintain appearances, a task at which they often fail through anxious overstatement. Given the general situation, there is not much ease, and it is therefore not surprising that the White community tends to be divided into a number of cliques banded together in much the same way and for much the same reasons as people elsewhere in Canadian society. Educational levels, class origins and ethnicity play very important parts in the formation of cliques, and there is abundant reason to think that the class position (or aspirations) of a White more surely determines his choice of friends than any other factor. This evidence includes the fact that the traders and police, who are usually from lower-middle or working-class backgrounds, have less status within the White community than other agency employees. Friendly relations may exist between these two and between them and the other groups, but the policeman is usually not invited to dinners and parties given by the more certainly middle-class Whites in the community. Although such generalizations are uncertain when based on so small a population it is perhaps all the more surprising that they do appear to fit the realities of settlement life and that I found surprisingly few exceptions to them.

More evidence for the discriminatory attitudes among Whites can be seen in their reactions to the transients who pass through the settlements. Inevitably there are numerous officials from regional headquarters who visit either the agencies or the Eskimos for whom they bear administrative responsibility.

Often officials pass quickly through the settlement in groups. A plane brings in a cluster of important people, meetings are arranged, issues are discussed, and the plane leaves again. Often these are one-day trips and very rarely do they last much longer than two days. They are, however, attended by much ceremony. To understand the nature of such visits, one must realize that in virtually all the small settlements communications with other settlements are entirely in the hands of Whites. Information about the movements of aircraft, like the aircraft themselves, is essentially within the sphere of White activity, and Whites usually arrange visitors' accommodation. When an official plane arrives, it is met by members of the White community, and the persons on it are escorted to one or another of the White houses within the settlement or to transient quarters. Then the officials are entertained, perhaps at a somewhat formal dinner party, and escorted to whatever encounter they are expecting to have with the local Eskimo people. Should they be staying overnight, it is likely that a party for all the Whites in the settlement will be arranged.

The more important the party, the more elaborate is the response of the White community. When the Commissioner of the Northwest Territories makes one of his official visits, for example, the White community feels collectively obliged to entertain him and his entourage. Less senior visitors find a less grand and less collective reception, but the tendency remains for the White community to affirm its solidarity with and before institutional visitors. So strong is this tendency that it persists even when it clearly interferes with the stated purpose of the official visiting, and it clearly inhibits and limits the possibility of official contact with the Eskimos.

It is of course perfectly normal for lower personnel in hierarchical institutions to show much enthusiastic hospitality to their superiors. Equally, it is not surprising to find junior personnel in one agency showing a respectful enthusiasm about visits by relatively senior personnel in other agencies. In a wide sense, all the personnel in all the agencies are colleagues, and are likely to welcome one another with generosity. More elaborate shows of generosity are, by the same token, the signs of a normal desire to impress senior officials as favourably as possible. These features of White social life exhibit conventions that are common in the south. It might, however, be argued that such conventions are misplaced in the northern settlements because their consequences widen the gulf between the representatives of White agents and Eskimos and therefore impede or prevent the proper achievement of many of those agencies' stated purposes.

To this last argument one could reply that the White community, which is so small and believes itself to be so isolated from mainstream satisfactions, would naturally enough wish to open its doors to any White visitors. And there is truth in that reply: many Whites are extremely hospitable and welcome any visitors to the settlement: the north has a reputation for hospitality to strangers. But there are respects in which this reputation is not fully deserved: two groups of visitors do not find a ready welcome, but are rather the objects of suspicion and unfriendliness, and come easily to be objects of quite startlingly bitter resentment.

French-Canadian construction workers constitute the first such group. Obviously the prejudices as well as social conventions of southern Canadian society as a whole will find full expression in the White communities of the Arctic. Problems that divide the larger society are not likely to be submerged or resolved by the abnormalities of small settlement life. Rather, they tend to appear there in stark relief.

Teams of construction workers arrive in many Eastern Arctic settlements in the early summer. Many of them are primarily composed of French-Canadians and range in size from one or two specialists to groups of ten. During two summers I was able to observe the reception given these workmen and heard the resident Whites' indignant complaints against them. In most settlements such seasonal workers live in a transient centre, where they provide for themselves as best they can. Usually they bring with them most of the foodstuffs they are going to need during their stay, and they are anxious to maintain a supply of liquor from the south. In these respects they are like all other Whites who work for regular agencies, but unlike the permanent residents, migrant workers do not exclude Eskimos from their quarters. Rather, they show a marked readiness to entertain visitors from the native community. The supplies the workmen bring with them are plentiful and, by northern standards, exotic, and Eskimos visit enthusiastically. The construction workers are often young, vigorous and socially extroverted: visiting them is good fun.

Social exchange between these workers and Eskimos is a common subject of fierce criticism by agency Whites. From their point of view the construction workers are profoundly deviant. They do not seek to maintain face and propriety in front of Eskimos; rather, their life is made more joyous and interesting precisely because they had abandoned those proprieties – or perhaps had never been concerned with them at all. So the permanent Whites are angered by the nature and scope of communication that quickly grows up between workmen and local people. They are convinced that the workers are feeding liquor to each and every Eskimo who visits them, and that the one purpose of this debauch is to persuade the girls to sleep with them. There is some truth in these allegations, for no one denies that such parties are indeed often drunken and that liaisons do spring up between workers and local girls, but the nature of permanent Whites' indignation reveals more about their own attitudes than about the realities of the transient workers' way of life. Any sign of a festive spirit is seen as abandoned behaviour; sexual relations between a worker and an Eskimo girl are seen as the result of cynical treachery that will result in the corruption of the girl and of the community.

Not all construction workers become involved with local people. Some are unable to overcome language difficulties, others have no interest in liaisons of any kind with Eskimos. Moreover, it sometimes happens that a worker is alone or with one colleague, and is not well placed to maintain a round of parties. Yet even in those cases, White residents tend to exclude such visitors from their social lives. More accurately, they remain aloof: construction workers are not merely looked at askance for their dealings with Eskimos, they are more generally looked down on. They are rarely invited to participate in the social events of the White community, and little interest is shown in who they are and where they come from. This reaction obviously contrasts sharply with attitudes exhibited towards official visitors. It is as if the French-Canadian workmen were not quite considered White, an attitude that evokes the outlines of class consciousness. Certainly that sense of superiority, combined with anxious nervousness, which is at the core of the attitude towards construction workers strongly resembles mainstream Canadian attitudes towards the French-Canadian working class.

An interpretation of these attitudes in terms of class consciousness and class antipathy is reinforced by internal qualities of the White communities that have already been mentioned. Although the community exhibits considerable solidarity, there is some stratification into cliques. Although these cliques are often bonded by considerations of common interest, or ethnicity, there is a significant division between the cliques of middle-class persons and those which are predominantly lower-middle or working class. The majority of Whites occupy positions which are essentially middle class. This is reinforced by the sense of solidarity in relation to Eskimos as well as by the sense of position in relation to important and more senior outsiders. It is also reinforced by association with the Government and its policies, which many of the agents see themselves as actively engaged in implementing. Yet the HBC and the RCMP have established traditions of ruggedness in their northern service, and have not fostered as much concern with the comforts of life. Both have recruited their employees from working-class sections of southern society, and there is a cult among their personnel even today of toughness and simplicity.[4] It is no coincidence that neither HBC nor RCMP employees are given northern positions if they are married and they have always

4. 'Five years before we met him, the Hudson's Bay Company had sent Bob Cruickshank to the Belchers to establish a trading post. He went alone, the first and only white inhabitant of the islands, living in close association with some two hundred chestnut-hued Eskimos, ready to be king, Socrates, Big-Boss White-Man, and great inspirer to any lazy hunters of foxes. Failing this, he was to keep his head if he could' (Twomey, 1942, p. 175).

been strongly discouraged from marrying while in the north. Those government personnel who tend to dominate settlement life regard employees of the less middle-class agencies with some disdain. There is a social gulf between them that seems to be based simply on difference in class position. HBC and RCMP personnel tend to enjoy a lesser status for reasons of social class: their positions as shop assistant and policeman are socially inferior to those of teacher, administrator, missionary and nurse. In understanding the configuration of social cliques within the White community, the class factor is important.

This picture of White social styles and self-valuation would not be complete without some account of how a visiting social scientist is received into the established community. While it is not easy to generalize about such a subject, most social scientists who have worked in the Canadian north have encountered hostility during field trips. Particularly in the case of social anthropologists, social scientists tend to stay comparatively long periods in one community, and they set out to discover details of social life that are usually not apparent to the settlement Whites themselves. The arriving social scientist has no clear relationship to any of the established institutions, and therefore he cannot be expected to take any predictable position in the social life of the community. His location in the informal hierarchy is as uncertain as his dependence upon the established agencies.

Two difficulties thus arise automatically. First, resident Whites become anxious about which circle of friends and colleagues (which clique) is going to adopt this newcomer. If the settlement is too small to form such groups, then anxiety can quickly arise about whether the newcomer will integrate into the White community at all. Secondly, and much more importantly, resident Whites know that social scientists regard full and easy relations with Eskimos as the *sine qua non* of their work and are therefore unlikely to pay much, if any, attention to prevailing conventions about the limits of inter-ethnic contact. Sometimes this anxiety is inflamed by the social scientist's competence in the Eskimo language. Obviously, anthropological field methods oppose frontiers between Whites and Eskimos and cannot be limited by how agency Whites see their roles as socializers of the Eskimos. The social scientist threatens to upset a number of local applecarts. If a distance between Eskimos and Whites is felt by the latter to be vital for effective realization of their purposes in the settlements, then a social scientist can quickly be seen as an enemy.

In this respect the social scientist is like the man who is bushed, or like the migrant worker who disregards middle-class proprieties in dealings with local people. But the social scientist cannot so easily be dismissed. He has at least two stamps of approval. In the first place, he is, by occupation, a *bona fide* middle-class person and commands some respect and status on that score alone. In the second place, he represents an academic tradition that is paid some respect by mainstream southern society; he is also in some measure invulnerable to the disapproval that is the principal weapon in northern social control. Moreover, Whites are conscious that a social scientist spends his time uncovering information to which northern Whites usually have little or no access, a fact worsened by the confidentiality of that information, which can act only as an irritant to Whites who love gossip and are already nervous at having such an investigator in their midst.

It is inevitable that social scientists should encounter ambivalence: hospitality and some friendliness from the middle-class Whites can be easily and quickly replaced by suspicion and hostility. If the social scientist slightly mismanages so complex and problematic a relationship, he can easily inflame local officials against himself and can find he is ostracized by the White community as a whole. He may also find that particular White officials can express their suspicion and hostility by obstructing his work. The mismanagement of the relationship typically takes the form of incomplete participation in the social life of the White community. I have already said that all the Whites in the settlement are expected to play their part in the round of parties and, in the course of these events, to demonstrate their fundamental solidarity. It is scarcely possible for anyone whose highest priorities include easy solidarity with the local Eskimos to fulfil those expectations.

Whites often criticize one another by saying that 'X just can't get on with the Eskimos' or 'the Eskimos don't like X at all'. In this criticism as in others, Whites have arranged each other in an invisible hierarchy, with positions determined by whether or not Eskimos like them. Since contact between most Whites and Eskimos is either minimal or absent, the basis for this judgement is uncertain. Quite simply, the Whites do not know whom the Eskimos do and do not like. The social scientist may therefore represent a very special and specific threat: he just might be discovering whom the Eskimos really do and do not like. Anxious on this score, Whites press investigators to say how they and others are judged by the local population. They know that social scientists carry on confidential conversations with the local people, and feel threatened by a refusal to disclose information.

Conflict within the White community is a recurrent feature of settlement life. Everything in this chapter points to the conclusion that conflict is likely and not easily resolved. Low tolerance for deviance from exacting social demands inevitably gives rise to difficult and uncertain relationships. The tiny communities are composed of people who do not necessarily have much in common. Indeed, there is a likelihood – given the variety of agencies for which they work – that even when they do have class position in common, they will still tend to feel in competition. Given also that appearances are a principal concern of the community, strains are many and are compounded by internal criticism. Some Whites are not at ease with their role in the community and criticize others for mismanaging their roles, or even for accepting them at all. This factor is assuming increased significance; northern Whites are no more impervious to criticism of interracial and colonial situations than to any other aspect of life in the larger society wherein they have their intellectual and social roots. Self-consciousness, doubt, and ambivalence about the kind of role they have are all likely to foment mutually critical attitudes.

It is the main argument here that factors of social class and class consciousness are important guidelines to understanding the social formation of the White sub-community. But it must not be forgotten that small communities of this kind are inevitably vulnerable to a range of social difficulties that go beyond those arising from class factors. Perhaps the point can best be made by suggesting that relevance of class factors will increase directly in relation to the number of personnel in any settlement. Small settlements will have difficulties that arise from smallness and from idiosyncracies of individual members of the community, whereas larger settlements will form cliques and develop internal problems more directly arising from the class consciousness of the various personnel. Yet the general thesis can stand: the Whites of the far north are class-conscious to a remarkable degree, and the nature and minutiae of their social life are informed by that consciousness. In a subsequent discussion, we shall see how orthodox middle-class consciousness informs attitudes that Whites have developed towards contemporary Eskimos and how these attitudes in turn mould relationships between Eskimos and Whites.

5 • White Attitudes to the Eskimo

> Behind this roomful of strange, intent men in a
> London auction room I seemed to see other men,
> the wild, uncouth men of youthful romance, out in
> the savage places of the earth ... Hunters! Trappers!
> ... We have all longed to be trappers, we have
> all longed ... to crack the ice on Great Whale River
> before we could catch our breakfast ...
>   'Any advance on £350?'
>   The howling of dogs, the pine trees in shrouds;
> and then – silence.
>   'Four hundred. Any advance?'
>   The green glitter of ice and the drama of a man
> battling the elements, fighting solitude; stark,
> primitive, his mind following the minds of beasts ...
>   'Five hundred. Any advance?'
>   Forty below zero! The cracking of whips, the
> racing dog-team with its laden sledge.
>   'Going, going, gone!'
>
> > – A story in the *Beaver*, magazine of the
> > Hudson's Bay Company, 1925

Social contact between northern Whites and Eskimos is minimal
or absent. There is scant basis for everyday sociability; cultural
and class differences are compounded by a serious language
problem. Circumscribed by the paraphernalia of material comfort and social influence, the White community is self-contained
and remote from the lives of the real northerners. Beyond the
material and political dimensions of the wall around them,
settlement Whites express a number of intriguing and initially
perplexing attitudes towards Eskimo people. A discussion of
these attitudes will review the northern situation in its most
general terms. This chapter, then, will proceed from small-scale,
quite straightforward factual matters to more abstract and
theoretical issues, from a sketch of actual details of behaviour
to some theoretical questions of colonialism and class structure.
    On those rare occasions when Whites and Eskimos do interact

socially and casually, on occasions that are not formal and ordered by the conventions of work situations, most Whites are excruciatingly embarrassed. They do not know how to talk or what manner to adopt; they become nervous and self-conscious; they suffer from a painful shame and confusion. They exaggerate their gestures and raise their voices, showing in every aspect of their social being an acute and pervasive unease. Language problems are well known to lead to agitation and raised voices, as though volume might eventually prevail against barriers to understanding. But shouting is only one of many ways in which a person strikes out against the confusion and personal disarray that so often arises in unknown or unfamiliar situations. Shouting itself does not reveal very much about the attitudes Whites have towards Eskimos in the Canadian north. It is the Whites' excruciation, their embarrassment, their general unease that indicate the nature and extent of these attitudes.

In such encounters, Whites show an urgent desire to please and to be sure that the Eskimo feels liked and respected. This is probably, at least in part, a consequence of Whites' anxiety about being liked themselves, and their anxiety receives many expressions. I have already said that Whites are often competitive over the Eskimos' affection. They frequently denigrate colleagues by saying, 'The Eskimos don't like him, you know.' And they are anxious to hear from any Eskimo speaker news of whom the Eskimos may have criticized among themselves. In a general, perhaps metaphysical sense, Whites are obsequious to Eskimos: what the Eskimo says and believes about them is a matter of great importance. This obsequiousness manifests itself in dealings between a White and an individual Eskimo, but it is a consequence of an attitude towards the Eskimos *in general*. Here, response to an Eskimo is moulded by a concern with or anxiety about phenomena that transcend the individual. The individual is, after all, the representative of a class or a race. But in most familiar social situations, through the recurrence of daily encounters a person's individuality becomes an effective thing in itself, temporarily qualifying the collective to which he belongs. But in the Arctic, in an *informal* encounter, the White is faced with an Eskimo outside any familiar context. Such an encounter is atypical, and its unfamiliarity effectively means that there is no formula for handling it, no procedure whereby communication can be established, and little or no exchange between the two personalities involved. It thus happens in such an encounter that the White sees an Eskimo only as an Eskimo. He is not employee, colleague or friend; rather, he is simply a representative of the Eskimo people; he is an abstraction. It is hardly surprising therefore that anxiety and unease should characterize such encounters.

This abstraction is bound up with the stereotypes that northern Whites have of the Eskimo, his personality and culture. Those stereotypes are worth detailing, although they are not coherent and their elements are sometimes mutually irreconcilable, and embrace now one and now another reconstruction of things Eskimo. But a number of features predominate: it is widely believed by Whites that fully traditional culture has endured essentially intact, but is suffering disorganization in the context of the present institutional situation. Whites respect the society for its effectiveness in adversity, an effectiveness built on physical and mental toughness, on endurance and on an ability finally to go beyond endurance to an actual indifference to privation and pain. Originally Eskimo society was, according to this stereotype, self-contained and nomadic, little bands of people drifting across immense distances, recurrently beset by starvation and disaster. There was no social organization, no leadership, no authority. This way of life created a people both tough and benign: they smiled and laughed, even as they struggled against all odds to endure. It is widely believed that Eskimos were indifferent to death or accepted it willingly, cheerfully; it was a world in which more tender human sentiment had no place; with calm acceptance of necessity, with the clear view of pragmatism, they abandoned their old and killed their female infants. According to Rasmussen:

Their habits and customs are so entirely different to ours, and, in particular, their time-honoured infanticide, or extermination of 'superfluous girls' – here [among the Copper Eskimo] as well as among the Netsilik Eskimos – is so diametrically opposed to all forms of society that the rivalry about women, and the many cases of vendetta which naturally follow in its wake, give birth to morals that are peculiar to these careless and temperamental children of nature.[1]

It was also believed that the weak and incompetent, being burdens on a group that was already (or always) overcome by adversity, were ruthlessly eliminated. The view is simple in its entirety: individuals in the collective adaptation of such a society would not develop moral or emotional subtlety or complexity. Nor could they develop any control or refinements of sexual practices. Innocent and simple-minded, the native was, according to this stereotype, in a state of nature until the Whites introduced them to the confusions and complications of civilized life. The 'real Eskimo' is thought to have been brutal, too, able to kill with equanimity and face death without fear. There was equanimity also in his deep reluctance to discipline children and in his refusal to become angry. But, we are told, such simplicity had its counterpart in naïve improvidence: surplus was never saved, and consumption in times of plenty was wasteful. Such improvidence revealed irrationality as well as naïvety: stories are told that illustrate how Eskimos would not deviate from traditional behaviour, techniques or movements even to avoid starvation. Such stories aim to reveal the degree to which such irrationality was irreducible: it would not yield even to the threat of death.

According to this stereotyped view, such traits were bred into the very marrow of the Eskimos, and they are not easily displaced by modernization. This is a direct counterpart to a familiar view that a White presents of his own circumstance: 'It took *us* 3,000 years to get this far.' And the corollary is implicit: 'How can you expect *them* to get there in only ten or even fifty years?' It follows that every Eskimo is believed to contain in himself, at the central core of his being, an essential Eskimo-ness, a quality that can be finally dissipated by evolution alone. Meanwhile, in the shorter run, for the present millennium or so, there must remain somewhere in the Eskimo the tough, smiling, naïve, ultimately irrational soul, which, animal-like, is deeply attracted to roaming the open spaces of the limitless tundra and ice.

1. Rasmussen (1932), p. 17.

Whites develop and maintain this view of the Eskimos, as well as broader theories of human life according to which such a stereotype might be reformed even in casual conversation. Discussion of the nature of the original or true Eskimo is a main preoccupation among northern Whites, and it reveals in some part their enthusiasm for the place and touches the monotonous repetitions of their everyday life with *some* magic. Many of the qualities they attribute to Eskimo society figure in books and articles, but the context in which the stereotype is given its real life is in the northerners' story-swapping. Conversational exchange of stories is a significant part of social life in any community, but in the north the frequency with which stories are told about Eskimos is extraordinary, and the common interest in them is a vital feature of social exchange among the Whites.

Those stories, usually second or third hand, dwell on the more exotic aspects of Eskimo life; they are filled with wonder at the Eskimo's bizarre ways and focus on revelation of his true character. They are *illustrations*. Repeated, retold, reworked, they are a confused form of folklore: each storyteller shapes events and meanings according to his own preoccupations. Too young and unformed to be true folktales (they have not yet achieved recognized stability in the telling), they are nonetheless mythical; their significance does not lie in whether, or the degree to which, they are objectively true or false. Considered alongside more reliable accounts of traditional Eskimo life, or viewed in the light of northern history, they must be judged to be inaccurate. But the teller of such stories does not attempt to judge accuracy, he is not concerned with the possibilities or niceties of objective validity; he has not studied the books and articles. The stories and views expressed by northern Whites are the product of a living social context; they inform and are being informed by it, although the causes may, at first glance, seem hidden and obscure. Although the views and judgements of social scientists and other students may be at odds with that context, the stories nevertheless have their place and give a special atmosphere to the distant social world of the Whites in northern Canada.

Stereotyped views of Eskimo personality and culture are much enriched by the Whites' view of the northern land and climate.

Indeed, it is in this context that the efficacy of Eskimo personality and culture are judged. And 'the land' is a further stereotype, as detailed and as mythical as the Whites' conception of the Eskimo.

Most northerners regard the north as the margin of the universe; it is at the edge of the possible extension of life, and at times and in places it seems to go even beyond the possibilities of life. Many believe that each degree northwards is a degree closer to the margins – or beyond them. Whites are accordingly preoccupied with how far north a particular place is and with who has been where; there is a special attraction in venturing even farther north, and there is pride in anyone's description of the farthest points north they have been. This preoccupation reveals a common acceptance of a worldview in which climate grades from south to north in degrees that are numerical and exact and are accepted as measures of harshness. Such a view of northern conditions does not correspond with Eskimo judgements nor with comparatively hard data on game-resources and temperature.[2] Such details, some imagined and some real, fascinate northern Whites. Officials from settlements all over the Arctic vie with one another in comparing the extremities of darkness, temperature, wind speed, length of winter, etc., that they have experienced.

In accounts of Eskimos and Eskimo life, however, storytellers emphasize coldness and Arctic wildness in their more directly human aspects: the snow, ice and blizzards, like the darkness and barrenness of the place, combine to make life barely possible. Whites like to recall journeys they have made, during which they encountered almost insuperable difficulties. Stories of death narrowly averted build up the impression that the treacherous Arctic is ever ready to claim its victims, that any intelligent, prudent person would hardly venture far from home in such a place and that such journeys in the wild are best left to the brave, stoic and insensitive Eskimo. The barren and unfriendly lands of the far north are regarded by most Whites as

2. Although it is true that the farther one goes north the longer is the period of winter darkness, temperatures in the High Arctic are higher than those of the mainland Arctic tundra and sub-arctic regions.

scarcely fit for human habitation and as plainly unfit for civilized life.

As Whites tell stories of the land and its people, they sketch out pictures that are broadly accepted by their colleagues. There is among them a general consensus on northern images and stereotypes. Newcomers are not likely to discover any other picture of the north for themselves, and the prevalent view is established by much repetition. Such a consensus is exactly what might be expected among persons who share so many common interests. The great social and intellectual distance between Whites and Eskimos is emphasized in the minds of Whites by the harshness of the Arctic and the intimate closeness of Eskimo life with the land: the harsher the environment, the closer to nature must be the people who are able to inhabit it. Newcomers to the north are continuously reminded of the distance between themselves and the Eskimos by stories woven out of these romantic and romanticized views. The people and the land are mythical – the 'real Eskimo', a strange and wonderful being, utterly remote from the familiar places of the storytellers, far off in the heart of the land, where he takes nature's rhythms and makes them his own, a figure invested with wild dignity and powers, a force of nature himself, leading a life that could scarcely be more different from the settlement and its warm, protective homes. In the minds of the Whites, far out there, on the bleak, windswept, rocky land lives the image of the real Eskimo; he was there, everywhere, in the past, and he lives on, reincarnated, in every Eskimo today. That is the romance conjured up by the stories, a romance that deeply affects Whites who are brought into any sort of informal contact with Eskimos.

The nature and intensity of these views has cast the presence of the Whites in the north into a curious relief. The latter are there as socializers intent on effecting changes or consolidating changes that have already taken place; yet they maintain an attitude of romantic awe towards the place and the people they are changing. That contradiction is embedded in many, if not most, colonial situations. It has been the subject of a number of speculative studies, and I shall return to it soon. At this point, however, I wish to offer a theoretical formulation that may give some insight into the whole pattern of the Whites' attitudes towards the Eskimo.

It is of course impossible to discuss White attitudes towards Eskimos or towards the north without some reference to their attitudes towards themselves and their own place there. The comment and response of anyone who has distanced himself from his home and background, is formed by his view of the contrasts: the things he notices as striking or significant are such simply because they are different from or even opposed to what he had, in the past, taken for granted. In a colonial situation, these differences are especially striking. Anyone with a definite assertive role today within such a situation sees these differences as obstacles, and to a considerable extent he sees the whole environment, human and material, in plastic terms and tries to see how and within what limits its elements are amenable to being re-shaped. Colonial situations in remote regions among non-literate and technologically simple peoples have some special features. Anyone with an official capacity in such a situation tends to disregard the humanity of the natives, for they evidently do not – at least not yet – subscribe to the conventions and code of conduct that the colonialist believes to be at the heart of civilized society. Indeed, he often regards the native as being without a society, savage, wild and heathen. This view has dominated the attitude of many colonialists especially when they have come from an urban technological society and when the natives have been non-literate and nomadic.

White presence in the north falls into this category of colonialism. Representatives of the world's most technologically advanced societies have gone, as agents of social and moral change, among a people who, according to their stereotyped idea, lived at the very edge of possible human life. That edge, as we have seen, is geographical and technological. Moreover, Eskimos often live on raw food, always live with great simplicity, and are highly mobile. They are therefore seen as an embodiment of nature, as a part of the land, beyond the reach of culture – which is what the colonialists bring to the colonialized.

There is a long-standing tradition among European colonizing nations which holds that the Eskimos, being the people the most remote from civilization geographically, are also culturally the most primitive. Lyon, a naval officer who was among the first to bring stories of the Eskimo to the English public, wrote in 1824: 'It is a generally allowed opinion that the farther North a man is settled, the more dwindled is his form, his intellect and his passions.'[3] And the following remarkable passage appeared in a London magazine in 1892:

Thus whilst many a lady dies in labour, a hop-picker will lie down under a hedge, and leave her new born baby there whilst she goes on with her work, and the Esquimaux woman (whose people take the prize for low intellect and want of education) brings her child into the world with a conical head of so soft a consistency that she is quite unable to understand the penalties her more civilized sisters have undergone. It would take years of civilization to bring the Esquimaux woman up to the standards of the English.[4]

The great Nansen wrote in the 1880s that 'The Eskimo forms the extreme outpost towards the infinite stillness of the regions of ice . . . The tracts which all others despise he has made his own.'[5]

In 1935 a missionary echoed the theme:

Here, as one proceeds farther from the frontiers of civilization, step by step the native cultures unfold themselves as though in retrospect, terminating among the Eskimos, whose contemporary existence represents in act and thought the behaviour of an early new-stone age.[6]

The opposition between culture and nature has long been a favourite subject of discussion in anthropological theory, and is central to all theory about society, from Rousseau's abstract State of Nature to the theoretical foundations of post-Second World War social philosophy. Modern anthropologists, especially Lévi-Strauss, have used the distinction or opposition between nature and culture to describe schematically the important features in the structure of the intellectual life of various peoples, features that are contained in myth, but are concealed

3. Lyon (1824), p. 355.   5. Nansen (1893), p. 4.
4. Marryat (1892).   6. Speck (1935), p. 13.

by detail and surface elements. The analysis of a people's myths, in the light of other related myths and of the details of the people's culture will, it is argued, reveal the structural oppositions that are embedded there. Use of such analysis focuses on the mind of the people in question, and, most ambitiously, on the nature of mind itself. Clearly, there are striking parallels between these formulations of structuralist theory and the way in which Whites in the north in particular and colonialists in general, regard themselves and their subjects. The culture–nature opposition may help to throw a new light on the information at hand.

The argument can be stated very simply: the colonialist regards his own society, or societies very like it, as synonymous with culture, and he regards the colonialized as part of nature. The colonialist sees the progress of civilization in the terms of overcoming nature. Within a culture, a man can protect himself against nature; his technology and knowledge are directed to that end. The colonialized are thought of as a people who can barely protect themselves against nature (hence the emphasis on 'the benefits of civilization'), and insofar as they *can* protect themselves, it is because they are part of nature. Many colonialists are nevertheless conscious of and enthusiastic about technological and other achievements of the colonialized, but do not regard these achievements as sufficient in themselves nor as substitutes for their own definition of culture. Whites in the north today, like many other colonialists, are also enthusiastic about the land: it is a place of wonder and they are proud to be associated with it. Colonialists do not denigrate the colonialized merely because they regard them as close to nature – but this theoretical question must be taken up after a closer look at the Whites' attitude to Eskimos.

The most coherent, most explicit, expression of that attitude is found in the way Whites talk among themselves about individual Eskimos, and it is evident that most Whites have definite negative feelings about most individual Eskimos. Usually, when Whites discuss an Eskimo, they find fault with him. A man may be said to be incompetent, good neither in settlement work nor at hunting, or to be untrustworthy, or simply stupid. Whites often pronounce judgements on areas of competence of which they can have only limited knowledge at best, and of which they are usually totally ignorant. Thus they are willing to discuss a man's effectiveness as a hunter, as a traveller, as the father of his family or how a woman deals with her children or manages her sex life. These judgements provide bases for criticism and complaint against individuals with whom the Whites have no daily association and, in many cases, with whom they can never talk. Furthermore, the range of criticism is so wide that an Eskimo can be condemned from any point of view: if a young man is uneasy in the settlement, unwilling to work there or inexpert at the jobs he takes, he is characterized as 'stupid'; yet if he chooses to live on the land and tries to make a success of hunting and trapping, he is scorned for trying to be a 'real Eskimo', or for attempting to succeed in a life that has no economic future. The same sort of double judgement is made about young Eskimo women: if they are friendly, sociable and eager to join in settlement life, they are often regarded as 'loose'; but if they are shy and withdrawn, avoid contact with Whites, and stay at home, they are likely to be regarded as 'nice, but stupid'. Many young Eskimo men speak English and are enthusiastic about modern styles in dress and music and try to introduce these ideas to the people of the settlement: they are usually described as 'the delinquent element'. Teenagers who are not interested in modern styles and fashion, who are retiring and prefer to spend most of their time at home, are also said to be 'stupid'. There is a sexual dimension to the Whites' attitudes to teenage girls and younger married women: the 'modern' girls are 'promiscuous' – although the shy girls are 'dumb'. The older men, who stay in the settlement and do not often go out hunting, but are happy to live off their families (often because they lack the cash necessary to make a hunting trip) are regarded as weak.

Behind all of the Whites' negative attitudes towards particular Eskimos lurks the spectre of the 'real' Eskimo. Whites seem to judge any Eskimos against that ideal standard and to feel dismay each time the standard is not attained. No Eskimo who lives in the settlement most of the time and who depends on a regular cash income can attain that ideal standard. The feet of these Eskimos are heavy with the clay of settlement life and ordinary economic activities. And so long as the Eskimos fail to be 'real' according to White standards, they will continue to be the focus of the Whites' hostile and critical attitudes.

Yet most northern Whites also express affection for Eskimos and emphasize the distinctive excellence they have found in Eskimo culture and personality. There is, therefore, a striking contradiction between White attitudes towards Eskimo-ness in general and towards Eskimos in particular: all Eskimos are touched with the magic of real Eskimo-ness, although any given Eskimo is likely to be criticized for stupidity, incompetence or delinquency. The source of the contradiction is obvious: the modern individual Eskimo fails to achieve the standard of excellence implicit in the Whites' ideas of the 'real Eskimo'. A majority of Eskimos, perhaps the vast majority of them, are therefore from the White point of view deviants in some degree – they deviate from the canon of perfect Eskimo-ness and fail to live up to part of, perhaps a great part of, the Whites' accepted stereotype. The paradox is brutal: Whites criticize those who respond to pressures the Whites' institutions are dedicated to exerting.

Not all Whites express hostile attitudes towards every Eskimo they know, but it is the older men, those who are still thought to embody traditional modes and disposition in some way, who receive greatest praise. A missionary, lamenting to me the passing of all that was good about the north, remarked: 'There aren't any Eskimos left around here any more.' But he spoke warmly of the older Eskimos he had known when he first came north ten years earlier. Whites are frequently patronizing and over-friendly when they speak with older people, but that particular uneasiness has its counterpart in positive attitudes that Whites express to one another in private. And, of course, they have minimal relations with the older Eskimo men and women. The older people have great difficulty understanding the pidgin Eskimo used by the few Whites who have any grasp of the language at all, and they must simplify their vocabulary and grammar so much that serious communication becomes quite impossible. In such conversations, both Whites and Eskimos resort to an enthusiastic repetition of 'Yes', as though by affirming goodwill in the abstract, they have magically transformed their communication into something real. There is therefore between the old people and the Whites who claim to admire them only the feeblest contact. This lack of contact makes it possible for Whites to attribute idealized qualities to old Eskimos without fear of contradiction. Old Eskimo men are provided with whatever qualities, dispositions, ideals, the Whites feel old Eskimo men *should* have. Whatever the truth of the matter, the old man is a living embodiment of the 'real' Eskimo that is so essential to the Whites' romantic view of the north. Moreover, given the significance to them of the real Eskimo, the Whites are not likely to be assiduous in seeking to know the older Eskimos' *actual* views or aspirations. Limitations to direct contact are therefore useful: they secure the White against possible disruption of his ideas and ideals. The old Eskimo is said to know the land, to understand its ways, and to feel nostalgia for the old days. The ways were those of a primitive mobile hunter, who had his own distinctive vision and peculiar excellence; they were the ways of a man beyond, or before, or above civilization and culture. A man steeped in such a past must be interested only in his own skills and values, and must accept only the canons of his own wisdom. He is a man with no place in the new world the Whites are making in the north. I shall show later that any real communication would have disrupted such views, but it should already be clear that such views are potentially dangerous.

The attribution of a mythical persona to the older Eskimos is not the only important exception to the Whites' preponderantly negative attitudes to the people. There are individuals who slip through the net of stereotype and prove exceptions to the generalizations that are applicable to one or another category. These exceptional individuals are usually men or women who have some institutional role in which they are judged to be successful and competent. In short, they tend to be 'good workers'. In the church, for example, persons of any age who are devout in their expressions of belief and reliable in their attendance are approved by the missionaries. Their devotion must be regular enough to overcome the missionaries' increasing suspicion of 'modern' attitudes. In the same way, a young man working in a government office, perhaps as assistant or clerk to the settlement manager, may through his willing enthusiasm and readiness to learn become well liked and respected by local government personnel. A teacher may grow to like a classroom assistant; an HBC store manager may develop respect and affection for a local store employee. By comparison with the general disaffection for and impatience with Eskimo employees in White institutions, however, such attitudes are uncommon; it is more usual to hear complaints of incompetence, slowness, or – a complaint that lightly shades into a half-complaint – the inability to work because of being 'too much of an Eskimo'.

Obviously each institution sets its own standards and judges employees according to their competence at specific and specialized tasks, and it is difficult to offer any soundly based generalizations about the nature of the Whites' approval, other than to indicate its restricted quality. But there are a number of values on the basis of which (or on the evidence for which) competence at specific tasks is approved. They are, of course, the time-honoured values: punctuality, compliance with work discipline, quickness of comprehension, dependability, sobriety. Broadly, an Eskimo employee is judged to be good insofar as he co-operates with Whites and expresses in his work or in his life-style southern ideas of the good things in life. Trivial as this observation may be, it points to a perplexing feature of the contradiction that has already been noted between the idealization of the real Eskimo (as an abstraction) and the denigration of real Eskimos (as individuals). While Whites tend to idealize older Eskimos in terms of their supposed traditional qualities, when it comes to evaluating Eskimos working for southern institutions approval and praise are meted out on the basis of criteria which are in many respects directly opposed to the traditional ideal. Vallee has pointed this out in relation to the missionary: he notes the irony in a missionary's lamenting the passing of tradition, although the whole reason for his living among the Eskimos is a commitment to effect such changes. That irony can be found in the attitudes of the vast majority of northern Whites.

As an illustration, consider a series of events that involved an Anglican missionary in an Eastern Arctic settlement during the spring and summer of 1971. This was the missionary quoted earlier in this chapter as saying, 'There aren't any Eskimos left around here any more.' He was obviously a man deeply involved with the romance of the north, an involvement that over the years had made him profoundly unhappy with the course of events among the people he knew best. He was hostile to the education of Eskimos, perceiving it to be a force thoroughly destructive of the life-style that Eskimos most desire and need, and he was inclined for the same reason also to be hostile to local government officials. He was therefore somewhat isolated from other Whites. He was also troubled by the trend he saw towards irreligiousness and deviance, modern phenomena that are, in his view, causally connected and worldwide. Evangelistic in style and belief, he devoted all his energy to reviving faith among the people of his settlement, preaching in the fire-and-brimstone manner, arranging extra services, and organizing special missions by other evangelists. Over a period of several months he inculcated a spirit of fearsome religiosity. Many people, young and old, were deeply concerned with the dangers of sin, hell and Satan, with which the missionary remorselessly and repeatedly threatened them. It became customary for Eskimos to attend church services or religious meetings four or five times a week; devotion turned into a passionate anxiety. There can be no doubt that this resurgence of religious feeling and practice was the result of one missionary's massive effort; the second missionary in the settlement, a Roman Catholic, certainly felt that was so and cryptically offered his view that his colleague was 'not so much an Anglican as a Protestant'.

Other Whites who had lived for some years in the community expressed their surprise and some alarm at the Anglican missionary's success in his revivalist endeavour, a success that eventually became most conspicuous among the younger people. They began to organize their own religious meetings; there were

Bible readings and an open struggle for comprehension of its messages; a group of men working on an extension of the settlement airstrip broke off from work each night to make direct contact with God; one young man, accompanied by his friends, tested the power of his faith and their prayer by attempting to walk on water. The intensity of their response to the evangelical call alarmed many older people; but even more troubling than their intensity was the extent of younger people's independence in their expressions of belief. The young had undertaken to seek their own relation to God and tended to dispense with the mediation of the church and missionary, at least in some of their religious activities. The old were accustomed to think of the institution and the missionary as the necessary means of religious expression; not so the young.

Eventually a number of older men confronted the missionary and complained of the way in which the young were so flagrantly disregarding the well-established conventions of Christianity – at least so far as they had understood them. Their anxious representations placed the missionary in a quandary. On the one hand it was these men whom he liked best and who had the strongest appeal for him: traditionalists, yet Christian, they appreciated the irony and contradiction inherent in the missionary's role. But as an evangelist, he was delighted with this new concern with evangelism; he was sure the young people's zeal was a sign of his success. Indeed he spoke of it as something beyond his own success and characterized it to me as 'a movement of God's Spirit' by which the young were 'driven to praise God themselves'. That movement, however, called into question the prior attachment of the older people and placed at risk some part of *their* attachment to the church. The missionary explained the older people's opposition by reference to their innate conservatism ('What is ingrained in the minds of the older people is that you've got to go in that church, got to have the English Prayer Book before you, before you can meet God. And that drives me up the wall'), and to their lingering memory of some religious murders in the past. 'They feel that the young people are being converted and saved and filled with great joy, and they seem to think – some of them –

that this is a bad sign. Now some of them had some bad memories of something that happened away back in 1946 or so, or '43, when something went wrong.' He dealt with the problem by assuring the old that all was well and by urging moderation on the young:

There is a bit of a reaction, not a fear, and a misunderstanding. But I have not squashed it [the new movement] at all. There are one or two things I have asked them to tone down on, but I certainly haven't squashed it by any means because I believe this is a healthy sign ... Simply to avoid a split which was imminent, I have told them to calm down some of the things which they were doing. But by all means I think it's great.

Behind the missionary's new satisfaction with the young lurked his unfavourable view of modern settlement life, specifically in its effect on the young. The salvation he saw was a delivery from the delinquency and deviance that he believed to be the most imminent dangers to youth – dangers represented to him by some individuals in the settlement and by the habits and attitudes of many, perhaps even the majority, in other settlements. Salvation consisted in a self-conscious, full repudiation of all things modern in favour of a religious life. The secular aspects of the repudiation were ordinary enough: abstinence from extra-marital sex, alcohol, tobacco and bad temper. These things represented a shift towards traditional Eskimo traits, specifically towards respectfulness and non-violence in interpersonal relations and against the adoption of southern styles. He saw salvation as a return to what was best in the 'real Eskimo' (the missionaries are rather strikingly able to reconcile the 'real Eskimo' with the Christian Eskimo). So long as there is an apparent revival of those particular traits, the missionary can feel encouraged. If such a revival incorporated the majority or the whole of a community, he could feel on a wider scale the enthusiastic goodwill that he normally showed only with the older people and with a few other individuals.

To a considerable extent, the same kind of change in attitude is basic to the psychology of other Whites who have grown to feel full-hearted goodwill to particular Eskimos. I have suggested that many Whites are inclined to feel negative towards their own roles in the north insofar as they consider that they contribute to the acculturative modernization that the Eskimos 'cannot handle'. That expression is often used to describe what are thought to be the consequences of Eskimo maladaptation to modern phenomena; these consequences include drunkenness, domestic violence, irresponsible spending and despondency. The few Eskimos who can 'handle' modern ways are said to be able to do so *either* by adherence to tradition, as with the older men, *or* by quiet and cheerful, cooperative and subservient participation, so that even some young persons may be said to have been touched by the virtues of tradition.

The same question can usefully be approached from the opposite direction, by describing in more detail the dislike that northern Whites so often express towards individual Eskimos. Probably the most striking feature of these expressions is their intensity: it is not at all unusual to hear an Eskimo criticized in fierce terms. Ferocity may sometimes be a result of the self-consciousness and tension that are caused by preoccupation with inter-ethnic contact and racist feeling in general. Northern Whites always fear that uninformed and inexperienced strangers, from a faceless civil servant in Ottawa to their superiors in regional offices, are watching for any sign of racial discrimination or oppression. They are consequently nervous, irritable and inhibited in their expressions of views about others, yet find relief from this strain in occasional bursts of complaint that are the more ferocious for having been suppressed. Yet the forcefulness of White criticism is not at issue here; for present purposes, it is more useful to focus on the type of Eskimo who usually gives rise to complaint. The categories of Eskimo who tend to be objects of negative attitudes have already been noted; it is now worth looking beyond these categories to specific illustrations.

Northern Whites pay close attention to drunkenness and cleanliness, and Eskimos who are known to drink are regarded as incipient alcoholics. So anxious is this attention that many Whites refuse to offer the ordinary hospitality of a drink to Eskimo visitors, sometimes in the face of an embarrassing situation, as when an Eskimo visits a house where a group of Whites are already drinking. In such a situation, I have seen Whites continue to drink, refilling their own glasses, but not offering any to the visitor. Such behaviour indicates clearly enough what many Whites feel towards an Eskimo who is a known drinker. But criticism of the 'drunkard' may be even more stylized than that.

Alice, a young married woman, left her settlement to work for the federal civil service, as a translator and special assistant to various senior permanent officials in the Department of Indian and Northern Affairs. She was qualified for such work because her spoken and written English, which she had learned in hospitals in the south, was excellent. During her years in the civil service, she acquired a reputation for good work; she was well known and much respected. But she also began to drink heavily, and gradually habitual drunkenness began to impair the quality of her work. She was eventually persuaded to move to another city, in the hope that a new environment might reduce this problem. (It was widely believed that her drinking was a direct consequence of the bad influence of her associates and friends.) The move was unsuccessful, and Alice eventually returned to her home settlement. She returned with the modest glory of having worked in 'high places' and of having gained the friendship and respect of 'important people'. Once back in the settlement, she was offered work as assistant to a White official: it was a job of no special importance and gave Alice no status higher than that enjoyed by other Eskimo assistants in the settlement. Her drinking lessened, and there now seemed no danger of her becoming an alcoholic. Nonetheless, she drank more than other local Eskimos, and she took a leading part in the drinking parties that aroused so much anxiety among the settlement's Whites. Nevertheless, Alice was still invited to occasional parties given by Whites, and she was not refused drinks if her hosts were drinking. She was, it appeared, exempted from the prohibition applied to most other Eskimos, although she was one of the few local Eskimos who had a serious drinking problem. Furthermore, when occasionally she did drink heavily and stayed away from work for days, and was sometimes violent, many Whites grew anxious and tried to offer support and friendship instead of just trying to enforce abstinence. Indeed, one or two White officials made a point of joining Alice in some of her drinking bouts to ensure that no harm came to her.

In contrast to Alice's story is the case of Annie Alook. She had never left the settlement for long periods, but had succeeded in acquiring good English and a professional skill. Annie was employed, like Alice, as assistant to a White official, and she received a series of promotions as a result of passing examinations. She was known to be good at her job and was expected to continue to do well. But she too sometimes drank heavily and, like Alice, would periodically stay away from work for a few days and was occasionally involved in fights. Her drinking never became a medical problem, nor did it seem likely to. Yet the Whites in the settlement criticized her for being a drunk; and invariably refused to offer her drink on social occasions when they might have done so. This refusal was obvious to Annie herself who found it insulting and resented it – a feeling she did not conceal from the Whites. So she came to be criticized also for her ill-humour and her tendency to become violent. The Whites showed no concern over the problems she might be facing; criticisms of her were not softened by kindly sentiments.

Whites consider an Eskimo's drinking to be bad if the drinker has none of the compensating qualities that carry weight in a middle-class environment. In much the same vein, the Whites criticize those they regard as 'dirty'. An administrator in an Arctic settlement told a social worker that he would obstruct an adoption because the prospective foster-mother was 'a slut'; she in fact was a hunter's wife, well known for her adherence to the traditional life-style. For the Whites, any public signs or the mere rumour of domestic disarray or the smallest evidence of 'deviance' form the basis of bitter complaint against an individual or family. This criticism is aimed at traits, dispositions and problems that are expected and common in overcrowded, poor communities, the people of which have little or no voice in the exercise of authority. But when Whites make such a criticism, what they are in fact objecting to is the way an Eskimo fails to exhibit a bourgeois life-style – and I emphasize the word 'exhibit': Whites who criticize drunken Eskimos are very often themselves heavy drinkers, but they restrict the evidence of their drinking and do it privately. Even those Whites who idealize the traditional Eskimo approve of the Eskimo who exhibits middle-class behaviour.

David Stern had worked in the north, in various official capacities, for several years, and by northern standards he was sophisticated, well informed and articulate in his hopes and attitudes towards himself in particular and the north in general. During his years in the Arctic, he had experienced a wide range of social conditions and had lived there when hunting and trapping were still the mainstays of the Eskimos' economy, and when Whites in the north were not yet so numerous, so wealthy or so conspicuously middle class. He had travelled with the Eskimos and had made some attempt to learn their language. It was not surprising, therefore, to hear Stern talk enthusiastically of the old days and of the 'real Eskimo'. He was proud to have glimpsed the remains of that life, he had enjoyed spending time in camps, and he valued his knowledge of the old ways. Nor was it surprising to hear him lament the passing of what had been good, and he criticized many features of the settlement life that had replaced it. He complained bitterly about the increasing 'delinquency' among the young, and was quick to call any young man a 'bum'.

But Stern also expressed some faith in new opportunities for the Eskimos, such as skilled labour and the benefits of social welfare. He remarked once, 'I would like a welfare officer to come in here because, with the new structures – all social assistance, unemployment, insurance payments and things like that – a lot of people are completely ignorant about their rights.' More generally, he indicated his faith in conventional middle-class virtues, not only by derogating people who lacked them, but by strongly approving any sign that they were making headway. On one occasion Stern heard that an Eskimo family had given a small dinner party at which a meal of meat with potatoes and peas had been served in southern style at a table

with knives and forks, followed by a fruit pie. In the Eastern
Canadian Arctic it is extremely rare for such food to be eaten
in accordance with southern customs. Eskimo custom does not
favour meals at which whole families eat together, nor is the
fork commonly used, nor are foods presented in courses. So
when Stern heard tell of the dinner he was alive to the unusual-
ness of the occasion. He commented: 'When I hear things like
that I feel that all our work up here is worth something, and
these people are really getting somewhere.'

It should be obvious that northern Whites hold contradictory
attitudes towards the north and towards Eskimos. But it is the
main argument of this chapter that there is a pattern to these
attitudes, a pattern bound up with the pattern of the Whites'
own activities in the north. It may now be useful to re-state
the bundle of attitudes that are most common and most apparent and that can often be found co-existing in a White
official's mind.

1. The old or traditional Eskimo is idealized.
2. The land is idealized.
3. Eskimos (and Whites) who are anti-middle-class in behaviour are keenly disliked.
4. Eskimos who are quiet, cooperative and considered to be
   partly modern and partly traditional are well liked.
5. Young Eskimos who want to go back to the land are generally scorned.

Favourable and hostile attitudes are both often expressed in
relation to a traditional and irreducible 'Eskimo-ness'. Thus, as
has already been suggested, the cooperative and quiet Eskimo,
who is in fact a good employee and exhibits some, at least, of
the middle-class southern virtues, is said to be 'good' partly because he is still 'Eskimo', that is because he is even-tempered
and friendly. But an Eskimo who is a bad employee, reluctant
to accept the discipline of office hours or inclined to be spend-
thrift and improvident, is said to be 'bad' because his irreducible
Eskimo-ness still asserts itself. And the Eskimo who is blatantly
anti-middle-class, who openly and loudly repudiates, con-
demns or in any way assaults southern institutions, is said to be

deviant, and his hostility is believed to have arisen inevitably from too-rapid modernization.

Mannoni, in a masterful study of the psychology of colonialism, argued that Whites who choose to work in colonial situations are especially attracted to a 'world without men'. It is a theory that emphasizes the extent to which colonialists regard the colonized as primitive and, therefore, not part of the world of real men. Such colonialists, runs the argument, find relief in their escape from the competitive and highly critical atmosphere that is typical of their home environment, of the 'real man's world'. He wrote: 'So, then, colonial life is simply a substitute to those who are obscurely drawn to a world without men – to those, that is, who have failed to make the effort necessary to adapt infantile images to adult realities.'[7] My own argument suggests a similar view. The northern Whites want to live in a world of nature, but they are dismayed by the discovery that the settlement they live in is increasingly a place where men *are* real, and they are the more dismayed because the 'reality' is often that of wage-labour. They express their dismay in hostile attitudes towards most of the local population. Mannoni also wrote,

> Civilized man is painfully divided between the desire to correct the errors of the savages and the desire to identify himself with them in his search for the lost Paradise (a Paradise which at once casts doubt upon the merit of the very civilization he is trying to transmit to them).[8]

In this observation Mannoni touches on a source of colonial confusion, on a fundamental contradiction that besets all colonial endeavour. To a limited degree, such an observation neatly fits with some of the phenomena described in this chapter. Many Whites do seek to identify themselves at some level with the 'savage', a desire that is revealed in their enthusiasm for the land, their keen interest in the history of Arctic exploration and in accounts of the explorers' first encounters with truly traditional peoples. And this interest does conflict with their desire to improve 'savage' customs. It is my argu-

7. Mannoni (1956), p. 105.   8. ibid., p. 21.

ment, however, that the Whites' determined efforts to improve the customs of the Eskimos spring primarily from their aversion to life-styles that are not bourgeois. 'The 'savage' is seen (at least in White fancy) only in the older men who, they believe, are still essentially Eskimo; when talking of them, the Whites seem to regret much of what they do and express, albeit implicitly, quite strongly anti-colonial views. The same views are revealed by Whites who lament the whole process of change and modernization in the Arctic, for they are horrified at the replacement of the 'savage' by the 'bum', of the proud and independent hunter by the down-and-out labourer. Once the Eskimo *is* a labourer out of work, however, his behaviour and attitudes inevitably become the focus of hostile indignation from Whites who are determined to effect yet more change, a change that not only brings the Eskimo more fully into the modern world but brings him some way towards the middle class. It seems to me that White hostility towards the Eskimo is better understood as the result of inter-class oppositions than as the living disappointment in their failure to realize infantile images. In support of this view, consider the Whites' attitude towards welfare.

If Whites are ambivalent about the persistence of the 'primitive', then we should expect to find an ambivalent attitude also towards welfare. After all, welfare *could* be seen as a means of keeping some traditional values alive – a man could be subsidized by welfare to remain a hunter, and thereby much of that form of life could be preserved. The old man who is thought to be a 'real' Eskimo is usually in economic difficulties, for no longer can one live by trading skins and by subsistence hunting. David Stern once said to me,

I think welfare is a problem . . . Sometimes there is an applicant who actually doesn't need welfare, but he comes in on the off chance that he is going to get it anyway. Going by the rule book, how can you possibly give it to a man who says, look, I want to go out on the land? It is very difficult. There is the odd bird who will say I've got a disability which prevents me from doing this, that and the other, yet with your own eyes you can see him do everything to the contrary. By and large, actually in this community I'm surprised at them because most of the people are pretty industrious and they are willing to look after themselves rather than sink their pride and come by and look for a hand-out, which in other settlements is prevalent. Most of the guys are aware that if they can't look after themselves by carving, hunting, fishing and casual labour, then [welfare] is available, although there isn't too much.

Welfare is widely regarded as a corrupting and degenerative force that makes independent men into despondent bums. But, it may be pointed out, welfare may be thought to be corrupting precisely because Eskimos are being urged into the life-styles of the middle class or upper working class. They hover between wage-labour and unemployment, between success and failure as proletarians. It is rare indeed to hear Whites urge that welfare should be more widely used to offset the Eskimos' economic dependence on an outmoded means of livelihood, for Eskimos are really seen as workers, not hunters.

Many Whites are manipulative and authoritarian in their attitudes towards Eskimos. They believe that they know what is best for them and, if the Eskimos themselves are not enthusiastic about the good things Whites have to offer, that is attributed to the Eskimos' misunderstanding or error. Eskimos are continuously being urged to be grateful for what Whites say Eskimos need. There is literally no part of Eskimo life that Whites have left outside the realm of southern responsibility. Eskimos are given houses, schools, beliefs, sex education, clothes and goods – all of White manufacture and design. That is inevitable, at least in its technological aspect, in a society experiencing sudden modernization. But if we consider the attitudes of the Whites who are implementing these changes, wider issues than technology come to the surface. Northern Whites come from a society that regards itself as liberal and disavows authoritarianism generally and, more specifically, persons or institutions that attempt to force their views on others. This society insists on the right of all men to the basic liberties that are celebrated in liberal social philosophy. Yet in their colonial activity, Whites do the opposite: representatives of White society insist on regulating the way in which Eskimos live and on identifying what it is that Eskimos should want.

These decisions are taken with minimum reference to the Eskimos' own aspirations and with scarcely any attempt to assess what local circumstances actually require. This may not be surprising at the Canadian national level, for the country is governed by majority democracy, and it follows that tiny minorities cannot easily maintain their own kind of social order. Most of the Whites in the north, the actual representatives or salesmen of the national system, are themselves committed liberals, but in their northern work they behave and think differently. The contradiction *does* exist in them. They treat Eskimos in a way that they would never treat one another, and adopt attitudes towards the Eskimo communities within northern settlements that they would never use towards their own communities within the same settlements. Indeed, Whites greatly resent interference and authoritarianism from their own superiors, yet at the same time they are themselves profoundly authoritarian towards the local people.

It is here that the nature–culture theory is valuable. Insofar as the northern White regards the Eskimo as a part of nature, he places him beyond the pale of 'cultured' values. If Eskimos eat raw food, then according to the stereotype they were driven by necessity to do so. The harshness of nature forces Eskimos to be non-men, and this same power is believed to have prevented them living in 'real' social groups. The Eskimo is, therefore, an embodiment of nature and in many respects a surrogate for it. He receives from the Whites a curious blend of approval and revulsion – approval because he has triumphed over nature (thereby achieving the essentially human), but revulsion because he is still part of nature (thereby remaining less than human). Northern Whites themselves are essentially human and seek to triumph over nature, despite their fear of its stark powers. So insofar as Eskimos are a part of nature, Whites seek, in spite of themselves, to triumph over them, too; just as mountains must be climbed, so must Eskimos be led to culture. The 'natural' Eskimo has no more claim to human rights than nature itself.

Even the writings of Rasmussen and de Poncins show the pervasiveness of these notions. Rasmussen wrote:

The inhabitants of Ukatdlit were uncommonly attractive people, and their manners betrayed that for years they had been accustomed to white men. Though in general I am no advocate of the principle that wild beasts should be tamed, it is undoubtedly pleasant to be among Eskimos who do not display too much contempt for ordinary tact and peaceful intercourse; at any rate one is able to work better.[9]

And De Poncins:

There is no learning to know the Eskimo through an exchange of ideas. Properly speaking, the Eskimo does not think at all. He has no capacity for generalization. He cannot explain himself to you, nor can he explain his people.[10]

In the writings of the missionaries these ideas are seen at their most gross:

In the Eskimo [the] primary impulses appear in almost absolute form, and the society which emerges is a tyrannical one that permits only the fittest to live, the useful to exist ...

Such degradation may be explained in a single sentence: 'They had forgotten God.'[11]

In the language of the missionary, the Eskimo must be 'saved'; in that of the administrator, he must be 'helped'; in that of most Whites, he must be 'civilized'. Each White justifies his own work by referring to the benefits, medical, moral, intellectual or material, that southern culture can give. And as the process gets under way, as the Eskimo slips from nature and is pushed towards culture, he is in a limbo between social classes, between worlds, and in the colonialist's mind becomes half man and half non-man. In the contemporary northern settlements, the Whites perceive a worker without work, a villager without land, an employee with few motives to work. In his socio-economic status, the Eskimo is a new member of the lowest class, a status that northern Whites are confused about because of the lingering traces of 'real' Eskimo: there remains an element, some fleeting glimpse, of the natural man. The Whites are unsure whether he is the natural man of Hobbes or of Rousseau. When 'naturalness' means violence, turbulence, anger, it is the natural

9. Rasmussen (1932), Vol. 9, p. 68.
10. De Poncins (1941), p. 114.   11. Buliard (1953), p. 95.

man during a difficult acculturation, the expression of social inferiority discovering itself. When the natural man is quiet, withdrawn, in retreat, there is the 'real Eskimo', the remnant of the ideal and of the stereotype. Whites are troubled because the acculturative drift seems to them to be towards a Hobbesian view of the world, where fear and confrontation are the ways by which individuals try to secure and defend their own purposes; it becomes even harder to find in Eskimos the embodiment of the old ideals, and it is consequently harder for Whites to find real excitement in living in the north. They therefore retreat into their own roles, though not silently. They complain about the failures of northern policies and grumble about the Eskimos. At the same time, they accept the customary benefits of their roles – material prosperity, influence and power, a highly social life, a certain amount of freedom, and all the other advantages a person with well-developed middle-class aspirations may discover in the north.

The Whites' satisfactions, therefore, are gained despite the directions of federal policy and despite disappointing changes in the people they have come to live among. In the larger northern settlements, this trend is well developed. Whites in Frobisher Bay, for example, like to live there for reasons that have little to do with the 'real Eskimos': they have retreated into their White middle-class world and a routine performance of their roles in the main institutions. In the small settlements that I have been describing, this has not yet happened, but it is likely to in the near future. Those Whites who cling to their ideals and cannot find sufficient satisfaction in the material and social benefits afforded by a life in the north quickly leave and return south.

6 • Local Government: The Local Reaction

'Just as the Canadians were born to look after
themselves, so the Inuit were born to look after
themselves too'

— Samwillie Annahatak, Vice-President of the
Payne Bay Community Council, 1974

Richard Travis, a new settlement manager, arrived in his village
in mid-winter. The Eskimos there had never had a settlement
manager before, and their only previous full-time administrator
had been an industrial development officer. Although the
Eskimos' attitudes towards the first administrator had been
critical, his enthusiasm and goodwill had inspired general confidence in the possible achievements of his successor. When Travis
arrived, therefore, he received a warm welcome. Among themselves, the Eskimos noted his kindly appearance, commented
favourably on his readiness to shake hands with everyone, and
approved his strong build. First appearances were evidently
good.

The first weeks passed happily enough. The large suspended-
basement house where Travis lived was much visited. Often he
and the Eskimo men played games together, tried each other's
strength, and devised difficult – and sometimes merely ludicrous
– tests of skill. There was much laughter. Since the settlement
was one of the poorest Eskimo communities and had suffered
much hardship, even in recent times, such visiting and games
gave rise to high expectations among the people. A settlement
manager, they knew, controls welfare payments and other subsidies. Moreover, he is the man to represent their needs and
wishes to the Government. Their needs and wishes were numerous, and they naturally expected Travis to provide a great deal
of new or augmented support. Even at that time, the Eskimos
recognized without illusion their dependence upon southern support.

When Travis arrived, there were both a settlement council and a clearly defined group of leaders. Besides these leaders (all but one of whom were members of the council), there were a number of other men who were conspicuous for their outspokenness. The community was known among northern Whites for the confidence with which its residents expressed their views. The reserved or shy manner commonly attributed to Eskimos, and which allegedly bedevils attempts at political and community development, was less apparent here, and certainly the council had little hesitation in voicing criticisms or expressing anger. But despite the council's and the community's confidence in themselves, most of the people in the settlement insisted that they badly needed help from the Whites. They perceived this need partly in political terms: they thought the council and cooperative could be strengthened if – and only if – Whites provided the information and taught the skills which these institutions so obviously demanded. In general, the people expected a good deal from the institutions the Whites had introduced, and they certainly were not going to be satisfied with tokens. Because the Whites presumably understood the ramifications of the institutions they had introduced, they could and should make them work. In other words, the Eskimo community had come to believe that these institutions could significantly enhance their lives and livelihoods. They looked to Whites for guidance. Specifically, they looked to Travis.

The development of these institutions needs some explanation. The settlement was one of the remotest communities in the Canadian Eastern Arctic, and among the last to receive federal housing, educational and medical services. Although a dire need for the distribution of welfare was evident in the 1940s, regular payments were not made until much later than that, and when payments were made, they were determined at first by officials who lived more than seventy miles away and subsequently by a local school-teacher whose competence in the matter was doubtful indeed.[1] Poverty and sporadic hunger

1. Distribution of welfare was, in many parts of the Canadian north, at first placed in the hands of Hudson's Bay Company factors. It was later given by the RCMP. In those early days (the 1920s in the western

continued into the late 1960s, but the hungry became aware of the possibility of federal welfare during lean periods. The Industrial Development Officer who had preceded Travis had regularized welfare payments and had finally confirmed people's entitlement to governmental support. By that time, however, hunters had discovered that the people of neighbouring settlements had far less difficulty in obtaining this form of support, and had come to feel that they had not been treated justly. This sense of injustice, combined with their greater need for support, was probably a cause of the assertiveness towards southerners which was already a feature of community life when Richard Travis arrived.

The payment of welfare had always been a delicate matter, but Travis was from the first determined to reduce the scale of what he regarded as a form of dependence. In fact, he measured his own success by the size of the settlement's welfare budget: the smaller it was, the better he felt he was doing. During his first weeks he tried to discover which men who depended on welfare might depend on some other resource. In a number of cases, he managed to encourage men to carve soapstone and in that way to earn enough money to support their families – or at least to stop their claim to welfare payment. In the beginning, his attack on welfare payments did not arouse any very great antagonism. In the early spring, after a few months in the village, he left for seven weeks to visit other settlements and attempt to learn a little of the Eskimo language.

It was during this absence from the village that I first met Travis. His enthusiasm for his position and the optimism with which he looked forward to working with his community were immediately striking. Less apparent at first, but troubling when noticed, was Travis's intense concern with the details of organizational matters; he insisted upon casting a net of exact arrangements around others' activities. Although this uninvited assistance was usually given with abundant bonhomie, in an evident desire to be helpful, again and again it was marred by

Arctic, and the 1930s and 40s in the east) it tended to be offered as if it were a paternal blessing, and very much as the benevolence of the agents who made the decisions.

lack of sensitivity to what others in fact wanted for themselves. Thus, he could and would arrange a few odds and ends of food into an excellent dinner, but the details of the dinner, its menu as well as its timing and style, catered for organizational principle rather than for the tastes or needs of others. Furthermore, Travis seemed not to notice the small signals put out by those who were irritated or troubled by his managerial ways. He seemed to have become strangely inured to the subtleties of interpersonal relationships.

Yet Travis overcame this inability to get along easily with others by virtue of other qualities: he was always willing to organize, he was not afraid of hard work, he showed great generosity, and he was usually good-humoured – qualities that deservedly are highly regarded in northern settlement life.

From many discussions we had at that time, it was clear that Travis was profoundly antagonistic towards welfare. His antagonism had two distinguishable aspects. First, he regarded welfare as money for nothing, and he subscribed to the conventional moral view that anyone who lived on hand-outs was liable to lose all self-respect and dignity, and was well on the way to losing all interest in work itself. (There were, of course, exceptions to this rule, and they included the old and the sick.) Secondly, he greatly admired the traditional Eskimo because he was able to look after himself in a harsh climate with a minimum of material support. Obviously, an Eskimo who lived on welfare stood in stark contrast to that ideal. Somewhere, at the back of his mind, Travis seemed to feel that he should consolidate and preserve that traditional independence against the erosive qualities of dependence on welfare. For Travis, an Eskimo more closely resembled his worthy ancestors if he scraped a living by carving and occasional wage-labour than if he asked for welfare to help him continue life as a hunter and trapper. When it was suggested to him that for many Eskimos welfare payments were the only means of obtaining the money they needed, and that perhaps they should be allowed to judge for themselves what they needed by way of support, Travis became indignant. And when a settlement manager was mentioned who did hand out welfare as if it were the right of each and every Eskimo, he scorned and derided such behaviour with fierce invective as though it were a betrayal.

Arguments about welfare are common enough in the Canadian Arctic, and these discussions with Travis were entirely ordinary. The positions he adopted were neither strange nor, from his point of view, unreasonable. Indeed, he was able to argue his position persuasively. Yet his discussions were tainted by a curious ferocity: Travis did not easily brook any difference of opinion. When opposed by a more liberal or generous position on the welfare issue, he quickly became enraged. Furthermore, when he described such arguments to a third party (which he liked to do) he heaped abuse upon invective, apparently willing to discount the very sanity of those who had disagreed with him. Given that in general he tended to be a man of constant good cheer, his anger on these occasions was doubly striking. The question of welfare obviously touched on something central to his very being.

During the weeks that I first knew Travis, I had little opportunity to see how he got along with Eskimos in his professional capacity. In a purely social context, he was always cheerful and ready to try to communicate, even where there was virtually no language in common. The barrier to communication did not seem to make him as uneasy as it did others, and he did not patronize or belittle the Eskimos he knew. Moreover, he was keenly interested in hunting and fishing, and those interests provided important points of contact. He was always ready to join Eskimos on their hunting trips and, while travelling with them, was quite prepared to subordinate himself to their knowledge and plans. Once again, these are qualities that are not common among Whites. At this time Travis was especially anxious to learn from and be friendly with the Eskimos he met. He hoped that such knowledge and friendliness would translate directly into an ability to be helpful as an administrator.

Some four months after our first meeting, I visited the village and renewed my acquaintanceship with Travis. Before getting to know any of the local people, I had a number of long discussions with him about his position and administrative role in the community and how he saw the settlement's and his own future. During these conversations, Travis emphasized what he considered to be his successes. Welfare payments were much lower than in the past, and would be reduced even further. The village itself was cleaner and tidier than it had ever been. A number of individuals were doing very well in jobs to which they had been transferred from welfare. According to Travis the community council was functioning well, and its councillors were rapidly assuming much greater control of settlement affairs. Travis contrasted his record with what he saw as his predecessor's bungling.

In these conversations, it was troubling to notice how far Travis had adopted a proprietary attitude towards the people. He spoke of the settlement and its residents as an extension of himself: 'I have a boy doing really well down in Winnipeg.' 'I'll send my long-liner over to fetch them.' 'My mechanic is no damn good at his job.' The boy mentioned had gone to Winnipeg for further education and had not been sent by Travis: the long-liner was the community's cooperative's boat and entirely at its disposal: the mechanic was employed by the Territorial Government and his work was not directed by the settlement manager. It was obvious also that the Eskimos had ceased to visit Travis except on specific errands. Even on those occasions, visitors tended to stay in Travis's office and appeared nervous of going into his living quarters. In the first few encounters I witnessed between Travis and local men, it was impossible not to be surprised by his assertive, domineering manner. In attempting to overcome the language difficulty, he raised his voice, sometimes to a shout, and he simplified his English to a bald statement of instructions. His willingness to be friendly, despite language and cultural differences, seemed to have evaporated.

In the following months, I heard people of the settlement talking about their settlement manager. Confidence in him was extremely low. They said that he refused welfare to people who needed it, but gave it to others whose immediate families adequately provided for them. Travis claimed to know who was and who was not being supported by their families, and would not listen to the Eskimos involved. And, whereas the local hunters claimed that only they could assess hunting possibilities, Travis sometimes refused to give a hunter welfare because he was convinced in his own mind that hunting possibilities were good. As one hunter said to me:

He looks out of his window and see all sorts of birds flying about, and he says to an Eskimo, 'There is good hunting out there, go and hunt, you are not going to get any welfare this month when there are many birds so close to the settlement.' But birds do not stay and wait for the hunter. They come and they go again. The settlement manager cannot know when the hunting is good by looking out of his window. If he had to live by hunting he would know better and would not say such things.

A second complaint concerned Travis's attitude towards the Eskimo cooperative.[2] Although the cooperative does not officially fall within a settlement manager's responsibility, the two institutions inevitably impinge on one another. In a multitude of small ways, any official in a settlement can show that he supports the cooperative. The people were convinced that Travis did not wish to support it, and they were troubled by his objections to cooperative directors' proposals and plans. Again and again, I heard that Travis had nurtured rivalry and opposition between government departments and the cooperative and that he would not himself assist its work. This contrasted most unfavourably with Travis's predecessor, who had, by all accounts, offered it every support within his power and had even offered the use of government facilities and equipment.

A third complaint concerned Travis's manner. He was said to be 'bossy', forever eager to prove that he and no one else was the boss.[3] Evidence for this criticism came from all sides,

2. Virtually every Arctic settlement has a cooperative that buys and sells furs, carvings and some general provisions. These cooperatives are controlled locally by a board of Eskimo directors, and their membership includes any residents who wish to join. They are capitalized by loans from a central fund. Many are successful business ventures; some are not.

3. The word used to mean a boss is, in the dialect of this settlement, *angajuqqaaq*, a word that seems traditionally to have been used to refer to a camp leader (though *not* to a shaman – *angakkuq*) and was commonly used to mean Hudson's Bay Company factor.

since he so often objected to suggestions from local people. The trait also revealed itself in personal idiosyncrasies: he often shouted, he would grow suddenly and fiercely angry, he usually disregarded the arguments or objections of community councillors or members of the public, and he generally treated the people as though they were children. The Eskimos believed that his behaviour and the positions he took on specific and important local issues revealed that 'he does not want to help the Eskimos'. Some of the Eskimos insisted that his very appearance, his facial structure, had altered since he first arrived. As one said: 'When he came here he was friendly, he was smiling. I thought: how good that this new settlement manager is going to help the Eskimos. He shook hands with us all. Then later I saw him, and his face had changed. He was not handsome any more. His nose had become much bigger.' Eskimos commented astutely on the extraordinary way in which Whites often change when they come to live in north Arctic communities. With reference to Travis, one Eskimo remarked that Whites who are all smiles and enthusiasm when they first come north are the ones who are the first to become troubled and angry, and the first to be anxious to leave.

By September, at the end of Travis's first year in the settlement, relations between him and the community council were approaching a crisis. The body of Travis's critics was beginning to include his interpreters, and few were willing to interpret for him. The chairman of the council, Isaàc Tullik, was also the chief interpreter, and he confided to me his despair. Because he translated all of Travis's important decisions, and painstakingly rendered into Eskimo the official rebuttals of one or another Eskimo plan, many Eskimos had begun to think that their council chairman was hand-in-glove with the settlement manager. This unfavourable opinion was aggravated by Tullik's dual role: as interpreter, he was obliged to say things in Eskimo that confused and annoyed the community, and then, as a comparatively sophisticated man and as council chairman, he felt obliged also to explain why the settlement manager had spoken as he did. As the tensions between the community and Travis increased, so Tullik's job became more and more difficult. Moreover, he grew to dislike Travis, and found personal association with him disagreeable. As Tullik's troubles increased, he tried to identify himself with the faction of the council that was most hostile to Travis. But the public continued to be suspicious of Tullik and hostile towards him.

During this time, Travis himself became increasingly nervous and abrupt. At successive council meetings he was angry and defensive. The councillors complained that it was becoming most difficult to have any useful discussion with him. At public meetings, his peremptory manner annoyed his critics more and more. Once, when the interpreter asked him to say a little more because his words so far did not seem to make sense, Travis angrily ordered the interpreter to say exactly what had been said. When the interpreter insisted that he could not translate what did not make sense, Travis grew indignant and repeated the order. The interpreter told the public that he could not make sense of what Travis had said; Travis believed that the Eskimo just spoken was in fact the translation he had demanded. Later in the same meeting, Travis said that he agreed with some of the old people who deplored the lack of discipline among the younger people; in fact, he said, he had spoken to some of the young people on the subject. At this point, an elderly man, who seldom spoke in public, said, 'I do not believe what you say, because what you say is never true. But if this time you are speaking the truth, then I thank you, because what you have said is right.' Towards the end of this meeting, in response to a speech by Travis on welfare, a question came from the floor that summarized the whole painful situation: 'I want to ask you one thing: What the hell are you doing here?' The man did not wait for a reply, but added scorn to insult by walking out of the meeting.

Travis reacted to gestures of this kind by criticizing his leading opponents and dismissing them as incorrigible troublemakers who fed on the misunderstanding and gullibility of the people. Throughout these difficulties he continued to affirm his faith in and affection for the people as a whole, although he expressed antipathy towards various individuals. By this process he discounted the seriousness of the criticisms themselves and never tried to come to terms with what was actually going wrong with his position in the settlement. Instead, he entrenched his position and dignified himself by claiming that he had the thankless responsibility of teaching the community and its leaders the meaning of self-government. Conciliation or concessions on his part would, according to this view, be tantamount to dereliction of duty. It began to seem to Travis that even good manners or a willingness to prolong discussion might be taken as a sign of the weakness that leads rapidly to incompetence.

As these attitudes became more and more evident to the councillors, they intensified their pressure on their settlement manager to give ground. At the same time, Isaac Tullik's job was becoming intolerable, and he offered to resign as chairman of the council. At a public meeting, he explained that he found it impossible to continue working with Travis; the burdens of his dual role as chairman and translator were making him worry and lose sleep, and he was convinced that he must resign. The question was put to a vote, but only three persons, all of them closely related to Tullik, agreed that he should resign. (Travis was at the meeting when this was discussed and voted on, but he did not understand what was happening, and nobody offered to translate for his benefit. When he spoke of the meeting later, he said that he had understood they were voting about who should be given the job of dog-catcher.) Influenced by the measure of support, Tullik agreed to reserve his decision until the next council meeting. At the same time he said he wanted to talk with a senior local government officer in Churchill and to ask him to visit the settlement and advise them.

Soon after this public meeting, the council met again with Travis and, this time, they walked out of the meeting in a body because he again had refused to listen to what was said to him and had become angry. The meeting lasted only three minutes, and the council argued they would not talk with Travis again until the local government officer from Churchill had visited the settlement. Tullik began trying to reach Churchill by radiophone. For a number of days he tried unsuccessfully to reach a particular local government officer whom he trusted and who was generally well-liked by Eskimo councillors. Meanwhile a message reached this particular government officer by another means, and his reaction to it was unsympathetic; officials in Churchill were convinced that all was going smoothly, that Travis was doing a good job as settlement manager. Eventually, Tullik reached the government officer in Churchill, who said that he would come as soon as possible, although his schedule was very full. However, before he had a chance to visit the settlement he left Churchill for a position in another administrative district. So no one ever did respond to the council's appeal for help, and the passage of time alone eventually eased the crisis.

This was aided by the Eskimos' pessimistic resignation in the face of indifference, as they saw it, of White bureaucracy. Some of them looked forward to a meeting between the councillors and federal administrators that had been scheduled for that autumn. This meeting was supposed to provide a forum for discussing and resolving difficulties in the local government programme. But that meeting never took place, either.

When things were at their worst, Travis left the settlement for about two weeks. As he was leaving, a rumour reached him: In a community in another administrative region Eskimos had beaten up two Whites, a settlement manager and a mechanic. This rumour, like most northern rumours, turned out to be entirely false, but like most northern rumours, in the telling it had the ring of truth. Travis was clearly affected by it, and it led him to talk about his own situation in a new way. During the last conversation I had with him that autumn, Travis for the first time asked himself what he was doing and raised the possibility that he was making bad decisions and creating justifiable opposition. He had glimpsed the possible danger of his position, once it had been presented to him as a threat of violence. He went further and raised the essential question: Were the Eskimos likely to gain anything from his work in the settlement? Travis was close to painful self-criticism. For a moment it seemed possible that he might realize his position and perhaps regain some of the good humour and balance he had shown during his first winter and spring in the Arctic, and that he might return to the village in a spirit of reconciliation.

The second winter was a little more harmonious. The community council once more met with Travis, and the welfare issue calmed down. Meanwhile, Travis himself went on a few trips with settlement hunters. There was some bad feeling locally after the official visit of the Commissioner of the Northwest Territories, which was regarded as too short, and because the Commissioner spent most of his time in social activities in the settlement manager's house. For the most part, however, life was superficially calm. Confrontation having proved unproductive, the community merely held its peace. One or two individuals found such restraint difficult, and there were a couple of violent episodes, both of which involved drunkenness. On one occasion, Travis found it necessary to punch one of his critics in the face. On another occasion a man decided to go and shoot Travis, but was prevailed on by his family to stay at home. The appearance of social peace in the settlement and the community council must, therefore, have been achieved at the expense of a significant degree of repression. Travis's critics were quieter because they now believed that little or nothing could be achieved by the sort of criticism they had expressed the previous summer. The harmony was uneasy and unreal.

During the spring and summer, I once again had some conversations with Travis. His situation had changed in some important respects. He was now living with his wife, who was making her first visit to the north. She felt deeply isolated and was lonely without her children, who had been left in the south, and she soon became antagonistic towards the north and its people. Naïve and ignorant though her antagonism was, it introduced new threads into Travis's own view. She felt that the Eskimos had been given too much, and she regarded northern Whites as an unappreciated group who had in some curious collective way given much and sacrificed much to help an ungrateful lot of primitives. In comparison, Travis's views appeared relatively moderate, but he began to direct his criticism towards the Eskimo community as a whole. He felt that the Eskimos were wrong not to regard the settlement's problems as their own social responsibilities. He complained of the absence of community spirit and of the fact that the Eskimos expected high wages for work that should, if they had any public spirit, be done voluntarily. He also criticized them for their unwillingness to take initiatives and for concerning themselves only with what he held to be petty and personal demands, especially for more money.

Behind this sort of complaint lay a more general impatience with the bureaucracy that employed him. During his eighteen months in the north, Travis had grown cynical about the policies and intentions of his superiors, and that cynicism was now turning to hostility. He began to think that the source of his troubles with the local people lay in the policies of Yellowknife and Ottawa. He charged his superiors with ignorance of northern conditions and with failure to adapt policies to the special needs of northern peoples. He thought that the educational services were overemphasized and he complained about teachers and mechanics with little experience and less ability. More generally, he felt that the administrators above him acted inconsistently and therefore made his own work impossible. And finally, he was convinced that at every turn and every opportunity they wasted money.

Throughout the spring and summer, the Eskimos continued to talk a great deal about Travis. His critics were now more numerous and their complaints more damning. Yet their readiness to complain to him or about him at public meetings had waned considerably. The general feeling was that the sooner he left, the better it would be. Some of the men had begun to discuss the possibility of the community's obtaining hamlet status, for then Travis would have to leave.[4] Even the settlement clerk, a young Eskimo who had worked with Travis since his arrival, was now outspokenly hostile to him.

In late July, Travis was informed that there would be a public meeting, and he asked to speak at it. The council told him that

4. The local government programme aims at shifting each community upwards through a hierarchy of local government levels. Hamlet status, the stage above a settlement, has among its benefits the absence of any direct supervision by southern officials.

they desired him to attend. The meeting was a long one. During the first hour, members of the council and others made brief speeches against Travis. Their fierce condemnations turned as much on his personality as on his role. All the settlement's difficulties with him were reviewed – but, once again, nothing was translated for his benefit. During these denunciations, he sat on one side of the room and passed the time playing with some small children. Towards the end of the denunciations, one woman pointed out that Travis could not understand what was being said. One of the councillors replied that he couldn't understand anything anyway, so there was no point in interpreting for him. These exchanges were followed by a councillor's speech in favour of hamlet status. A vote was taken, and the suggestion was opposed by a two-to-one majority.[5] The meeting then moved on to other issues and, after almost two hours, Travis was finally asked what he wanted to say.

Travis spoke about the children. They had broken windows in the school, they had damaged a small dock, they had thrown rocks at the government truck. All this was interpreted into Eskimo, but the interpreter did not translate into English the comments and discussion from the floor. Travis spoke into a curious void, and he had no idea of the effect his words might be having. During the speech he elaborated an argument that I had heard him use before: School windows were expensive because special glass had to be used. Each pane cost $15. The community would have to pay for the windows, $15 for every broken pane. This would come about indirectly: the Government would run short of money because it had to pay so much money for new windows, and because it ran short of money it would have to economize in other ways. Therefore, money would not be available for houses, and people would have nowhere to live or at least would have houses that were in bad condition.

5. Rejection of the proposal was not surprising, given the people's extremely negative attitude towards the problems of the settlement. The people as a whole felt that the Whites should deal with the problems Whites had created, so it was surprising that this rejection was by so narrow a margin.

When he came to the end of these warnings, there was no reply. The total lack of response was emphasized when a local trapper followed Travis's speech with the statement that he intended to use a boat that had been lying on the beach for some years. His statement was not translated into English, and the chairman of the council then closed the meeting.

Soon after the meeting, a rumour circulated through the settlement that Travis wanted to leave. It was eventually an open secret that he not only wanted to leave the settlement, he also wanted to leave the Northwest Territories altogether. The secret was open because Travis began to devote much time to filling in applications for jobs in southern Canada. This news brought about two more changes in the local situation. First, even Travis's most assertive critics began to withhold their expressions of disapproval, and second, Travis himself began to express openly and vehemently his complaints against the local government programme. In the north there is a strong, if unwritten, rule that Whites should not criticize one another in the hearing of Eskimos. Travis began to break this rule and, on one occasion, announced to his interpreter that as far as he, Travis, was concerned, the new local government programme was 'a crock of shit'.

Travis eventually left the settlement just two years after arriving. I do not know what he felt when he left, but the people there were certainly pleased to see him begin his journey to the south. His last summer had been marred by a severe shortage of gasoline. The supply had run out in the spring, and most of the settlement's hunters were seriously hampered until late summer, when the ship finally delivered a new supply. During most of that time, Travis still had a supply of gas, and many Eskimos felt that he should sell some of it, at least, to hunters who needed it. Every time he was seen using his canoe and outboard motor, criticism flared anew. His explanation that he needed it to maintain his own service to the community throughout the summer was discounted as an outright lie. Finally he refused to discuss the matter any more.

Before continuing, it should be said that some criticisms of Travis were without foundation. He was not a liar, nor did he wish to subvert the cooperative and undermine the authority of its directors. His attitude to dependence on welfare payments was rigid and conservative, but he would not see families go hungry. The opprobrium he received was chiefly the result of an abrupt and unsympathetic manner. If he had a moral flaw, it was self-righteousness and an exaggerated confidence in his own judgement. But it is also fair to point out that the Eskimos often expressed their complaints and criticisms in an obscure way; understanding them required patience and some ability to interpret an unfamiliar idiom. It was easy enough for Travis to misunderstand such criticisms and, mistakenly, to dismiss them as confusion on the Eskimos' part. Nor was it easy for him to be patient and to find time to understand, when he was burdened by endless paper work. Scrupulous in his formal duties, Travis did not feel able to neglect his desk jobs to listen attentively to his petitioners. In this way little troubles led to major crises, hostility accumulated, and the chances of any proper communication steadily diminished. Moreover, Travis was the type of man who, whether from previous experience or by disposition, found communication in a confrontation extremely difficult. He was suspected of hoarding gasoline because no one believed the reasons he gave. In fact he really had offered all the gasoline he could spare to the cooperative and was holding the government supply at the lowest level he dared.

He inherited the welfare problem. For over a decade welfare had been managed inconsistently and capriciously. Eskimos in the region had sometimes received less than 50 cents in a monthly cheque, and they also remembered the humiliations of those seeking help from the school-teacher who had formerly been charged with the responsibility of assessing and distributing payments. This man had kept them waiting in an anteroom, told them not to talk, not even to sniff loudly while waiting, and had treated them to long, moralizing lectures on the wickedness of accepting welfare money and the sin of indolence. At another time, welfare had been the responsibility of officials who lived many miles from the community. During that period, the officials' interpreter became so unpopular among the people that he eventually became literally sick with worry and left the settlement altogether. Against this background, it is not surprising that Travis's every move and every decision were regarded with suspicion. He was expected to continue the unpopular tradition, and he inevitably found that reactions against his decisions were, as far as he could see, hostile out of proportion to the decisions themselves. He did not know the history of welfare administration in the community, and he was in no position to discover it.

As well as these local and individual reasons for some of Travis's difficulties, there was another problem – the nature and scope of his work as a settlement manager. These were institutional difficulties, and some of them Travis saw clearly enough himself. Some consideration of these difficulties may provide not only a more sympathetic view of his professional failure, but may also offer an insight into the workings of the local government programme in the north.

There is an essential contradiction at the heart of much administrative endeavour in the Canadian Arctic. There is, on the one hand, a conviction that Eskimos are in need of this and that material or social provision, and therefore the Whites must provide it. On the other hand, it is said that the Eskimos should not have everything done for them, because such a dependence is morally and socially corrosive. The provision of goods and services by Whites to Eskimos presupposes that the Whites really know what the Eskimos need. But that presumption is plainly at odds with the fact that all other Canadian citizens supply leaders from among themselves and direct their own political and social development. Eskimos must therefore assume greater responsibility for their own problems. Political institutions must be created for them and local political leadership encouraged. Then and only then, the argument runs, can the residents of an Eskimo community influence the quality and course of their lives and thereby exercise the acknowledged right of all Canadian citizens.[6] This argument is presented to the Eskimos by way of

6. This view is of course reinforced by a fashionable concern with ethnic cultures, especially that of the Eskimo, as well as by an equally fashionable rejection of western culture and technology. A false inference

encouragement; they are told that through their participation in local government, they will shift control from the Whites to themselves. In practical terms, the message is clear enough: if you (Eskimos) adopt these political methods, constitute the necessary elected bodies, demonstrate adequate leadership qualities, and all this by following a number of relatively uncomplicated procedural rules, then we (Whites) will turn the government of local affairs over to you.

All the evidence at my disposal demonstrates that at least in the Eastern Arctic, the Eskimos received this idea with enthusiasm, for they were anxious to change local circumstances and to reverse a number of trends. It often happened, therefore, that a leader or a council or perhaps an individual asked for some change to be made. In the nature of things, these requests for change turned on important aspects of the community's life: a family should be given welfare; liquor laws should be amended; prices at the store should be lowered; a particular White should leave the settlement; their children at far-away residential schools should not be allowed to go to bars. But in all of these examples, the Eskimos have been told that the issues are beyond the range of even their newly enlarged jurisdiction. Community councils cannot decide liquor laws, nor can they interfere with rules governing children in residential schools. Such matters remained in the hands of the Whites.

The administrators thus find themselves in a curious position. On the one hand, they urge the Eskimo community to believe that every effort is being made to give them responsibility for their own affairs. On the other hand, they insist that many of the affairs that the Eskimos regard as most important cannot be included within their sphere of responsibility. They soon realize that all fundamental decisions are still to be made by Whites. It seems likely, therefore, that the local government programmes, in the context of the Eskimos' sense of subordinate status, have accelerated that withdrawal and indifference which the local government programmes are specially aimed at preventing. A

---

is easily made that the establishment of local government will preserve an essentially Eskimo life.

settlement manager is in the unhappy position of having to translate these ironies into daily political realities. The ironies are not lost on the Eskimos.

The problems of a settlement manager or of any other White administrator can be formalized in this way:

1. The prescriptive context in which the administrator works asserts: 'Eskimos must take over the roles and responsibilities at present in the hands of Whites.'

2. The Eskimos agree and say: 'X should be changed.'

3. But in his educational role the administrator replies: 'You *cannot* change X; that is not within your authority.'

4. The recurrence of 2 and 3 undermines 1.

5. The Eskimos identify the administrator with the negation of 1.[7]

Of course, the contradiction originates in confusion about areas of responsibility and authority. Such confusion also works the other way. Whites in the north have their own ideas about Eskimo responsibility. Teachers, for example, feel that parents are responsible for putting their children to bed at night; settlement managers feel that apportioning the settlement budget is the responsibility of the community council. Sometimes the Eskimos do not agree or consider that they do not have relevant skills or knowledge. Obviously, their tendency to leave difficulties to the Whites can be intensified by withdrawal from conflict with White authority, or by resentment against Whites for maintaining their dominance, or by concluding that the settlement is in itself a White creation and its administration should be left to the Whites. In Travis's settlement a number of the older people considered that the need for an administrator had grown alongside the difficulties that beset the community. One woman remarked, 'We are in a fog. The Whites have led us into this fog, and it is their job to lead us out again.' The Eskimos' attitude towards the school was similar. The educational institution and its rules, together with everything taught inside it, were a White creation: the Whites should therefore bear responsibility for its daily routine and for the problems it caused. Given

7. In broader terms, of course, the entire White or southern society is identified with negation of 1.

the extent to which a northern settlement, in its material, ideological and economic structures is a creature of southern intrusion, it is not at all surprising that many Eskimos assume that the Whites should bear not only the costs but also the responsibility.

Travis confirmed these assumptions, if only because he made the problems of the settlement his own, and was gratified or felt rewarded to the extent that his ideas or suggestions were accepted. The settlement people, for their part, hoped that they could secure changes they wanted; they hoped that Travis could be tempted or persuaded to dispense favours according to local aspirations. It was obviously necessary to believe that their settlement manager was a man of real power, and that he personally would make the changes. But Travis's position was made uncomfortable by local rejection of his ideas and suggestions, and he began to assert his role as a 'man under orders'. It was in that role that he often vetoed the local council's suggestions.[8] Generally speaking, the settlement manager must define and interpret the rules that emanate from the central government and limit local authority and responsibility. No matter how effectively local councillors may denounce the settlement manager's policies or how accurately they expose contradictions or errors in government rulings, the administrator to whom they present these arguments is in no position to take practical heed of them. There are real limits to his authority. In reply to the critics, he can only assert his junior status: he may argue that certain rules are of doubtful use, but they are nonetheless rules.

The situation would seem less strange were it not for the fact that the settlement manager has usually begun by giving the impression that he possesses real power. Travis certainly did this, and his later and sudden assertion of limited power was therefore seen as dishonesty at worst or humbug at best. As relations between him and the community deteriorated, Eskimos charged him with using the rule-book only when it suited him. More seriously, they believed that what suited him best was to prevent the Eskimos from doing what *they* wanted to do. In essence,

8. This has implications for theories about patronage. See, for example, Paine (1971), who develops such a theory in relation to the Canadian Eastern Arctic.

they accused him of having power and refusing to use it, and they refused to listen to his excuse that his role was really very limited. The trap that can so easily isolate a settlement manager behind a wall of suspicion and resentment is a pitfall built into the position itself. Travis might have lessened the danger by a conscious definition of himself as a junior, despite the historical and institutional elements of the situation that urged him to act as if he were a real power. But it is virtually impossible for a White administrator not to enhance his prestige by encouraging aspects of the situation that give a very misleading impression of his place in the bureaucracy.

In Chapter 2, I argued that there is an essential continuity in the history of White–Eskimo relationships in the Canadian Eastern Arctic. Political incorporation, following economic and ideological incorporation, is the latest attempt to change the social and economic life of Eskimos to a form more like that of Canadian society as a whole. This political incorporation would lead to the settlement manager's 'working himself out of a job'. Even if the aim is achieved, the continuity of northern history will have been preserved. Settlement managers, such as Travis, are caught in the contradictions that are the price of this continuity. The people of the far north may be told that the resolution of their social and economic problems will become their own affair, but the degree of autonomy that such a suggestion implies is not at present countenanced by the persons who continue to make the rules.

Of course it is not impossible to give reality to some of the Federal Government's stated objectives for Eskimos and Indians alike, but little or nothing practical is being actually done in this direction. People are promised a voice – a real voice – in local government, but they are not given it. Without it, the Eskimos will remain a tiny minority in the national electorate and a weak pressure-group in the context of an advanced industrial society. The economic and social developments in northern settlements that everyone – native and White – say they want have so far been no more than high-sounding but empty words.

The continuity of Canadian Arctic history is at the level of overall White and southern objectives. There is discontinuity in the history of Eskimo reactions to these objectives and, accordingly, to the individuals and institutions that represent these objectives in the settlements. Although Eskimos throughout the Eastern Arctic admit without hesitation that they are dependent on White society and the Government in the south, they are beginning to grow hostile about that dependency. An Eskimo woman from the settlement where Travis had worked expressed to me the form and direction of this hostility:

Some of the people are still doing whatever the Government officials and the White men tell them to do. Maybe that is why Government officials think that the people are stupid, because people here sometimes do things for the Government even though they are against them. So I think that in the future this should be done: the people here should just decide to go ahead. If the cooperative or the council want to do something, and not do things *this* way or *that* way, or want to quit doing something, then we should just tell the Government to stop coming here because they are not really trying to help. The people should tell the Government to go away and try and fool people somewhere else.

7 • *Inummariit*: The Real Eskimos

Inuk is Eskimo for an Eskimo. The plural, *Inuit*, means 'people', and is the Eskimo word for Eskimos as a whole.[1] By a process of adding middles and endings to a root, the Eskimo language uses single words that, when translated into English, can form long and grammatically complex sentences. A simple example is the Eskimo word for the Eskimo language – *Inuttitut: Inuk* (a person, an Eskimo) + *titut* (in the manner of).[2] The same word is used to mean both 'Eskimo language' and 'like a person' or 'the way a person does'. Another simple example is *Inummarik*, 'a genuine Eskimo' or 'a real person': *Inuk* (an Eskimo) + *marik* (genuine). The plural is *Inummariit*, 'the real Eskimos'. The combination of these two examples shows the structure of a third term, *inummarittitut: Inuk* (an Eskimo) + *marik* (real) + *titut* (in the manner of), hence 'in the manner of a real Eskimo'. Some people are said to eat, work, talk or even to walk *inummarittitut*.

Not very long ago, the *Inummariit* lived in camps, close to the land. They were people of distinctive skills and personality. Many of their ways – economic, familial and individual – are remembered and respected by the Eskimos of today – and even

1. In Eskimo there is a dual as well as a three-or-more plural form. *Inuuk* (with a long *u*) means 'two people'.
2. When infixes are added to stems or to one another, the final (linking) consonants are modified. That modification explains the doubling of the *t* and *m* in *inuttitut* and *inummarik*. In effect, in both cases the final *k* of *inuk* is changed by the first consonant of the affix. Here and elsewhere I use Standard New Orthography as devised by Raymond Gagné for the Canadian Federal Department of Indian and Northern Affairs.

by the young men and women who live under the hegemony of Whites in the new northern settlements. The attributes of *Inummariit* can be readily discovered in Eskimos' accounts of life as it used to be and of certain famous individuals. And there are epithets, phrases and remarks to follow these stories, brief comments on traditional ways, such as *Inummariugamik*, 'because he is a real Eskimo'. Or, less happily, something of the customs of the *Inummariit* can be gathered from complaints now made against opposite qualities, especially against modernity that is plainly antagonistic to the 'real' things – for those real things are, in the conscience of most Eskimos, representations of human goodness, honesty and strength.

Inuit conceptions of tradition lie, therefore, within the compass of the meaning of *Inummariit* or *Inummaritut*. The common use of these terms displays a strong consciousness of tradition. And tradition is the right word: the Eskimos of the Canadian Eastern Arctic are acutely aware of the passing of a way of life, and they tend to see in its passing the disappearance of what was best in their past. Nostalgia for these older ways is characterized in the same words, attitudes and moods that are used in other societies to express regret for the loss of traditional elements: there is sadness, a feeling of inevitability, and wavering between nostalgia for the past and acceptance of the new. Regret is deeply ambivalent.

Many Eskimos are very aware of their ambivalence about old and new. If their traditional life was hard and occasionally brought hunger and distress, many of its qualities and some of its dignity depended on a patient resistance to hardship. For this same reason, many of the older, most traditional-minded men and women warmly accepted the new ways. Now that they find these new ways are not what they had hoped, they wish to recover their own tradition. There is no naïvety in this desire. Those Eskimos who had lived on the land are not eager to return to total dependence on the land alone, for they have not forgotten the dangers of such dependence. Their ambivalence will be evident enough in the next pages. In this chapter, I shall try to describe the traditional life of the Eskimos as they themselves recall it. Most of my discussions of the old days – which were often only about ten years ago – arose in the context of 'Was it better then?' The quotations and anecdotes given below move back and forth between the past and the present.

In the old days, permanent Eskimo camps were small, usually with no more than two or three families, rarely as many as ten. They were scattered along the northern coast of North America and some of the Arctic islands, but, with the exception of the Caribou Eskimos, they were rarely sited inland. They were essentially base camps from which the hunters made long journeys inland or along the coast that lasted weeks or even months. When the Federal Government introduced its low-rental housing programme in the 1950s, some families chose to have their prefabricated timber-frame house built at their base camp, rather than in one of the administrative centres. These houses were sometimes as far as 100 miles from the nearest settlement. Settlement Eskimos still identify themselves as the people of some place or other and, in answer to the conventional question, *Nani nunaqarpit?* ('Where do you have land?'), a man will give a résumé of all the places he *has* 'had land'. Some hunters were evidently more mobile than others and they might be vague about their base camp, but most of the people would answer that question with 'In such a place I had land', and that place was a permanent camp. Even today, the people in settlements know very well who comes from where, an awareness that is often a sign of social divisiveness. Many groups of families, having been camped at or near the same place over a long period, have become interrelated by marriage.

In many communities of the Canadian Eastern Arctic, the move from camp to settlement has only just finished. In a very few places, there are still some families who continue camp life during part of the year, and who definitely feel that they do not belong to the settlement. However much they may depend on settlements, or have near relatives who finally moved into low-rental housing in a government village, whatever their problems of isolation as the last to stay on the land, such men as the *Inummariit* still keep many or most of their possessions in the camp and try to spend as much time there as possible. Some families who have been forced to move into a settlement will still insist that the move is temporary, the consequence of some passing adversity such as sickness or poverty, and that they will soon be back in camp again. Such individuals are widely respected.

One elderly man moved from his camp to the settlement during the spring of 1971. His camp was close to the village, and he could walk to it in a day. He had, over the preceding four years, divided his time between his camp and the houses of his relatives in the settlement, so this final move into the settlement might have been thought to represent only a slight readjustment. Indeed, it was thus described by the White settlement manager who oversaw the move. For the man himself, however, it was a difficult and important decision. He felt that he had given up his real life for a foreign world. He often insisted that he knew little of the settlement and could have few opinions about it; 'after all,' he said, 'between 1944 and now I have been in Ikpiarjuk and so I cannot talk much about life here in the settlement; I want to talk of only things I know. I am not involved in things happening here.' Yet, during the next two years, that man travelled with his dog-team to exactly the same places as before, he hunted for the same animals, employed the same techniques and technologies as he had always used. What, then, was the crucial difference for him between living in camp, where he was a 'real' hunter and trapper, and living in the settlement, from which he also hunted and trapped? Here is a part of his answer.

In camp each year, every year, sea animals were there. They were there all the time. Now there seem to be fewer of them – especially the harp seal. The harp seal can no longer be readily found. I am sure that there used to be more animals along the shore, farther along the shore. When I used to travel a lot I would notice that the caribou were few: now I think that the caribou are more abundant. Recently, inland between Pond Inlet and Clyde River, there seem to be many caribou. In that land there is a place called Anaulirialik, the place where you should club. It is a narrow spot by a river. We travelled there from camp, and could find caribou. Today there are caribou all over the land; the hunters do not need to go to special places.

In the past we used to hunt, particularly for seals. Once we left the camps that became harder. There is as much game as there was, but it is much harder to hunt than it used to be. Yes, it is harder; there is a long journey to the seals. In the camps we could simply stay and wait for the animals. Even the narwhal would just come to us. During the summer it was not necessary to go out of the camps at all. In the settlement the journeys are long, long at all times of the year.

In the old days we Eskimos used to live only on wild animals. The old people were brought up on wild country foods. Their stomachs are used to that, and even today there are many who can buy good things at the store but still prefer to eat the wild animals with the blood and everything, so that they are really satisfied. It is only with the wild country food that they are satisfied. They get weak on store food, and these men as old as I, we have to try and hunt for other old people. But there are today men who do not really bother hunting; they have to stay in the settlements. In the old days we all had to be anxious about hunting, we could hardly wait. Today the men do not seem to be the same way. They have got better equipment, but I wonder how come they do not seem to be able to get the same amounts of good wild country food.

Camp life, then, ensured that most hunters were as close to the animals, especially to the sea mammals, as they needed to be. The Eskimos distinguish very clearly between sea and land mammals, using distinctive terms for the 'skin' and 'fat' of these two categories, and a set of taboos once militated against any blurring of the distinction.[3] In aboriginal days, the camps for hunting sea mammals and those for land mammals were kept firmly apart. Preparation of caribou meat or skins on the sea ice was taboo. But the permanent camps of the *Inummariit* were on the coasts, and sea mammals were the focus of most hunting from them. The closeness of the people to the life of the sea mammals recurs in accounts of camp life. Movement away from camps has been a movement away from the *Inummariit*'s closeness to the sea mammals, on which they had been profoundly dependent.[4]

3. A land mammal's skin and fat are *amik* and *tunnuk*; in the case of sea mammals the words are *qisik* and *uqsuq*. This distinction is preserved today.
4. We shall see that for cash they depended on the Arctic fox, which they needed as primary trading skins. Trapping and skinning foxes from shoreline camps thus constituted a violation of the land–sea opposition,

This dependence was expressed in their attitudes to food. The *Inummariit* preferred sea-mammal meat to all others. They delighted in fresh seal meat and whale skin and made the distinctions of a gourmet between the meat of various kinds of seal. Indeed they distinguished between the various cuts, bones and entrails of any one seal and knew how to blend one item with another to give each mouthful the best richness of flavour. The *Inummariit* preferred their food raw and enjoyed it rotten. In the settlement, many Eskimos still affirm these preferences, and a group who are expressively enjoying what they consider to be *real* food will comment on how good it is to eat *Inuttut*, that is, 'as an Eskimo'. When there is a dearth of such food, or when a visitor comes to a house that has no such meats, there is a familiar expression of regret, *Aittak niqimariqangitualuq*, 'Oh dear, there's no real meat at all.' The same view is often pragmatically expressed in discussions about food in general: only the meat of sea mammals can protect a person against cold and hunger; other foods, including caribou and wildfowl, leave a man vulnerable to those dangers. As for the southern food they buy, delicious though it may be said to be, it lacks all the essentials of true food and is widely regarded as no more than an appetizer. When no food, no wild food, is available in a settlement, the Eskimos grow depressed. One summer, I saw some settlement hunters, who were well able to buy food at the local store, trying to shoot seagulls near the garbage dump to supplement store food with some *real* meat. It is a matter of pride, among Eskimos who take themselves seriously as hunters and trappers, to carry with them a minimum of 'unreal' food, thereby acknowledging their dependence on the hunt and on the food of the land – food that will keep them warm and well-fed.

Their continuous talk of country food can be somewhat misleading. In the camps, Eskimos did not devote their whole time to hunting sea mammals, and they did not maintain an economy that focused exclusively on them. Although the value of such meat was considerable – equivalent to the income needed by a

and may well have defied taboo. If so, it is an outstanding example of how economic readjustment erodes deeply entrenched belief systems and transforms the social practice which was moulded by such beliefs.

southern family to keep well-fed on high-quality foods – their economic life spread beyond subsistence. How the *Inummariit* earned and still earn their living is revealed in recollections that show the ambivalence of contemporary attitudes towards camp life. Since this ambivalence focuses on material hardship and the struggle for livelihood, they reveal much about how the *Inummariit* made their living.

The thing I really miss about camp life is the good health that came from hunting and walking and travelling by boat. The thing I think was really bad about camp life was when there were very few seals and perhaps there were no fox. Well, sometimes you were almost starving. That was really the problem. Only if you were in excellent health, really in the best condition, and only if there were foxes and seals around the place, was it possible to have a good life in the camps.

It is a good thing to bring up the question of living in camps and I am always happy to talk about camp life, about what it was like there and how we lived there. It is good to talk about the ways we had when we were in camps. My life was more difficult and less happy because it forced me into a life which I found hard. You had to work all the time. You had to make important decisions which were not easy: either you went hunting or you carved. For instance, one day I go hunting and manage to kill nothing. On my way home I think like this: if I had stayed at home I would have spent the day carving and I would have carved, and I could have sold what I had carved, and then I would have been able to buy oil at the store. And that oil would have kept us all warm. That is disappointing. And I was always having that kind of problem.

I have heard some opinions. Some say that in those old days it was better, living in the camps, when there were not many people, even though it was sometimes difficult to get food. That is one opinion. Another opinion is that it is a lot better living here. I myself think it used to be much better in the camps. So long as the prices at the store were all right, so long as it was possible to sell fox skins and seal skins and then buy all that we needed for camp life. Then it was really good to be there.

The economic life of camps at least since the 1920s was a blend of subsistence and trade.[5] The Eskimos of today regard

5. In his account of the Copper Eskimos, a particular isolated group, Rasmussen describes 'a young woman in a magnificent caribou-skin jacket,

that blend as the essence of *Inummarik* life, and it is a combination of activities that many people in the settlements still pursue. Yet the *Inummariit* of the camps are significantly distinguished from modern settlement Eskimos by their hunting technology. Certainly the *Inummariit* trapped foxes, but they followed their trap-lines by dog-team; they hunted seals by kayak in summer, by stalking them on the ice in spring, and by waiting at their breathing holes in winter. The *Inummariit* certainly had guns, but the settlement Eskimo of today wonders at the crudeness of those guns and respects the success achieved with an old-fashioned rifle much as southerners respect a hunter who had only harpoon and bow. The principle is the same: these old-fashioned firearms, which had no telescopic sight, only a single shot, and were loaded with hand-made shells, made it necessary for a hunter to be close to his game. That ability was the surest measure of a hunter's knowledge and skill. Of course, the conditions of *Inummariit* camp life demanded competence in traditional technology. There was no cash surplus to acquire more sophisticated equipment, and there could be little improvidence in the use of purchased equipment. In a story about caribou hunting an old man told his children what *real* hunting was like thirty years ago:

We walked far on the land every summer. The first day we walked a short way, and then each day a bit further. Then, after some days, we walked very far without being tired, until we came to the place the caribou were ... When we shot a caribou we would line up two animals side by side and kill them both with one shot. In that way we would usually find the bullet lodged in the second animal, then that bullet could be used again. It could be used again because we mixed some grit with it, to make it the right size.

Of all the Eskimos' hunting skills, those involving caribou had probably changed least. But caribou never achieved commercial value and were of only marginal interest to White

though its beautiful colour effect was entirely concealed by a red overall of calico. Her hands were weighted by gaudy "shop" rings, and between two fingers she held a fragrant "Lucky Strike" cigarette with almost blasé nonchalance' (Rasmussen, 1932, p. 38).

traders. To Eskimos, of course, they were essential for clothing, and at certain times and places they might be as important as food. Once the trade period began most of the *Inummariit* were based at shore camps, and hunters usually had to make long journeys inland to reach caribou herds. The narrator of the story I have just quoted left his shore camp each summer with his entire family and walked hundreds of miles in search of caribou. Once that family had left the coast, they were beyond any assistance that traders or trade might offer; they had taken a step away from the mixed economy back to that of true subsistence.

It was trapping that broke the Eskimos' economic self-reliance, trapping for the fur trade. Before the traders began demanding fox skin, that resource lay at the very edge of a hunter's life. The *Inummariit*, however, were and are excellent trappers; they knew and know how to set the steel traps which they bought at the store, and how to place the best bait in the best position. They learned how to skin a fox in one piece without tearing it, and they learned how to clean, dry and pretty a skin.[6] They learned how to do all these things to secure good prices for the skins at the trading post.

Stone-carving came to be important in the economy of camp-life, and continues to be so in every settlement. The manufacture of tools, amulets, toys and talismans out of ivory, bone and stone predates the fur trade. But the sale of semi-artistic trinkets and momentoes to whalers and other White adventurers became important in the 1800s: cribbage boards, canes, scenes of Eskimo life scored on walrus tusk, small-scale dog-teams and the like had found their place alongside other souvenirs in some south-

6. There are stories of *Inummariit* who were able to pretty an Arctic hare skin in such a way as to convince a greenhorn trader that it was in fact a white fox. Trapping foxes and preparing the skins was man's work; women prepared the less valuable seal skins, which were at times important as trade items. The older *Inummariit* remember two sorts of stone fox-traps that pre-date the fur trade. It is probable that fox-trapping was originally part of a woman's activities, and that its new importance to the man was a result of the development of the fur trade: by taking over this kind of woman's work, the men maintained their dominant economic position as the primary producers.

ern homes long before the commercialization of soapstone carving.

That commercialization got under way in the 1950s, when soapstone – which had long been used for making cooking pots and blubber lamps – was urged on Eskimos as a medium for artwork that might have great value in southern markets. Some of the motifs of these soapstone carvings are distinctively Eskimo, but their size, and many of their forms, have been conditioned by the marketplace if not by the somewhat idiosyncratic artistic sensibilities of one or two of the scheme's White pioneers. Eskimo carving, as it is now internationally known, is a consequence of southern domination of Eskimo economic life. Nonetheless, it is, like fox-trapping, held to be among the *Inummarik*'s traditional skills. The *Inummarik* is said to have carved soapstone and trapped, and to have done both for trade.

Many recent reports on Eskimo life have stressed the importance of a mixed economy for a people whose special skills are directed to land-based activities. This literature emphasizes the possibility that, in the future, the hunters, trappers and carvers of today will be able to carry on their life, at least in part, despite the fact that (or, on some theories, precisely because) they live in a settlement and work occasionally for wages. Whatever the outlook for the future, most Eskimos in the Canadian Eastern Arctic today are engaged in hunting and trapping at least part of the time. However, the *Inummarik* is admired not only for these skills and for his ability to survive hardship, but also for an immensely detailed knowledge of the land itself. The *Inummariit* recognize very many species of plants and birds that no longer have, and in many cases never had, any importance for subsistence or trade. They also know of species that only rarely visit their lands and of some that are now unknown in the regions familiar to them. Such knowledge, which was once of enormous interest to all of the people, has only very recently begun to fade.

Knowledge of this sort has a specialized vocabulary. It is a form of knowledge that consists primarily in *naming*. The *Inummariit*, however, use a vocabulary with a special richness beyond the names of creatures undifferentiated by others. They also use a host of refined terms and phrases and complex grammatical forms. The younger Eskimos in the settlements sometimes cannot understand what the *Inummariit* are saying. The best interpreters, when translating between an older Eskimo and a White, often encounter difficulties caused by the richness and subtlety of the language of the *Inummariit*.

Southerners who try to learn the Eskimo language are encouraged by their teachers to get beyond *surusirtitut*, beyond 'talk ing as children do', to *inuttitummarik*, 'the way real Eskimos talk'. But these teachers distinguish between *inuttitummarik* and *inummarittitut* – 'the language of the *Inummarik*'.[7] The former is correct Eskimo, spoken with respect for grammatical rules and a vocabulary range that goes beyond children's talk; the latter is a sophisticated and elegant manner of speaking that includes vocabulary and constructions that have come with long experience of camp life and a long period of learning. An example of this kind of enrichment can be seen in the vocabulary of shamanism, which was once known by all of the older people. The vocabulary did not consist in special concepts or in specialized words but in specially imaginative ways of naming familiar concepts and objects. For example, the shaman did not refer to the caribou by its everyday name but by an expression that literally meant 'lice', and so evoked abundance.

This difference in the use of the language is very clear to people in the settlement, and is perhaps the clearest indication of who is and who is not an *Inummarik*. I discovered the significance of this difference in a revealing way. Many of my best Eskimo teachers were older men and, as I progressed, they began to play a game with me. They taught me the meaning of certain expressions and told me when and how I could use them. Then, when one of my teachers was visited by another older man or woman when I was also visiting, the teacher would

7. The formation of the two terms depends on the order of infixed phonemes and shows how each infix modifies whatever has preceded it. Thus the root, *inu(k)* (Eskimo), is in one case modified by *mari(k)* (real, true), and in the other case the root *plus* first modifier (*inuk* plus *titut*) (in the manner of) are both modified by *marik*: *inu(k)-(t)titu(t)-(m)marik*, *inu(k)-(m)mari(k)-(t)titut*.

ingeniously manipulate the conversation to ensure that I would use these expressions. As soon as one of them was used, both visitor and teacher burst into delighted laughter. At first this laughter confused and embarrassed me, for I was sure that I had unwittingly slipped into, or had been cunningly led into, a *double-entendre* and probably an obscene one. But I was re-assured eventually by their repeating over and over to me '*Inummarittut uqarputit*!' 'You talk like an *Inummarik*!' It became obvious that some expressions and words are so distinc-tive of *Inummariit* that to hear them said by someone who wasn't even an Eskimo caused excited delight. Once reassured as to the nature of the game, both my teachers and I played it with success.

In reminiscences of camp life, of the days when everyone spoke *Inummarittitut*, there are many references to the quality of life. To the Eskimos from the camps, the settlement seems crowded, impersonal and full of problems. In the camps, a group of families lived together by choice; anyone who felt oppressed by discord or tension could easily move to another place. Families that stayed together felt a mutual loyalty. Mem-ories of the camps invariably recall the togetherness of life there.

When I lived in camp, living the camp life, I always noticed how friendly people were towards one another. Of course, it was bad when we had to sit there, all of us, in difficult times, and could not get help from outside. If only for that reason settlement life is better. But the way we lived in camps was by living together – and that was a better way of living. Food – country food – was easy to share: when just a few families were in camp one small seal could mean a lot to them. It was always possible to share out game killed by one hunter, to share it out between all families of the camp.

The disagreeable thing about not being in camp is rumour. In camp there were no rumours and stories going about, no untruths that caused trouble. Now there are stories about people, and those stories are usually not true. But there are too many people here. In camp there were few people, and we knew one another, and we knew what was being said, and everyone knew what was true and what was not true. The same thing affects the sharing of food. In the camp we would know who had got what food, and could always share it out. Here [in the settlement] you do not know if someone has got food, you only find out if they have it after other people have finished it all up. Even if you could always find out in time, there still would not be enough to go round all those who wanted or needed some food. I think that in those small camps people were friendly and cheerful – more friendly to each other. We shared everything – even store-bought supplies. When a man came back from trading, came with his supplies from the store, he would share them with all the families in his camp.

There is one thing that I want to say about camp life. In the old days it used to be difficult for someone to get food. For the best hunters it was not too bad, however, so they would share whatever they killed with others. And if we heard that in a neighbouring camp a family was having difficulties, hunters from our camp would go and fetch them. They would move the family to our own camp, and so make sure that we all shared whatever had been killed. Today these things do not happen. But, in general, today everything seems to be better for everyone. We are all getting food ... I do not remember many things from the past, from the old days. I do not think about those times very much. What is the use of thinking about the past? But I can tell you one thing; in those small groups who lived in camp, one family helped another.

The smallness of the *Inummariit* community conditioned the relationships that existed among the families in it. They looked to one another for help. Indeed, they had a strong right, almost a legal right, to each other's help. In a camp, the Eskimos were their own masters, neither directly supported nor manipulated by outsiders. This sense of coherence and integrity was felt most strongly in family life. Eskimos today talk of ideal family relations; they recall a pattern and code of relationships that were distinctive and in many respects at odds with family life in the settlements. *Inummariit* have strong views on two closely connected aspects of family life in the camps: relations between generations, and marriage. The *Inummariit* hunters were men of great influence and authority, equipped by experience and ability to make decisions that affected the community and their own families. They expected, and they usually received, obedience; they did not assert their authority forcefully, but presumed it would be accepted. Younger and dependent persons were not bullied into accepting that authority, but they were expected to recognize its value for themselves.

In the old days the girls used to be forced to marry someone. A young man would go to her parents and ask if he could marry the daughter; the parents might say it was all right, and if they did say that, then even if the girl herself was against the marriage she would be forced to marry that man anyway. In those days, when you think about it, it was a good way of fixing marriages. The girl was sometimes forced to marry a young man. She might not be happy for a year or so, but as she got older and more mature, after a few years, her marriage worked out well – much better than the marriages people have today.

From this distance, it is impossible to judge how often a girl was coerced into marriage, and to what extent parents took account of their children's wishes. Probably the move from camp to settlement, together with other recent disruptive changes, have combined to create a situation in which opposition and discord within families are much more frequent and in which the authority of older men and women is systematically called into question. Whatever the sociological and political truth of this important matter, Eskimos in the settlement now feel that in the camps the *Inummariit* properly held complete sway over their families and that, in those days, marriage was undertaken only with the approval of the older people. There was a clear line of authority passing from parent to child even after the marriage of the child. Respect accrued to age, for only with age and long experience did the *Inummariit* gain all their accomplishments and skills.

Present-day concern with marriage indicates the importance of Christianity in the camps. When Eskimos talk of marriage today, they usually mean it in the Christian sense; at least they mean that there has been or will be a Christian wedding ceremony and that the marriage vows of fidelity and eternity will be taken seriously. Because the practices and beliefs that prevailed in the camps are now regarded as elements of traditional Eskimo life, Christianity has been absorbed into tradition as an important part of the *Inummariit*'s system of beliefs, and they try to guard it against erosion by modern influences. The case was put clearly to me by an elderly Eskimo in these words:

It is happening that the young are beginning to lose their belief in the church. They seem to have stopped wanting to believe in it. But older people are trying hard to make sure that the church does not fade away like other Eskimo traditions are fading away. A group of women here is trying to keep interest alive among the younger people, interest in all things which are really Eskimo things. If that group gives up its work, it might happen that the church and other traditional things will just fall away.

Moreover, many Eskimos feel that they were better Christians in the camps simply because camp life was more conducive to religious practices. A woman once said to me:

In the old days when the families were scattered in camps it was not really possible to have a church service. So we did not have a church service every time we should have had one. But in a way it was better then: we used to pray in our homes, every morning and evening. Nowadays, in the settlement, they have long church services – sometimes a long service is twice each week. I think that is not as useful as the way we did things before. Too many people are going to the same place at the same time, so the preaching does not really reach them. It is not person-to-person any more. And the way people act in the settlement, you can tell that the services are not really getting to them; those long services are not so useful. In the old days it used to mean a lot to people, when we held services in our own homes.

With their anxiety about the dangers to Christianity in Eskimo tradition, they also worry about the possible disappearance of Eskimo writing in syllabic script. Virtually everyone in the Canadian Eastern Arctic was once literate in syllabics, and that script is still widely regarded as an important aspect of the things that are essentially Eskimo.[8] But almost the only literature that existed in that script, until very recently, was parts of the Bible and *The Book of Common Prayer*. This is not sur-

8. In fact a number of different orthographies were used in different parts of the Canadian Arctic; the Labrador Eskimos, many of the Netsilik Eskimos and the Eskimos of the Western Arctic have used a Roman orthography since they have been literate.

prising, because the script was in fact devised by the Rev. James Evans, an Anglican missionary, for the Cree Indian language in the 1840s, and was adapted to Eskimo only in the 1870s. Both syllabics and Christianity were features of camp life, and *Inummariit* were well-versed in them. They are included in the same association of traditional knowledge as hunting techniques, richness of language, geographical lore, animal behaviour and clearly defined authority in the family.

To these qualities and aspects of camp life can be added another abstract conception, one that is implicit in many of the traditional ways already described. There exists a definite notion of the ideal Eskimo personality, a notion that people are surprisingly ready and able to describe. The $\overline{good}$ man or woman never interfered or appeared inquisitive; he never interrupted, but let anyone come to the end of what he had to say. Such a person did not become angry and was never moody. (In the dialect of north Baffin Island, there is a term of disdain that falls just short of abuse: *Ningasaqaituq*, 'He is quick to anger.') An elderly Eskimo man, one generally regarded as an *Inummarik*, once tried to explain to me just what a good man should be by offering two contrasting caricatures. In both he pretended to be walking from his home to the Hudson's Bay Company store and, on his way, inevitably passing other people of the community. In the first illustration, he stopped to talk with the persons he passed, laughing and joking with one and another, and plainly taking great pleasure in the walk. That man, I was told, was 'without wisdom' (*silaituq*) and deserved little respect; he was not behaving as an Eskimo should. The second man, on the same imagined walk, behaved differently. He moved surely on his way, without haste and without delay; he acknowledged the greetings of those he passed, but he did not talk to them, nor did he find any cause for laughter. That man was indeed wise (*silatujuq*), and had behaved just as an Eskimo ought to behave.

These qualities of the ideal Eskimo personality are often mentioned in the context of the hardship and misfortune of earlier times, when discipline and good temper were of supreme importance. On only one journey did I personally experience serious difficulties, the worst of which were a week without food and several days stormbound in a snow house. During those days, neither of the two Eskimos with me showed discomfort, hunger or anxiety about our predicament, but they repeatedly asked me if I was all right. After all, they said, I was merely a *Qallunaaq* (White) who did not realize that such difficulties were nothing new or unusual. I was likely, therefore, to be afraid and uncomfortable, and I might even become angry with them for having allowed us to get into difficulties. On the penultimate day of our journey, when we were all weakened by hunger and finding it hard to keep the sledges moving through soft snow, the older man turned to me suddenly and with a quick smile said, 'It is a good thing that you have made this journey, for now you know how the *Inummarik* must live, and the way we have to be when things go wrong; we know because we have had to be like this many times, but for you it is the first time.' I do not mean to imply by this example that such self-restraint is justified only by explicit reference to its usefulness in adversity; Eskimos have praised the same characteristics to me because they think they ensure happiness in the home also. But there is today a continual mixing of modern life with the life of the *Inummariit*, and it is not surprising that the qualities of a good man are often revealed or remembered in difficult times.

This extended discussion of the *Inummarik*'s life-style and characteristics may seem to concentrate on the periphery of contemporary social issues. After all, Eskimos nearly everywhere are now living in settlements, and the changes that have accompanied the shift from camp to settlement have disrupted the old basis of authority and respect. Again, it may seem that this chapter is only a historical reconstruction of the *Inummariit*. Discussion of Canada's native peoples has often begun with the axiom that there remains at present only a lingering trace of traditionalism and that in future there must be an even more complete absorption of the natives into the mainstream of national life. According to this axiom, signs of modernity are signs of an ineluctably disappearing tradition. Behind the axiom, however, lies the fallacy of defining tradition in the terms of classical social anthropology as the customs of pre-contact culture. To contemporary Eskimos, tradition has nothing to do with pre-contact culture. The *Inummariit* are a small group, but it would be wrong to think that the present size or the likely future size of this group is any indication of the value of the tradition that the group embodies.

All Eskimos in the Canadian Eastern Arctic, and no doubt in Eskimo communities throughout the world, are interested in the traditions of their people. I noted at the beginning of this chapter the frequency of reference to *Inummariit* as a standard. Here are two examples that are representative of the attitudes of many, if not most, settlement Eskimos and show that the *Inummariit* tradition is important to Eskimos now living outside of that tradition.

Luke is a man of 30. He works in a small settlement as an assistant mechanic – a regular skilled job that is comparatively highly paid. Living in a government staff house with his wife and three children, he is among the most modern young men of his community: he speaks simple conversational English, spends his annual holidays in southern Canada, and plans to buy a car. He likes to hunt at weekends and on occasional evenings during the summer. But he hunts with the most modern equipment: high-power snowmobile, expensive rifle, new canoe and the best outboard motor. Luke is proud of his job, his house, which he has equipped with a refrigerator, expensive hi-fi equipment and other luxuries, and of his hunting gear.

Although Luke was born in a camp and spent most of his childhood and youth in its environment, he is often aggressively unlike the *Inummariit*. He makes little effort to conceal a quick temper, and certainly does not maintain a tolerant and quiet distance from others. Moreover he likes to drink and, when drunk, is subject to fits of both moroseness and anger; although he is not inclined to fight physically, he is, when drunk, extremely forthright in what he says. And what he says returns again and again to the question of his being an *Inummarik*. On numerous occasions, Luke told me of his knowledge, experience and skill as a hunter, trying to convince me that he was in all those respects a 'real' Eskimo. Luke always began these lectures with some discussion of the Eskimo language; he had noticed, he would say, that I spent much of my time learning from old men and women, and that I seemed to want to learn about the old days and how to do things *inummarittut*, 'in the manner of the *Inummariit*'. But why was it, he asked, that I did not come to him to learn the language? He knew the real words and how to express things in the real, full way; he was not one of those young people who was willing to speak like a child, nor would he teach others only children's talk. I would do well to spend my time learning from him, and I could be sure that he would teach me the *real* language. And I should hunt with him, also, for he could show me how to kill, skin and butcher caribou and seals the *real* way; he would teach me how the *Inummarik* hunted.

Drunk and somewhat incoherent as he often was when he railed at me in this way, Luke nevertheless always showed a profound reverence for the ways of the *Inummariit*, and he was plainly anxious not to appear to have lost those ways. It is possible to see beyond the irony of a drunken Eskimo's assertion of the traditional values, to the Eskimo who, although he is one of the most successful men in the settlement, still wishes to appear to be something other than he is. In his terms it is *not* enough to be an assistant mechanic on a good salary, to live in a good house equipped with a fridge, and to hunt with the help of the most sophisticated technological devices in use.

The same syndrome can be seen in the case of another man of similar age from the same settlement. David, a fully qualified powerhouse operator, had a more important job than Luke and, to most of the settlement youth, David represented the social and personal success that comes from full and competent participation in southern ways and institutions. Admired and trusted by White officials, sure of himself in dealings with them, David carried much influence among the Eskimos of the community. Like Luke, he had equipped himself with every kind of modern hunting device, and he was a famous killer of narwhals, but he nevertheless seemed opposed to the older people and to the more traditional life-style. David was, moreover, a non-believer and preferred hunting to church on Sunday. He also found time for some hard drinking. These facts were of course well known to everyone, and were sometimes commented on in that quietly critical way that the older people used towards successful men who seemed to repudiate tradition.

But David's view of tradition was not unequivocal. He had a plan for the future, which he expressed to me in these terms.

It is no longer possible to make a good living as a hunter. Gas and ammunition are expensive. And sometimes there is too little game, or prices for skins are too low. So I want to do this: I am going to work here in the settlement and make some money. Then with that money I have made from working, I shall go back to camp life – maybe for a year, maybe for more than that. Then I shall be able to be a real hunter and live all the time hunting from the camp.

It is evident that, although David was, to his peers and elders alike, the very symbol of modernity, he nonetheless held the life of the camp and the ways of the *Inummariit* in reverence. He valued tradition so far as he saw himself as part of it, and he valued the *Inummariit* whom he held to embody it more fully. Few as the *Inummariit* are and further threatened though they may be, they are still seen as the representatives and spokesmen of a traditional life that almost all Eskimos – the Davids and Lukes among them – identify with and admire.

8 • *Qallunaat*: The Whites

'They tell that John Ross's ship was first seen early
in the winter by a man named Aviluktoq . . .
But when he saw the ship's high masts he thought it
was a great spirit and fled. All that evening and
night the men considered what they should do,
but as they were afraid that the big spirit might
destroy them if they did not forestall it, they set out
next day to attack it, armed with harpoons and
bows . . . They saw at once that the strangers must be
the famous white men of whom they had heard so
much talk and who were said to have come from
the offspring of a girl in their own country
and a dog. All the Arviligjuarmiut now wished to
show that they were not afraid, and came out from
their place of concealment'

> – Netsilik folk history of an encounter with Whites,
> recorded by Knud Rasmussen

Qallunaat is Eskimo for southerners or Whites.[1] The south is
known, in the Canadian Eastern Arctic, as *qallunaat nunangat*,
the Whites' land. The origin of the word is obscure: the Eskimo
word *qalluk*, meaning 'eyebrow', is often said to be its root, and
Whites are supposed to have been initially impressive for their
bushy and prominent eyebrows. More plausible is the view that
Qallunaat was first used in West Greenland, where there is a
word for 'south' that closely resembles *qalluk*, and that the
term for 'southerners' originated there, and was carried west-
ward – probably ahead of the Whites themselves – into Arctic
Canada. In this chapter I describe the Eskimo's preoccupation
with *Qallunaat*, the Whites – as individuals or as a race, apart
from their institutional contexts.

1. The term *Qallunaat* has most often been written *Kabloona* (see, e.g.
De Poncins, 1941, and Vallee, 1967). In some eastern dialects the '*bl*' is
replaced by '*dl*', and, according to Standard New Orthographic convention, is written as '*ll*'. In Eskimo, vowel length is of crucial importance,
and the '*oo*' of *Kabloona* is wrong.

Whites come north from some far-away, unknown place. Even if they spend many years in the north, they are never thought by Eskimos to merge into the Eskimo world. They maintain close links with the south and – in the Eskimos' view – remain a part of the south. Because Eskimos regard Whites as racially and culturally distinct, they do not expect ever to know them as they expect to know one another. They may know something of a White in a local context, but that context – his work, life-style and professional character – is very little in comparison with what they do not know of him and of the background in the south that has moulded him. A White is therefore seen as something more than a particular man doing a given job. He appears to them as a complex, strange and unaccountable being that has been formed by places and processes that the Eskimo feels he can never know.

An elderly man once conveyed to me his sense of distance from Whites in a striking image. Sitting by a table on which lay a number of pencils, he was talking about the difficulties he and his contemporaries have with Whites. He picked up one of the pencils, then carefully replaced it on the table, saying, 'That is a white man; he has come to work with the Eskimos.' He took up another pencil and said, 'This is another white man, who has never been to the north, but is in charge of the first one.' Taking up a third pencil, he said, 'Here is the boss of this one who is the boss of the man I know at home.' He took up a fourth pencil, set it beside the first three, and said, 'This one is the man who decides things.' Then he elaborated:

The first man, living here, tells something to the second, who tells the third, who passes it on to the fourth. But each of them can change what they say, and the man at the end of the line will not hear what the first man said. But that man at the end will decide what the others should do just the same, because he is the real boss. And he lives in the south, far away. He will think he knows what is best, so the man who lives here in the north, close to the Eskimo people, will be doing what a man who lives far away in the south would do.

The point is of course political – Whites have the power and their power is based on the south – but it has cultural implications: both policy and character are formed in a place that is remote and entirely different from the north.

The Eskimos have many memories of Whites they occasionally encountered when they were still living in camps. Some of the missionaries spent time in camps when they first arrived, but most of them built a mission house and church near a trading post, and the two institutions eventually became the nucleus of a settlement. Very often the locations favoured by trader and missionary were not camp-sites, and the Eskimos had to travel to them. Memories of these visits remain vivid and tell much about the Eskimos' early attitudes to southerners.

The most common and revealing of these memories centre on the traders. As trade rapidly became important in Eskimo life, their interest in the journey to the trading post and in the traders was naturally great. Eskimos quickly realized that trade and trading involved a confusing combination of motives and values. The confusion often led to keen resentment. Traders evidently had access to unlimited quantities of provisions, but they exercised personal control over their distribution. By Eskimo standards, Whites were astoundingly rich and powerful, but their use of this wealth was governed by customs that were entirely unfamiliar.

The very first Whites I remember were Hudson's Bay Company traders. I think they were the very first to come here or to stay anywhere near us here. They used to be good men, good to the Eskimos, if the Eskimos were successful hunters and trappers. Only if you were good at hunting and trapping would those first traders do anything to help you. And the only good thing they did, even then, was to supply each man with a supply of ammunition for the early winter. They did that before freeze-up to make sure that a man would be able to go looking for foxes during the winter. That was credit. If a hunter or trapper did not have much success and got only a few fox, then the credit could not be paid back. And if credit was not paid, then the traders did not want to give any more credit. So I know that those traders were only interested in making money for the Company; or maybe they were interested in making money for themselves working for the Company.

People here used to feel angry about those fur traders because they were only here for the best hunters. I remember that there was one trader who stayed around for quite a long time; he was a trader when I was still a young boy, and lasted here until I was married and had children. He stayed a long time in one place. That particular trader was quite fair to the Eskimo – and good to the good hunters. But he was really bad to the Cree Indians. Many Indians starved to death while he was the trader.

Traders have changed a lot now, and seem to have got better. In the early days those traders were like this: if a trader learned that an Eskimo who had come to trade did not have many furs, then he would not even bother going to the store; he would not let the Eskimo even look at the things inside the store. The traders today are different: today it is easier to get things, and to get money, and the traders stay in the store all day each day. In the old days they would not bother walking to the store if you did not have much with you to trade.

*

Now this is my story. I would like to tell just one story about one particular winter that I remember: a very hard winter [1940–41]. I have never recorded this story, either on paper or into a tape-recorder, so I am anxious to tell it now. When we were young we did not spend our time together, even though we were about the same age. I want to tell this story to you because you were not there when it all took place. In those days, before either of us were married men, it used to be very difficult here: there were not many Whites at that time, and it was sometimes difficult. There were some Whites in a village 100 miles away, and I have heard since that time that the Whites were not coming to the north so much because they were fighting among themselves.

This story took place when my parents and I were living in Aluk. It was early winter. I went along with my parents because I was not yet able to move around by myself. We went to Aluk, and we were planning to stay there all through the autumn and winter. There were two families; in the other family there was an old lady who could not even walk, but she had two daughters. That family camped with us. The old lady was blind. The daughters had children – I think one of them had three children. So we were all camping there, and as the ice formed out at sea we were able to hunt seals and eider ducks.

When winter came the two families were hungry – very hungry. There were no seals and no ducks, because it is only a really good place for hunting during early winter. When the ice gets thick the animals move farther out, so that winter we got very, very hungry. So I sometimes used to walk to another camp, on a near-by island, to get some seal fat, for we had none left in our camp. When I walked to that island I was able to bring some seal fat back home with me, but I had to carry it on my back. We did not have any dogs. If you had a dog-team it was possible to go long distances, but we no longer had a team. Even my step-father did not have a dog-team.

But after the seal fat I had brought from that island had been used up I had to walk once again to another camp – once to a place quite far away. So I walked to *that* camp and I was able to carry some fat home from there too. One time going there I managed to get a ride with a dog-team which was making its way to the trading post; the post was located on the island. But after that the seal fat ran out once again, and I had to set off on another walk, to another camp, and there my brother and his family were camped. And that year my brother was not able to go and trade at the trading post because he had done something wrong, something against the trader, and was barred from trading. Even if he had seal skins, or even if he had good fox skins to trade with, he could not take them to the post. The trader would not trade with him.

Even though it is true that Uppik – my brother – did do that thing at the trading post, even though he had acted wrongly, it is all right now. It is a thing of the past. What happened was this. One winter night Uppik went to the trading post and took one of the small window-panes out of the store and went inside. Because they were so hungry Uppik had to do that; it was the only way he could get food. He went through the window, into the store, and once inside there he began packing tea and tobacco and other things into a box. But while he was in there the white manager discovered that there was someone inside the store. Now Uppik had a companion, and his name was Simonik. That companion is no longer alive. While Uppik was inside the store packing the things they needed, Simonik stood outside the window which Uppik had removed, and watched to see if anyone was coming. And when Simonik saw a flashlight coming towards the store he warned Uppik by whistling – the signal they had agreed to before – that someone was coming towards the store. Uppik had to rush out through the window, and as soon as he was out he began running away.

But the flashlight was shining on Simonik all the time. He was not able to run away; he just had to stand still until the manager got to him. He was very scared because a gun was being fired, and the

bullets were going round him – Simonik thought that they were trying to shoot him. The manager got to Simonik. There were two
Whites – the manager and his clerk. That clerk was a rotten guy; he
took hold of Simonik and began to beat him up. That clerk was trying to injure Simonik in the liver; Uppik was running away, and
being shot at – though he was luckily not killed. The manager was
not all that bad to the Eskimos, but his clerk was different. As
Simonik lay on the ground, that clerk kept beating him. Simonik
was saying all the time that it was not his fault, that he had not taken
anything. But the Whites could not understand the Eskimo language,
and did not know what Simonik was trying to say to them. Simonik
just covered himself up as they hit him, and did not try and fight
back at all. After he got up off the ground, they took him into the
manager's house and beat him some more. Then they let him go.
But he died a month or two later. I do not really know, but
maybe he died of his injuries. After that beating he was never well
again.

The following day I walked to the trading post from our camp
at Aluk to buy some things, and when I arrived there I saw the
manager's clerk walking towards his house. He was carrying a rifle,
and when we met he was shaking all over; I noticed that when we
shook hands. And he told me that there was an Eskimo man, a small
man, a very bad man, whom he had chased with a rifle. After I went
into the house, the manager told me not to be like that small bad
man. He did not tell me the man's name, but I guessed it was Uppik,
my older brother. Happily, the clerk's five shots all missed. After I
had traded, and got the things I wanted, I went back home and told
my family, especially my mother, what had happened. After I had
told my mother she recognized who that small man was, because
there was only one small man around here, and that was my older
brother Uppik. My mother told me it must be him. So it was all very
bad. It would not have been that bad, except that Uppik could not
go and trade any more, and since he had a wife it was hard on him.

Now that wife of Uppik's – his first wife – went to the trading post
after Uppik was no longer able to go there. She went that same
winter. And when she arrived, the manager asked her who she was,
and she answered: Mary, even though her name was Sara. She said
she was Mary because she knew that Mary was getting assistance
every month – she used to get some food and clothing for herself. So
Sara used that name, hoping that the manager would give her the
things Mary usually was given. And after Sara had said she was
Mary, he did give her some food and clothing. And she walked home

with those things. Then they ran out of food once again, and she went back to the trading post, and once again said she was Mary and got the things. But after she had left the store she was seen by an Eskimo woman there, and that woman who saw her went to the manager and asked him who the woman taking the things had been. And the manager said her name was Mary. But that other woman said it was not Mary, but Sara. So a month later when they again were without food, and Sara returned to the trading post, the manager there asked her her name. She said the same thing again, saying that her name was Mary. But this time the manager knew that her name was not Mary, but Sara. He told her not to come in.

At the same time there was the box of things which Uppik had got together when he had been in the store. The manager did not put the things back on the shelves, but left them on the counter, in the box, all the time. Then everyone who came to the store saw those supplies in the box Uppik had put them in, just sitting there on the counter. He left them there all through the rest of the winter, and through the spring too. After break-up he took them out in a boat, and threw them into the sea. He seemed to prefer those things not to be used by anyone; instead he threw them into the sea.

That is what it was like that winter. I could not stay at home because Uppik and his family were experiencing those sorts of things, hunger, and troubles with the store. It was a hard winter for that family, and for me too. But when I went to the post I used to take some of Uppik's furs, and just not say to the manager that they were Uppik's, saying instead that they were mine. Then I could take some tea and tobacco and other things to Uppik and his family. That was the only way my brother's family were able to get anything from the store. All that winter I had to make long walks to other camps, searching here and there for food. Once when I was at a camp called Naujak and then went back to our camp, some of the people camping with us had died. If a hunter had no skins to trade, the managers at the posts would give us nothing. Some of the people camping with my parents starved to death that winter. It was a particularly bad winter for everyone. Some people in another camp starved to death. It was the same thing. They did not have any skins to trade, so the manager would not give them anything, and so they starved to death. And from the cold, too. We did not have any proper clothes any more, and the hunting kept on being bad. For one whole month there was no open water, and they could not melt snow to drink because they had no fuel left for lamps. They could not even find wood, so where there was no seal fat to melt the fresh-

water ice they could not get enough to drink. Luckily in our camp
we did find some wood, and we would sometimes make a fire and
get something to drink.

That clerk at the store did not last long; he did not stay here very
long. After break-up the Hudson's Bay Company boss came here
and took him away. I think that the manager reported him one day,
when he had gone hunting. That clerk loved hunting, and maybe the
manager got tired of him being away too much. But I do not really
know whether he reported the clerk to the boss or not. But the rest
of my story is true; I remember it all very well.

The Eskimos of today do not believe that Whites came north
simply to be helpful. They see the Whites' arrival as bound up
with their self-interest. Nonetheless, on balance the Eskimos of
today view the Whites' coming as a good thing and say it was
essential that they remained. Survival in the camps depended
on trade and traders, even if relations between trader and
trapper were often uneasy or hostile. And even if that amazing
abundance of provisions was not spread freely among the
people, there was no doubt in the minds of the Eskimos that
they depended on these curious and difficult strangers from
the south.

The Eskimos' attitude towards these strangers was compounded of awe, nervousness and hostility, but outright conflict
was rare. The traders' own accounts, many of which have been
published, suggest that they believed themselves to be living
among a friendly, tolerant and good-natured people. True, Duncan Pryde, in his romantic saga of drama and strife, *Nunaga:
My Land, My People*, has described a different sort of behaviour,
but even he believes that the expressions of anger he so proudly
remembers having suppressed were not typical of the Arctic,
even of his especially violent corner of it.

The Eskimos of today recall that, in face-to-face dealings
with traders or other Whites, they always felt acutely nervous
and tried to present at least an appearance of compliant friendliness. The Eskimo's ready smile is really the mask for a host of
conflicting feelings and thoughts. The Eskimo of the camps
certainly knew that a trader's power was great, that, as the last
story reveals, during hard times he could hold the power of life

and death, and that he should, where possible, be appeased. Indeed, it is the general view of older Eskimos that most Whites are emotional and unpredictable, and they illustrate this view with many good-natured anecdotes about men who showed irritation or anger and therefore made themselves ridiculous. But they also remember Whites who had made themselves feared because of their irrational angers and who had been killed by Eskimos. Price recounts two such stories.[2]

An old man once told me that it is always easy to see what Whites are thinking because they show everything in their faces. Because every White who comes north is conspicuous among and important to the Eskimos, it is not surprising to find that older people readily recall each of them.

I have already said something of the transformation of Eskimo–White relations with the appearance of government agents in the north. The influence of the trader, whose primary interest was in a commercial relation with trappers, was partly displaced by Whites who claimed that their sole concern was with Eskimo welfare. We have come, such officials said, to help the Eskimos, to make sure there is no more hunger and starvation and that everyone has the material things they need.

At first these men persuaded the Eskimos that these were indeed their motives for being among them – or, at least, the Eskimos believed that the Government had sent these men to help the Eskimos, and that they had undertaken their mission honestly.

Then the administrator came, the first we ever had. He came and said that he was going to help people, and that he would really try and treat people all the same way. I was trying to support a family, and others were not. That administrator agreed with us about who did and who did not need help. It was like that when he came – we were all treated the same, and he said he would give us all the same kind of help.

But the Eskimos' attitude towards this offer of help from the south was soon revised, and they realized that although the Government in general and some Whites in particular wanted

2. See Price (1970). Price tells these stories entirely from the southerner's point of view.

to help the Eskimos, in practice they did not always do so. Some of the ways in which this new White presence affected the lives of Eskimos is illustrated by the reminiscences of a man, who was 31 when he told me this story.

I have a very short memory, not like my father – *he* can remember being on his mother's back . . . I was very young when my mother died, maybe a little older than 10; that is when I start remembering things, when I was about that age. I remember just after my mother's death that I was sometimes hungry and quite thirsty. Life was difficult for me when my mother died. I was thirsty, and I used to think that when I grew up life would be easy again. I used to think: when I grow up I shall be able to look after myself, and not be hungry and not get thirsty. The person looking after me did not really look after me properly when I was small, and I would think: I'll pay her back when I am an adult. But I do not pay her back, I do not make her hungry or thirsty. When my mother was alive I was looked after much better, even my clothing was better, even my seal-skin boots. I remember my good footwear when my mother was alive, but after she died I can remember my footwear being made from flour sacks full of holes. My feet were not taken care of and those sacks on my feet would wear out quickly; I sometimes walked around with the skin of my feet sticking through the boots. That went on until I was 18. And then, when I was 18, I was taken to hospital. I had a general sickness, I had tuberculosis.

I was away in hospital for about two years. That was my very first time away from the family. And that was when things in my life began changing. Since then life has been easier; when I was away in hospital I learned a few English words, so that when I came home again I knew a little English. I was the only person here who knew a few words of English, so when the Whites came here I was taken by them, to try and help them talk with the Eskimos. That seemed to make things easier, because I was finding jobs. You know, going out to hospital seemed to make life better when I came back.

I went into the same house as before and there were some pups there, which I was able to take. I got four pups then, raised them, and so got a dog-team for myself. When those four pups grew up, and were working as a dog-team, it was possible for me to go hunting for myself. Also, I asked the Hudson's Bay Company manager if I could have some credit – if I could have a rifle on credit. It was K. [an Eskimo] who was working in the store at that time, and he gave me the credit for a rifle. Getting that rifle started things rolling for me: I was able to feed myself and my team. It seemed this way with my step-mother: she used to be hard on me before I was 18, but since I came back, from 20 on, she has been treating me well – for I have been able to achieve things since then. I used to think, when I was under 18, that as I grew up my step-mother's attitude would change.

But when I was about 22, that rifle I had got on credit was worn out, and I had to get hold of a new one somehow. Fortunately, the Government gave me a new rifle, and some new clothes, and even supplied all the ammunition I needed then. I had enough ammunition to last through one whole spring. I did not ask for those things; I saw some men going to the office and getting things from the government official, and I just went along to see what they were all doing, asked, and was given those things. I used to get welfare from the Government from time to time, but when I was 22, that was when I stopped getting welfare completely. I do not know why that was. But those early administrators from the Government were good to me. The one who gave me the things once gave me some bits of advice too. He said: The Government is here to help people, so if you have no source of income to buy guns and ammunition you should never be afraid to ask. Even when that administrator left, and was followed by another man, I still got the same kind of help. Although in those days there was no administrator living here all the time, there was one who came from many miles away, making visits to the Eskimos here, seeing who needed Government help.

Here, then, is one man who found real benefit in the new concern of the Federal Government, and of course the new agencies reinforced the Eskimos' belief that Whites control countless riches. But now they seemed willing to use their power and these riches to help the Eskimos; southern claims were backed by the realities of welfare payments, medical services and some opportunities for wage-labour. These services are all provided in the settlements, and they are central in the Eskimos' view of Whites today.

The Eskimos do not always agree about the purposes and motives of individual Whites. Some say that *all* Whites are trying as hard as they can to bring southern benefits and a truly good life to the northern native people. Men with such a conviction are emphatic in their support of each White who comes to work in the village, irrespective of the way in which he carries out his work. But such uncritical support is rare. Most Eskimos distinguish between basic purposes on the one hand, and individuals on the other. Even those who see the presence of Whites in a broad political context as a consequence of decisions taken by men who never, or very rarely, come north, are nonetheless ready to express indignation at the behaviour of a particular White and even to be critical of Whites in general.

Most Eskimos have a charitable view of southern purposes, but they are critical of individuals: because their standards and expectations are high, individual shortcomings are duly judged harshly. In Chapter 6, I described the keen animosity that a majority in one settlement came to feel towards the local administrator. But many of those same persons believed that the southern presence in the north is good, and they criticized Travis for not helping the people, for not doing what he had been sent to do. Many in that community expressed gratitude to Whites in general for having been, and promising to be, of so much help to Eskimos. Yet criticism of individual Whites is rarely addressed to the Whites themselves. Eskimos feel a deep reluctance to confront Whites, even when indignation is keen and widespread. Even in the case of Travis, the confrontation was slow in happening and the work of only a few of those who were angry. The Eskimos agree that they avoid such confrontations, and point out that Whites are intimidating persons who take criticism badly. Moreover – many Eskimos say – Whites do not notice the subtle, quiet expressions of criticism they generally prefer to use.

Eskimo reluctance to criticize Whites is reinforced by a deep anxiety about how dependable they will be in the long run. Whereas Eskimos agree that southern support is essential and a matter for gratitude, they often say they fear the south will eventually abandon them. Some older people recall having had this fear since the earliest days of federal assistance. They reason that, even if the Whites are here now to help them, they will not continue that help unconditionally nor indefinitely. They will withdraw their support and leave the Eskimos to their own resources, and that is particularly likely to happen soon if the Eskimos do not cooperate fully with their laws. Many thoughtful Eskimos, realizing their dependence on southern support, cannot avoid this lurking apprehension. This fear underlies the Eskimos' reluctance openly to confront and criticize Whites. In the course of my field-work, many persons asked me how I intended to use what I was learning and asked for assurance that I would not tell southerners things that might make them think ill of the Eskimos, for (and this fear was often explicit) should they think ill of the Eskimos, then the Government would surely stop providing services. A dependent and politically impotent group reveals its weakness by its unwillingness to risk protest.

This central problem can be amplified by consideration of one word in the Eskimo language. Eskimos often say that they do not wish to criticize Whites, or even to visit them, because Whites are 'frightening'. They also say that it is 'frightening' to be among people whose language they do not understand. But they use different words for these fears: in the first instance, the word used has the stem *ilira*, and the expression often has the form *iliranarmat*, 'because it is *ilira*'; in the second instance, the stem is usually *kappia*, and thus the form *kappianarmat*, 'because it is *kappia*'. The first of those terms, *ilira*, is difficult to translate, and for a long time I was puzzled by it. Because it often came up in discussion of Whites and was used to explain why contact with Whites was avoided or was unsatisfactory, it was obviously important to unravel its connotations. Most translators render it as 'afraid', and do not distinguish between the two roots mentioned and a third one, *irqsi*. One excellent interpreter told me that he knew no word in English that could capture the central meaning of *ilira*.

The unravelling of the puzzle began in a way that surprised me.[3] For about five days, I had been avoiding my principal Eskimo language teacher. During field-work, there are times when a feeling of despondent pessimism makes conversation even with one's best friends seem impossible. Uneasy, and feeling so little confidence, it seemed either foolish or pointless to be with those who had helped me most: the Eskimo language

3. Had I read at that time Jean Briggs's study of Eskimo emotional expression (Briggs, 1968), I should have resolved the puzzle sooner.

seemed too difficult for me, and I felt I would irritate patient
friends. Five days passed in this way, then I happened to be
walking by my teacher's house, when he came to the door and
invited me in. Once inside, he told me that he had prepared
our next lesson and he was ready to teach it that very minute.
Sitting down at the table, he pulled out two sheets of paper on
which he had written a series of sentences. But before passing
them to me, he said:

My wife and I have seen you walk past our house, and have seen
you through the window walk past, not visiting. For some time you
have not visited us. My wife saw you walk by this morning and she
said to me, 'There he goes, he is not going to visit us. Perhaps he is
afraid (*ilirasuggamik*) to came here.' You do not know that word,
ilirasuggamik? Here, I'll explain to you.

Then he passed the papers to me. The sentences all used one
of the two principal words for fear – *kappia* and *irqsi*. A man
was hiding in a hole in the snow beside which an enormous polar
bear was strolling: he was terrified (*irqsi*.) A man was walking over thin ice of early winter: he was afraid (*kappia*). Others
were in the same vein.

Once I had understood those examples and had written sentences using the same roots in appropriate contexts, my teacher
spoke again. He said that when I came to visit I need not be
afraid (*kappia*) nor terrified (*irqsi*), because there were no dangers in his house. He knew I would not have such feelings. But
sometimes he thought I felt *ilira*, and he understood that I
might have this feeling, for I was a stranger and sometimes
would not understand the ways of the house. But I was wrong
to feel *ilira*, because there was nothing to feel that way about
(*iliranangituq*). When he, my teacher, went to the house of a
White, he sometimes felt *ilira*, and when he was a small boy he
thought that his father was very *ilira*-inspiring (*iliranalaurtuq*).
Gradually it became clear to me that the context that revealed
the root meaning of this word most clearly was the feeling that
a strong and authoritarian father inspires in his children.

Armed with this basic discovery, I began to grasp refinements of its meaning. The word seems to have at its centre the
feeling of nervous awe that comes from being at an irreversible

disadvantage, a situation in which one cannot modify or control the actions of another; it can also describe unpredictability – one is *ilira* of a person whose actions cannot be predicted, nor understood. It is therefore a term that neatly describes situations in which a person is in contact with a culturally dissimilar group, such as the visitor to a household that speaks a language he cannot understand. The term captures the feeling of the dominated towards those who dominate them, and may also connote dependence. Eskimos frequently use this word to characterize their feelings about Whites, and the range of its meaning is nearly co-extensive with the range of their attitudes towards Whites.

Eskimos sometimes refer to one another as being or not being particularly *ilira*-inspiring. When I was urged to visit someone said to be unusually interesting, I was often assured that such a visit was *iliranangituq*, 'there's nothing to be *ilira* about,' and I understood that I might expect a ready welcome, conversation and warm hospitality. But it was also made clear that the *Inummarik*, good, strong, admirable Eskimo of the old school, did indeed inspire some feelings of *ilira*. Young Eskimos sometimes confided to me feelings of *ilira*, a maximum of respect, towards some older person. If someone said a man was *kappia*-inspiring, then he would be criticizing that man, suggesting that he was given to anger or violence and might perhaps be dangerous. But if he were said to be *ilira*-inspiring, the man might be receiving a compliment.

Jean Briggs has discussed the term *ilira* and has contrasted it with *kappia* and *irqsi* (*iqhi* in her orthography) in terms similar to those used here. She writes, 'The term *ilira*, is used in situations in which a person fears that his request will be refused, or that he will be scolded or criticized . . .' and continues:

Children are said to feel *ilira* towards their parents, that is, their 'leaders' . . . Strangers especially, both Eskimo and kabloona, are *ilira*'d by everyone, and people of uncertain temper are also *ilira*'d, I think, whether or not they are strangers. Thus, one man told me: 'People who joke frequently are not frightening (*iliranaittut*) – implying that people who do *not* appear happy *are* frightening.'[4]

4. Briggs, op. cit., p. 32.

In my understanding of the word, Briggs's observation needs
some qualification. A person who appears unhappy will be
ilira-inspiring if, and only if, he is someone who also inspires
respect. Otherwise he may arouse *kappia*-feeling, or no feeling
of fear at all. My qualification is in fact implicit in two other
passages in Briggs's discussion:

> The following kinds of behaviour are all noted on occasions as
> signs that a person feels *ilira*: silence and constraint; a loss of
> appetite (or at least an unwillingness to eat) in the presence of the
> *ilira*'d person; a tendency to smile and agree, if the latter speaks,
> and a reluctance to disagree or to admit that one does not under-
> stand what the feared person says . . .
> Feelings of *ilira* make a person reluctant to ask favours. The
> woman in whose household I lived said that her early *ilira* feelings
> about me had made her reluctant to use my primus without express
> permission, and reluctant also to ask for food from my supplies.[5]

Because I am arguing that the most respected Eskimos inspire *ilira* in others, then it may appear that Whites who cause
so much *ilira* are being complimented. But *ilira* of Whites is
typically compounded by *kappia*: Whites inspire simple fear as
well as the blend of respect and nervous apprehension indicated
by *ilira*, and because the Eskimos believe that Whites are prone
to sudden anger, the element of such fear can be large. Whites
who are even-tempered, forthright and friendly can fairly
quickly dispel some of that fear, but the mixture of fears remains. If the feeling of *ilira* never gives way to ease, then the
one who inspires *ilira* is not only a person who commands
respect, he is also a cause of unremitting anxiety. To say of a
man, *iliranattuq*, is ambiguous praise indeed. I was told that,
by comparison with the Whites of even the recent past, those of
the present-day inspire both more *kappia* and more *ilira*. An
elderly man said to me,

> In the old days the Whites who came here were always writing
> things down, even when they were not at work in their jobs. Today
> they only write in their offices. In the old days traders and mission-
> aries and government officials wrote down Eskimo words and stories

5. ibid., pp. 32–3.

and learnt about them. Today they do not learn such things. Today the Whites are not seen to be writing.

That gulf between peoples created by common ignorance is bound to increase the *ilira* that the dominated feel towards their dominators. And as Eskimos have recognized the increasing intensity of that domination, so they express fear and unease about Whites more readily among themselves, but ever less readily to Whites.

Some of the Eskimos' unease centres on aspects of their life that they believe Whites are disposed to criticize, and the anticipation of criticism is closely related to the Eskimos' sense of the irreducible difference between Whites and themselves. Some commentators, including many social scientists, see modernization as a series of social changes that increase the similarities among the different parts of a larger society. For example, they would anticipate that the urbanization of peasant villages will bring the social culture of the villages closer to that of the urban centres of the nation and, in some cases at least, will lead to the disappearance of local traditional culture.

This process may be regarded as a reduction of boundaries: the changing or acculturating group gradually loses its sense of difference and discreteness, a change that facilitates or causes assimilation. The fact that this phenomenon is widespread has led many to expect that Eskimos, in the course of rapid modernization, will lose or blur their ethnic boundaries. That expectation would, however, be radically incorrect: in the case of the Eskimos described in this book, their ethnic boundaries are strongly felt and have been generally maintained despite modernization. The assimilation of individual Eskimos by White society is minimal. Most Eskimos are emphatic about the differences between themselves and Whites.

Eskimos consider that the concepts and words, the ways of thinking and the attitudes of Whites, are all distinctive. Whites even have distinctive causes of worry and fret about trivial things, such as punctuality. Furthermore, Whites are known to disregard literal truth and will say that a thing is going to happen when there can be no certainty of it or when it is no more than a personal judgement. Then, if the event does not turn out as expected or predicted, they are openly troubled. Whites are also different in many physical details: they walk, lean and sit in a distinctive way. One old man, talking of a government official we both knew, insisted that the man could not be a full-blooded White because he did not walk like other Whites. Although the official was typically Nova Scotian, tall, blond and English-speaking, the old man was satisfied only when I told him that the official had once been a Hudson's Bay Company clerk and had probably done a good deal of snowshoeing. Whites are also thought to lack physical endurance and strength. Eskimos who take Whites on hunting expeditions are attentive to their every need and anticipate their slightest discomfort, always fearing that they might collapse from cold or exhaustion.

Social and dietary habits bring out many differences that are subject to criticism. Eskimos believe that most Whites despise Eskimo food and are reluctant to be seen eating raw food, especially raw seal meat. Whites are believed to find such food disgusting and thought never to eat it. Elderly men who had, over the years, travelled with many Whites, including old-timers who lived hard and rough, told me they had never yet seen a White eat raw seal meat. On my first long trip with Eskimos, an old man and his teenage son, we had no food on the return journey except fish, which the old man boiled at every meal. Even when we stopped for a travelling break in the middle of a day's sledging he took out a stove and went to the trouble of cooking the food. Months later – when I had learned to enjoy many raw and frozen foods – we laughed together about that journey, for by then I had discovered that they much preferred to eat their fish raw, but had been afraid of disgusting me. Similarly, young Eskimos often express a distaste for raw meat, hoping thereby to impress others – especially Whites – with their modern and sophisticated views.

In the few settlements where Indians and Eskimos live as neighbours, the Eskimos feel the same defensiveness. In Great Whale River, for example, Eskimos told me that they always drew their curtains when eating raw seal meat, for fear of being seen by Indians. A preference for raw food is therefore an important trait of Eskimo self-identification, but it is also felt to arouse hostile criticism in others.[6]

Eskimos are also self-conscious about the ways they eat. They do not have regular mealtimes, which determine the pattern of daily life, but they eat when it is convenient (before setting out on a journey, on returning, when there happens to be food), or when they are hungry. Nor do the members of a family necessarily eat together; they often eat in succession or at different times. Most Eskimos prefer to eat standing or squatting on their heels around a carcass or some frozen fish, each cutting a chunk with his own knife, eating it, cutting another. Such a procedure does not require plates, cutlery, tablecloths, or any of the paraphernalia with which Whites dignify the transformation of raw flesh into food and culture. Of course, most Whites regard the Eskimo way of eating as messy, unhygienic and uncultured. Conscious of this view, Eskimos are defensive and nervous about their own food habits; if a White happens to visit an Eskimo home during a meal, it is assumed that he will not join in, and anyone who is eating becomes tense with embarrassment. Conversely, Eskimos are apprehensive about visiting a White's home when a meal might be in progress there, for the Eskimos recognize that eating is, for Whites, a strange and exclusive ritual invested with a formality that is entirely foreign to Eskimo manners.

I often visited the home of an elderly man. The visits had become one of the most relaxed parts of my work; the old man, his family, and I talked, drank endless cups of tea, and often ate together. I learned how to eat Eskimo foods in the Eskimo manner. Once the first embarrassment had passed, I felt that the old man took a special delight in teaching a southerner ways which Eskimos so often feel are distasteful to southerners. One day he suggested that we visit a relative of his. We went there, accepted the offer of tea, and the wife began to wash a cup for me. My friend called out, 'Don't wash a cup for him. He has been taught not to live like a White.' On future visits there, no

6. The word 'Eskimo' derives from an Algonkian word (*Eskimantik*) meaning 'eaters of raw flesh'.

further attempt was made to ensure that I had a specially clean cup. Those cups on the table were not dirty, merely in use.

When strange Whites visit an Eskimo home it is not surprising that they usually cause consternation and disquiet, for the Eskimos are sure that many things about their homes and their way of life will be criticized. Since such visitors are likely to be men of power, representatives of the authority that has been and still is changing the Eskimo way of life, Eskimos are very sensitive to such criticism. The Whites' dislike for raw meat, their bizarre way of bending forwards when eating, their preoccupation with clean cups and their vast wealth and political authority are all blended together.

This sense of difference is inevitably bound up with the Eskimo's feeling of *ilira* in any confrontation with Whites. The Eskimo assumes that all Whites are more or less the same, even though one or another trait may be relatively prominent. That assumption is poignantly revealed by the questions Eskimos frequently ask the occasional Whites they know well and like, '*Angajuqqaaraluulaarputinnai?*', 'You're going to be a powerful boss, eh?' The optimism of the question (after all, it would be good to have a comparatively agreeable man in power) is touched with resignation (after all, a White is a boss and an alien).

It is important for Whites to recognize the extent of the powers the Eskimo attribute to them, and the following anecdote may help to demonstrate the point. An Eskimo recounted to me a series of troubles that had led to murder. At this point, the RCMP had intervened, and eventually the police took a number of men to jail. One of the men died before completing a prison sentence. The cause of his death was unclear to me, so I asked some questions.

'What happened to the man in prison, before he died?'
'Nothing. He died there.'
'Was he sick?'
'No, he was killed in the prison.'
'Who killed him?'
'The police killed him. They knew he was never going to be a good man, so they had to kill him.'

'Do you know how they killed him?'

'They killed him. They knew he would be bad always. It was God's wish that he die, and it was the police who did what God wanted. The police always do that; it is their job. They knew the man must die, so they decided he should die, and he died.'

'Did they just wish it? Is that the only thing they did?'

'Yes, they wanted him to die. If the police want someone to die, then they decide it, and wish it, and the man dies. That is, if it is God's wish, and nothing can be done, then the police do it. They are God's helpers. They know what has to be done, and they do it.'

Few young Eskimos would today subscribe to this view of the police, but all Eskimos are awed by the extraordinary range of power and wealth possessed by government and medical officials, just as they were once impressed by the missionary, trader and police triumvirate. But new attitudes, which contain elements of hostility and resentment, are also growing even in the remotest and least developed communities. Many, perhaps most, Eskimos feel that the Whites have not always treated them honestly, fairly or generously, and many young Eskimos are indignant at such treatment.

No Eskimo is in any doubt that the Whites have ultimate authority, and very few, if any, can disregard the differences that have, over the years, come to be seen as a vast cultural divide between two radically different peoples. The one group, small, poor and troubled, is socially and economically dependent on the other group, which is numerous, powerful, assertive and critical. The prevalent attitudes of Whites to Eskimos and of Eskimos to Whites is fundamentally based on the Eskimos' awareness of this imbalance, and on the Eskimos' part it leads to a curious but understandable blend of gratitude and respect, defensiveness and anxiety, withdrawal and – increasingly – hostility.

9 • The Settlement

In many communities of the Eastern Arctic the transition from camp to settlement was effected in stages. Often the children were first sent to a residential school in a settlement while their parents remained in camp. As building and services in the settlements increased, so Eskimo families had more and more reason to spend time there. Moving back and forth between camp and settlement became a normal pattern of life. Yet despite a gradual shift of intent towards the settlements, with a gradual increase in the time that camp people spent there, nearly every Eskimo family can say precisely when they decided to move into a settlement. After the move, many hunters still returned to their camps for parts of the year, but that fact did not for most families obscure their sense of having moved.

The Eskimos themselves see the move as having been a definite choice, and they remember the factors that determined it and their feelings once the choice and move had been made. For many families the choice was recent, and their vivid memories of it provide a good starting point for a discussion of settlement life today.

A young man who in 1971 was still trying to live by hunting and trapping, described the move in this way:

It was 1966 when we came here. I decided to move because of the children. When we were in camp, we were always being asked when we would be moving. Everybody was always asking. One year there were two women teachers who taught in the camp, and they asked again. It was summer and they said it would not be possible to bring our children to the settlement and for us then to continue living in camp. But we anyway did not want to live like that; we would not want to live away from our children, without children at home with us. Now it is not too bad in the settlement, but I was happier in camp, only coming here to buy things we needed. Sometimes I regret the move. In the camp there was no rent to pay.

At first I did not like settlement life at all. We were all worried about being able to get Eskimo food – but then we found we could still hunt and eat good food sometimes. Then there is the problem of rent. We are asked to rent houses because it is supposed to be better for our health. People from the south told us that we would no longer get sick if we lived in a rented house. But sickness does not come only from housing; the people were fooled. In the old days we were isolated. Nobody was moving about among us. So sickness moves with them.

An older man told me:

I moved here because I was asked to move, and because I am ill sometimes and have back trouble. On the whole I am well looked after here. I do not think I had any real difficulty making the move, though some of us were sometimes unhappy when we wanted to hunt, but could not hunt as easily, as freely as before.

A middle-aged man thought the move was harder:

It was very difficult moving here from camp. We moved in 1967 because the children had to go to school. There was a hostel at that time for children whose parents were living in camp, but it always seemed to be full. The children in the hostel were well cared for by two couples, but we wanted to be with them. I would have stayed in camp if the children had not been a problem, and if my step-father had not moved. And what I noticed on first being here was the long road from our house to the school.

Most observers feel that great pressure was put on Eskimos to move, that the Whites were anxious to draw people into settlements. The pressures were informal and diverse, both as attractions (medical services, housing, proximity to store and church) and threats (no camp schools, illness in the camps). Once made, the central feature of the move was a new relationship to the Whites and their institutions: the move was acknowledgement both of the Eskimos' dependence on the Whites' goods and services, and White hegemony over social, economic and moral life. The move was made in full consciousness that, whereas camp life offered privacy and some sense of integrity and independence, settlement life must be lived under White domination – this consciousness at once described the terms of settlement life and assumed that the fundamental responsibility for them was in the hands of White administrators.

In *Kabloona and Eskimo*, Vallee states that the population of Baker Lake was readily divisible into *Nunamiut* (people of the land) and *Kabloonamiut* (people of the Whites). The latter were mediators between Whites and *Nunamiut*, occupied a prestigious class position and had adopted a whole range of southern customs.[1] Vallee considers the social position of the *Kabloonamiut* to have been important in the progressive acculturation of the Baker Lake Eskimos: the *Kabloonamiut* were distinguishable for their economic life and were employees of the southern agencies. But Vallee was in fact describing a brief and transitory period; today virtually all Eskimos are, by his definition, *Kabloonamiut*, and no longer does a small group of more acculturated Eskimos anywhere dominate community affairs. This differentiation in class and status is typical of the early stages of colonial development, but now there is a uniformity of class and status, not simply among the Eskimos themselves, but in their relation to Whites in the north and to Canadian society as a whole.

Eskimos view their move to the settlement as a move *to* the Whites, even though most of them would be deeply reluctant to call themselves *Qallunaarmiut*. And there is no doubt that Eskimos throughout the Canadian Eastern Arctic have become superficially more like Whites – hence the social scientists' interest in what they like to call acculturation. In the last chapter I argued that a keen sense of ethnic boundaries made it impossible for an Eskimo to change into a White, but the Eskimos are acutely conscious of and at pains to describe the changes brought about by living in a settlement.[2]

1. See especially Vallee (1967), p. 140 ff. '*Kabloonamiut*', as written in the orthography used here, is '*Qallunaarmiut*'.

2. Vallee, op. cit., p. 141–2, says: 'It should be emphasized that the *Kabloonamiut* are not simply regarded as the White man's Eskimo in the

Life here has definitely changed now. Eskimos have changed and they are in ways almost like Whites now. Some more, some less. They have been living for some years under the government administration. Already there have been five administrators in this settlement. Those administrators have been pretty good to the people here, but they are all carrying orders from bosses far away, and those bosses have decided how the Eskimos should live, what they should do. So the administrators here are not free to do what they need to do. Some people like the administrator we have now, and some do not. I do not know. He seems to be good to me all the time. The administrator's clerks are really good when they first arrive. When they get here they really go to work and do things on behalf of the people. Then they change, after they have been here longer. The present one has changed like that. You see, sometimes the clerks stop caring about people, and just carry out orders. Without trying to help. Maybe they get too tired from writing so much.

I think it is possible for Eskimos to do these jobs, being administrators and clerks. If they had to do it, they could. They could be happy doing everything here if they had the equipment – tractors, machines, everything, all the equipment. The Whites have the equipment now, and they do the jobs, and their bosses make all the decisions.

Resolution of the settlement's problems are considered to be the Whites' responsibility. A settlement's economics focuses increasingly on work provided by Whites, and the social and family problems created by settlement should be solved by them too. After all – many Eskimos say – Whites created the settlements, encouraged the Eskimos to move to them, and now should resolve the difficulties of life there.

---

sense that some Americans refer to the white man's Negro. Attitudes towards the *Kabloonamiut* vary, but they are regarded as Eskimos first and foremost. Although they have rejected the way of life which requires an acute dependence on the land, they have not given up the skills associated with the land.'

It is my argument that being an Eskimo, in self- or other-ascription, goes far beyond 'skills associated with the land'. That is, an Eskimo can live in a settlement, much or more as the *Kabloonamiut* Vallee characterizes, and *still* be quite sure of himself, and in the views of others, that he is an Eskimo. Vallee seems to underestimate the intensity and complexity of an Eskimo's sense of Eskimo-ness.

Among the most serious of these problems is the whole matter of White–Eskimo relationships, especially as they are concerned with the settlement's institutional problems. The Eskimos are not troubled by the manners or cultural traits of the Whites as such, not even as these manners and traits affect themselves as individuals, but they are troubled by the extent to which White–Eskimo relationships hamper the development of settlement life and interfere with realization of the aims of local institutions. This point is clear in the following remarks from three conversations:

I have thought a great deal about the church, about the Whites and the church we have here. Not one – not even the Hudson's Bay Company manager – not a single teacher – not the administrator – goes to church here. I know that it depends upon the religion that they belong to, what they believe in and have been taught. But if they are Anglican it would be better if they went to church – even if they could not understand. It would show that they had some interest in what is happening in the settlement. Sometimes they go to other activities, and they have jobs here, so why not to church? Why not worship together with the people here? They would then show that they were really interested in helping people. Perhaps some problems would not arise if the Whites bothered to go to church with the Eskimos; maybe they would understand things better. It would make the older people think that the Whites *belong* to the settlement, because they would see the Whites being involved in our activities. The Whites are sent here to help, they do try to help older people. But sometimes they seem to try and help people in some other way, trying to lead them into worse ways – instead of trying to make it better, have a better settlement.

*

A man needs a companion. The last administrator had a companion, his wife. He was happy with his wife, so he treated people the way he treated his wife. When someone came in to see him he would say something, or at least smile. But you can see a great difference with the present administrator, whose wife is not with him, who has no companion. It could be that his emotional problems are bothering him; it could be that if his wife were with him he would be happy. If you are to be an administrator you should be a complete man, a whole man. If you are only half a man, it is no good. If you are dealing every day with the public, you have to treat them like a family. So being married can make a lot of difference.

*

As you know, there are quite a number of organizations in this settlement. A White can come to the settlement, and people not know what he is doing here. When that happens it is possible for one of the organizations to run into a war, because the White might say: 'I'm doing this job, so this or that cannot be done.' That can happen. And the Whites do not always tell people what they have come here for. Most of the young people today can speak a bit of English, so they can talk to the Whites who come here to work. In the old days very few Eskimos could speak English, but Whites tried to explain what they were doing when they came here in spite of that difficulty. Also, government officials who come here for just a day or two days, they usually do explain what their jobs are. Those men are alright. But the ones who come here for a while, or come here to stay permanently, they do not bother to explain. So when they are here, the Eskimos sometimes want to work with them or want to do things with them, but the Whites tell the Eskimos, 'I do not do that; that is not my job.' If the Whites explained themselves, the Eskimos would not bother to ask them to do things they are not here for. I feel anxious about the Whites who come here to stay because they might start a drinking problem . . .

There are Eskimos who feel uncomfortable about having a neighbour and not know why he is a neighbour. At least if they told the Eskimos why they [the Whites] came here, then the Eskimos would feel more at ease having a White neighbour. If a White comes here and starts living in the neighbourhood, and if he is a really heavy drinker and makes trouble for himself, then the Eskimos feel bad. It is because they do not know anything about their neighbour, about his habits. It would be much better if as soon as he came here a White tried to explain why he had come here. The Whites and the Eskimos should always consult each other if they are going to be neighbours to each other – and if they do not want to cause too many problems in the future.

Towards the end of conversations about settlement problems and relations between Eskimos and Whites in the settlement, I was often asked questions unrelated to the discussion. I was asked what reason I had to be in the Arctic and whether I knew anything about other northern communities. One of the most frequent questions concerned the duties of settlement managers, a surprising circumstance since local government programme officers have devoted considerable time and effort to explaining that role; indeed, the whole programme of local government depends so much on that role that the one must be understood to grasp the other.

Eskimo concern over poor communication between Whites and themselves reveals the local government programme and its officials in a different context. Here are two comments on this concern:

These traders today, and administrators, they seem to be alright. What I would like to ask is this: What is the function of the administrator? I do not think that there is any communication. The administrator has never held a meeting simply to outline to everyone here what he is supposed to do and what his job really is, and how he is supposed to do it, and all that he is supposed to be doing with the people. I am sorry to say these things. If there is no communication there can only be bad things for our settlement. I think many people here feel this.

*

For quite a few years Whites have been sent here. In early days, when only a few of them were sent, they explained themselves, explained what their jobs were. They were quite easily understood. But these days the Whites just walk in and nobody knows what they are doing. A lot come and stay in the settlement. We do not get to know what it is they are supposed to be doing here. For example, Fred has been here some time but most of the Eskimos do not know why he is here, because the Whites do not explain themselves the way they used to in the old days. And the present settlement manager, we do not know what he is really doing here. I do not go and talk to him, so I do not find out what he is working for. I think that the only way to find out would be to go and visit him every month, or every second month, and talk to him. But I do not do that, so I do not know what his job is or how much he is involved in the settlement.

The failure of communication between Whites and Eskimos contributes to confusion and uncertainty about settlement activities as a whole, and Eskimos complain bitterly of Whites who seem, by going their separate ways and leading their southern life-style, as well as by their attitudes to Eskimos, to aggravate this confusion. It is evident to them that housing conditions, social life and economic circumstances are all being transformed by southerners and their various agencies. It is deeply troubling to the Eskimo, therefore, that Whites in the settlements appear to cut themselves off from the settlement and its people; this is regarded as disrupting to the community in the present and a threat to its future. Since the outlook for the future is judged to some extent by the resolution of problems in the present, and since those problems are said to be exacerbated by many settlement Whites, White behaviour inevitably inspires profound anxiety. It would appear to the Eskimos of such settlements that Whites have created a milieu in which a range of new difficulties are arising, and are now all too often failing to attend to those difficulties.

Among those difficulties, government welfare payments are perhaps the most frequent source of bad feeling towards individual officials. In Chapter 6 one case illustrated how welfare can easily become a focus of much discontent and indignation. But that difficulty also illustrates the whole question of Eskimo poverty.

It is a commonplace that modernization is often in effect a change from self-reliance to dependence on outside provision. That has happened to peasants under the impact of urbanization and capitalism as well as to hunters and gatherers under the impact of colonial administration. In sociological theory the general nature of such changes has often been described by a model of new needs – needs for goods and services which cannot be secured within the home economy, and purchase of which compels groups of people into new social and economic formations. The generation of such needs has often, however, been a consequence of other and earlier changes in socio-economic structure, for example in situations where groups have been drawn into labouring or slavery, or where disruption of traditional resources forced dependence on alternative (new) resources. Some classical sociological theory has tended to see these changes as equivalent to a revision in aspirations, as events which primarily have a place in the minds of those people undergoing change; attitudes, beliefs and hopes are transformed, thereby precipitating new social mores. In fact, disruption of social mores and impoverishment are frequently direct consequences of outsiders' intrusion: revised economic practices have usually been urged on people as part of colonial or developmental strategy. In its more modern versions, many examples of such change can be described in terms of shift to a money economy. In those cases shortages of cash provide a barometer of actual dependence, and are a measure of impoverishment. Cash is needed for acquiring new items; new items are needed because old ones are either inadequate or unavailable; therefore inability to acquire new items causes material deprivation; anxiety about securing money reveals the scale of such deprivation.[3]

Contemporary Canadian Eskimos worry a great deal about money. Although hunting provides food, which has a financial value, at least in the calculation of economists interested in living standards, hunting itself has to be paid for: guns, ammunition, knives, ropes, sledge-runners must all be bought, and a snowmobile, which most hunters now own, depreciates at a rate of at least $600 a year and must be supplied with fuel. The money earned by trapping goes towards the expenses of hunting for food and to buy the multitude of other things, including clothing, commercial foods and consumer durables that they need.

Eskimos who can buy all these requirements usually earn regular wages from permanent jobs, and their earnings spread through extended family networks. Without a cash income of some sort, no one could buy his family's needs – including what they need to go hunting. It follows that Eskimos who do wish to devote much or all of their time to hunting and trapping are forced into some sort of dependence on those who are able

3. Thus the subjective element, or psychological states, figure only at the end of the process: the initial or primary factor – which has the status of a causal factor – is established objectively.

and willing to work at low-level clerical or labouring jobs. Because such a dependence is unwelcome and is not always reliable, even the most devoted hunters among the older men periodically welcome a chance to earn cash. Moreover, trappers who have no success over a period of weeks or months are likely to experience real hardship and poverty. From the preceding chapters, it should be clear that Eskimos' fundamental loyalties are to a land-based life and its skills and activities. Yet the use of those skills and the taking of traditional wild food are restricted, hampered and sometimes made impossible by financial difficulties, or commitment to wage-earning.

It is therefore inevitable that many Eskimos have looked to welfare as their protection against poverty. They have often been told that the provision of welfare to protect them from hardship, and the principles of successive administrative experiments, have been based largely on an expressed wish to help. So, from the Eskimos' point of view, what more important help could be forthcoming than money for those who needed it? Many Eskimos, probably most, feel that they need it badly. Many of them live from week to week, often from day to day, in an eternal round of trying to find cash for immediate and short-term requirements. A carver who needs something that costs $30 will find a piece of stone of just the right size and carve an object worth just $30.

Families are large, prices are high, and it is not easy to save. In any case, Eskimos still try to provide for one another's needs, and shortage of ready cash is part of everyday life. Such concern causes anxiety for the future: if money is hard to earn now, what will happen when one is older? Because welfare is *not* given to everyone, and certainly it is not given to many who consider themselves to be in sore need of it, there is unease and confusion about the whole purpose and operation of welfare. What does this state of affairs forebode?

In the last few years, from 1968–70, a lot of southern goods have been coming to the community here, things for us to use. It is only in those years that a lot of goods have been coming here. So the people here want to get welfare, because of all the stuff that is coming here; it makes people think more about getting welfare money. Then the Whites began taking care of welfare,[4] and I ran into a wall. Since that time I have never bothered trying to get welfare, even though I sometimes think that I should be given it. I think that if I were disabled I would be able to get welfare, but not now that I am healthy.

Also, I understand a bit about the way the welfare system works. The previous administrator used to love talking to people here, and one time he talked seriously to me about what the Government is here to do, how it was going to try to help me when I had certain disabilities. Then the Government would try and help me feed myself and my family – that is, if I were seriously disabled. But the Government cannot help until then. Since I am young and healthy, the Government says that I can provide for myself. The Government is not going to help me now. I got that understanding from a previous administrator. Of course it might have been that the administrator was just saying those things. It is difficult to understand the welfare system, and how it is supposed to help people. Maybe that administrator was simply interpreting the laws his own way. Maybe another man will interpret the laws a different way.

I feel that if I one day get really disabled I will go and ask for assistance. The welfare officer of that time may refuse me. I do not know if the welfare officer who spoke to me was speaking for every welfare officer there would ever be; I do not know if he meant that I would be able to get help from other welfare officers even if I were disabled. But I think about it this way: if you are healthy and try to go to the welfare officer for help, then you are not being sensible. That is because the officer will say: welfare is meant for the old and the disabled and widows. I think that if you are not disabled and can try and feed your own family, then it does not make any sense to seek welfare.

*

I once got really angry with the administrator who was here. I tried to get welfare; I tried to ask for welfare. Before I went I knew that the administrator was not going to give it to me, for at that time my husband was earning dollars. But I had read in a newsletter that even if someone is working in the family, and earning money for the family, if you have a lot of kids to feed and your husband is not

4. At first, welfare in this particular community was largely handled by a welfare officer's Eskimo interpreter who travelled every month to the camps.

getting enough money for the family, then you should go and ask for welfare. That is what I read; the purpose of welfare is helping those who need it. So that month I asked the administrator, but he did not seem to want to hear anything of my case. The reason I went, you know, is this: there are a large number of children in my family, and on top of that there is the rent to pay. The income my husband was bringing in was simply not enough for all the things we needed. But no persuading would make the administrator talk to me about the case.

I know quite a few families that have had the same kind of difficulties. The welfare officer is very careful to account for all the money you make from little jobs, but he is not careful about listening to those people who are trying to explain why they still need welfare.

I disagree strongly with the way welfare is given out. Let us take two different cases. In one family there is a man bringing an income into the house and in the same house there is a widow, an old lady. So the officer gives welfare to that old lady. So the man who has both the income and the welfare cheque gets rich with food. And in another house there is only one man with his wife and children; there might be more people living in the second house. But the welfare officer gives the cheque to the lady in the first house. In another house a man brings food and is healthy; then he loses his job, and does not have regular work any more. But *he* does not get money either, because he is able to earn money. I also disagree with giving money to unmarried mothers. It encourages other people to do the same thing. Maybe they should be given a cheque only every other month.

*

These days in the settlement people are heading for problems, and these problems are getting heavier and heavier as the settlements get older. Welfare is becoming one of the heaviest of those problems; it is becoming a burden on all the people here. It is especially a burden for those who are elected – those who are elected representatives of the people. Those who are elected know the conditions in this settlement. They have to know, for they understand all about hunting conditions – they are themselves hunters. They must continue living by hunting, and they therefore know what others in the settlement are facing when they try to live by hunting. But the officials, since they are Whites, cannot see the problems. They have never hunted; they have never lived by hunting, so they are blind on that side. But that is the side they must work on for doing the welfare, looking after the welfare of the people, especially those people who try to live by hunting. The Whites do not know what it is like to be just a hunter and trapper, so do not know that hunting is sometimes hard and sometimes good. These Eskimos in the settlement, especially those who are elected as representatives, know exactly what others have to go through, but they cannot convince the Whites who have never hunted for a living, that one thing is true. So welfare is one of the biggest problems.

Neither these excerpts nor the evidence of Chapter 6 can by themselves convey how deeply the question of welfare preoccupies and troubles Eskimos. Discussion returns again and again to the subject. The provision of welfare differs from settlement to settlement, from official to official, and from time to time. But variations apart, the Eskimos do not understand what the system itself is intended to accomplish. Because the system is, in fact, rooted in the welfare officer's inability to distinguish between incapacity and indolence, Eskimo hunters everywhere are vulnerable to accusations of indolence, for the officer may think that here is a fellow claiming that he cannot feed his family. This feature of the system is exacerbated by availability of wage-labour as an alternative to hunting, for this alternative puts pressure on hunters and trappers to supplement their land-based activity with wage-labour in the settlement, whereas hunters and trappers, if they are serious, must wait on weather and game, not on the chance of work around the settlement. A man who determinedly pursues land-based activity is likely to be faced periodically with poverty and then to have to seek welfare; an administrator faced with such a man in such a situation is likely to see other ways he could earn a living in the settlement.

The Eskimos' preoccupation with the provision of welfare naturally centres on examples that are regarded as irregularities and injustices. These injustices are all the more acutely felt because the language problem makes complaint or appeal so extremely difficult. The general attitude of Whites further aggravates the problem. An Eskimo may think he is just as entitled to welfare as someone who has received welfare, but he may feel unable or unwilling to insist, being nervous of the White official, or suspicious of an interpreter, or perhaps feeling that he really has no rights after all. For these reasons, Eskimos generally acquiesce in decisions that in fact they think are wrong and, although angry, fall back on whatever resources their family and neighbours can offer.[5]

This failure of communication is general. It is not surprising that the Eskimos' ideas of how welfare should be administered are uncertain and often actually wrong. An example of one family's difficulties in this connection will show how serious that confusion can be.

Neither Annie nor her husband Kuutuq came originally from the camps tributary to the settlement they now lived in; she was born and had lived some 200 miles to the northwest, and he came from a camp over 400 miles away. There was nothing unusual in this, for the people of the area are famous travellers, and many families have relations in distant quarters. But Kuutuq, a man in his thirties, was unusual in having remained mobile up to the present; he would spend several months or a year in one settlement, and then move with his wife and younger children to another, comparatively distant settlement. In this way, he had divided the previous five years among four villages, strung out over a distance of 600 miles.

One consequence of this mobility was the difficulty of finding adequate housing; administrators familiar with Kuutuq's habits were reluctant to hand over to him one of the new low-rental three-bedroomed houses the Government had built, for such houses were then and are still in short supply.[6] When I first met Kuutuq in 1971, he and his wife Annie, a year-old son, two small children of about 5 and 6, and a step-daughter of 17 with an infant of her own were all living in a one-room house that measured approximately twenty-five feet by eight feet and

5. This reaction is a feature of a 'culture of poverty'. But far more significant is the harmful influence this acquiescence has on attempts to introduce local government or to adjust to the wide spectrum of White activities.

6. For details of Eskimo housing, epecially in the Eastern Arctic, see Thompson (1970), and for discussion of the housing programme in general, see Thomas and Thompson (1972).

was divided by a four-foot-wide partition into sleeping and living areas. Even by the standards of contemporary settlement conditions, that house was crowded. Moreover Kuutuq supported his family on traditional foods, with a minimum of cash. He had no regularly employed close relative in the settlement, and so he could not subsidize his household by making claims on his extended family.

Kuutuq's household lived by the rough-and-ready routines and habits of camp life. To the administration it appeared a squalid failure, a blight on the community, for most of the Eskimos there lived in 'better' conditions – or less conspicuous poverty. But Kuutuq and his wife were on the whole satisfied with their life; they occasionally lamented the limitations of their small house, but they preferred to continue hunting, trapping and travelling rather than concentrating on improving it.

One difficulty they had faced was adoption: they wanted another child, a boy. Kuutuq was anxious to have a son to follow him, and support him as hunter and trapper in his old age. For some reason that role was not assigned to his own son, perhaps because he was at school and could not therefore learn a hunter's skills; Kuutuq probably planned to keep his adopted son away from such influence. The difficulty was that adoption required, so Annie had heard, a formal procedure and the local administrator's approval. And she had the impression that the administrator would obstruct the adoption. She may have been right, for others in the settlement had heard the administrator say, 'Annie will get her adoption over my dead body,' and he had called her 'a slut'. Most of the settlement Whites joined the administrator in disapproving of Kuutuq's life-style, but in the end Annie and Kuutuq were able to adopt the boy.

It is no exaggeration to say that Kuutuq lived in poverty. He was a competent but not outstanding hunter and although he used a snowmobile and moderately good rifles, he could not buy the best equipment nor replace his equipment as often as required by rough hunting conditions, and during the summer of 1972 he had to borrow an outboard motor from a neighbour. His poverty often made it impossible to go on long hunting expeditions, for he could not afford to buy enough supplies, especially gasoline. He often had to hunt less efficiently than he wished, and he could not therefore trap as many skins as he needed to alleviate his poverty. That vicious circle is common to everyone who tries to live as a full-time hunter and trapper in the north today.

One day I received a message from Annie asking me to visit as soon as I could. Since I often visited their family I knew that the message had some urgency, and I hurried to their house. The problem was not unpredictable: they were short of money. When I arrived at the house, Annie was alone with their newly adopted son, but Kuutuq was out visiting. Their situation, she told me, was serious. Kuutuq had no money to buy ammunition and therefore could not go hunting. Even more seriously, the adopted boy had diarrhoea and fever. She was sure his sickness was caused by their poor diet, but they could not afford to buy more food at the HBC store. She wanted to know if I could think of any way to get help from the settlement's officials.

Annie and Kuutuq were obviously alarmed, and the child was indeed very ill. The settlement nurse had seen the child, had prescribed some medicines, and had given some reassurance. Had they asked the settlement manager for money? It appeared that some months before he had offered them a small loan. They believed that government officials would give hunters nothing but loans, and because they could not repay the last loan, they did not want to ask again. They could not get welfare, she said, because Kuutuq was young and strong. Kuutuq had tried very hard to get a labouring job, but had been told that single men who spoke some English were preferred, and Kuutuq was ineligible on both counts. They seemed to have reached a dreadful impasse where no help at all was available. Their feeling of helplessness was aggravated by their nervous fear of the Whites in the settlement and their reluctance to confront them. Annie, normally a confident and outgoing woman, was pathetic and abject; pleadingly, she explained their position to me a dozen times, simplifying her Eskimo each time, desperately wanting me to understand.

A month before this discussion and before Kuutuq's patch of bad luck in hunting, a social development officer – with special responsibility for welfare and family problems – had arrived in the settlement. He was the first of that title to work there and had recently taken over responsibility for welfare from the settlement manager. I suggested that Annie and her husband should discuss their circumstances with him. She hesitated. Were they, she wondered, really eligible for financial help? Would the new officer offer only another loan? They had heard that he did not speak Eskimo, so it would be difficult to ask for anything. Why should he give them money or food when others had refused?

I was myself unsure of the criteria used at that time to assess an applicant's claim to welfare, so I offered to ask the new man what the rules were and to mention the Kuutuq case. Annie greeted this offer with enthusiasm; evidently she had hoped I would do just that. And when I did speak to the officer, I learned that Annie and Kuutuq were unquestionably entitled to welfare for that month at least and that part of their payment would be a food allocation at the Hudson's Bay Company store.

The next afternoon I again found Annie alone with her little adopted son. Evidence of much eating lay about the room, and Kuutuq had left an hour ago to go seal hunting.

Although this episode ended happily enough, it did not end Kuutuq's troubles. Later in the year he was still in financial difficulties. He and Annie had decided to move back to his family's settlement, but had realized that they probably could not save enough money to buy fuel and supplies for a 400-mile journey. Kuutuq was again trying to get work as a labourer but could not find a job. Like many other Eskimos, he felt pressure to leave his life as a hunter for a life in the settlement that neither he nor his family desired. Welfare had helped him over a bad patch, but not enough for him to continue as a hunter. The southern view that full-time hunting is not a viable profession had prevailed against local occupational aspirations. And indeed, full-time hunting could not be a viable full-time occupation in or near a settlement. Anxiety and confusion over these realities has focused everyone's attention on the question of welfare, which may well be called, in the Eskimo phrase, 'one of the heaviest problems' that face today's settlement Eskimos.

This confusion is aggravated by the attitudes and behaviour of the representatives of the other principal institutions in the settlements. The old missionary–policeman–trader triumvirate has been displaced by a range of associated federal services, the nature and scope of which the Eskimos do not understand. And, so far as my observation goes, no one else in the north or in Ottawa can clearly distinguish the fields of competence and authority of these several services, among which there is often rivalry and dispute. The settlement itself, from a purely administrative point of view, represents a set of institutional problems. The old trading post has changed into a handsomely provisioned store; but the store's position is affected by the local cooperative, and the two are often seen as rivals. Government officials, especially settlement managers, are often believed to regard the cooperative as a threat to their own authority. For the Eskimos this situation of tension and rivalry is awkward, for they depend upon each of the main institutions, and their dependence inevitably results in their feeling threatened by the officials who represent these institutions, as well as by strained relations between them.

As long ago as I can remember, back to the time I was a small boy, I used to hear that traders were often difficult to deal with. But since I have been hunting myself, since I have been grown up, they seem to have been much better. So long as a man does not ask for too much credit at the store, the traders seem to be good enough.

As for the present trader we have got here – well, it is not easy for me to say how he compares with all the others who have ever been here, since I have not lived in this place all the time and can therefore only judge the past four traders. The first seemed good: you could wake him at any time of the night and trade. Even late in the evenings, when we came in from the southern camps, you could go to his house and get him to trade. The second was about the same. He did not really like to get up late all the time, but he would still trade with those of us who had travelled a long way. The third was like the first, willing to get up even in the middle of the night and trade with those who had come from the south and who needed to trade quickly so they could set off for home again in the morning.

The fourth one is the present one. The people thought he was really bad when he first came here. People used to talk among themselves: we must get him sent away. But then they got rough back with him when he got rough with them – and that is when he began changing. This present manager used to be so rough with the Eskimos here. He had been working in another settlement before he came here. I think he might have thought the people here behaved the same way as those people over there. He believed that people here were trying to take things off the shelves and steal things. We knew he thought that, because when Eskimos picked things up from shelves he would want to fight them or kick them out of the store. Maybe people from that other settlement used to take things from his store. One man here, last year, was in the store. That manager had not been here long at that time. The man was looking at some things on the shelves; he was trying to see what they were like. Then the manager suddenly wanted to fight, and tried to throw the man out of the store. That was because the man was touching things he did not really want to buy. After that people here ganged up on the manager and said: We are not going to put up with this, and you had better be more like other managers; you better let us look at things even if we do not want to buy them; we do not have enough money to buy everything, and so we have to choose the things we are going to buy. Then the manager's attitude began to change. Now I think he is about the best manager we have had here.

*

At one time the administrator worked to help the government and the co-op; he worked in the one office, but he was doing other jobs besides the government job. Like looking after the co-op. Then the administration changed, and things became entirely different. The two organizations fight against each other now. The settlement manager wants to fight against the co-op because it is different from his job. For example, when the ship came last year there were two gangs. One was unloading co-op stuff, and the other was paid by the government to unload government stuff. Why do that? Why not get them all to unload everything together? When the supply ship came in, carrying both government and co-op stuff, the administrator wanted to do it like this: there were two camps, like camps in an army, but the barge brought things all mixed up. So the two troops would rush into the barge and look for their stuff. When the barge did not bring much for the co-op, the co-op troop would go home. The government had only three men, while the co-op had a whole lot of men. With things happening that way you get to think that the government wants to fight. It did not used to happen that way before; then people used to try and get everything on land as quickly as possible, and then sort it out when they had done that, when they had got it all on shore. Last year was completely different; last year you were labelled as to which things you could carry.

Maybe the administrator was worried that the government was going to lose a whole lot of money if men carried stuff for the co-op; maybe he thought that if everyone spent all their time carrying co-op supplies he would end up paying too many men for other work. But then he must have found out that it took very much longer having only three men working for him; their time was always adding up. About the time that ship came in, I was very anxious to work and make some money for myself, but on the day of the unloading I was late arriving at the shore. As I walked along the road another man was coming from the shore, and when I met him I asked what he was doing; I asked him if there was no more work to be had. But he answered me, 'I am a co-op man, and there are no more supplies for us on this barge, so I am going home to wait for the next one.' That was the sort of thing that was happening with the men. With that sort of thing you get the idea that you have to fight against the government or against the co-op. But all these supplies are for us all, and we should all try and work together to try and get the stuff on to the shore. All the things we put on the shore were for all of the people here. When I saw that there were two troops doing the unloading I did not bother to ask for a job. I did not want to be working when we were working against one another. I wanted us to work together.

In the first of these anecdotes, the trader is a problem to the community; in the second, the relation between two local institutions is seen as a problem. There is, of course, a tradition of difficulties with Hudson's Bay Company managers: in the old days a trader was feared because he could directly threaten the livelihood of hunters and trappers. Today no such direct threat could exist. Nevertheless, the trader who interferes, as in the anecdotes, with the Eskimos' way of spending the little money they possess is a problem. Present difficulties between Eskimos and their White institutions may well develop and become more disruptive in the future.

Eskimos are poorly informed about the nature and scope of

existing institutional arrangements. They strongly feel that, with the partial exception of the cooperative and church, the settlement's institutions are controlled exclusively by Whites. This view extends to local education, to the day-school and to adult education.

In many settlements, the establishment of day-schools was preceded by a system of residential schooling. I have already mentioned the importance of residential schools in some families' decision to move from camp to settlement. Many children were sent far away from home, to towns which their parents regarded as part of the south. The children received part (often the main part) of their schooling in Ottawa, Churchill, Great Whale River or Frobisher Bay. The use of distant residential schools was characteristic of an early phase in northern education, and they firmly established in the Eskimo mind the connection between education and subjection to the influence of White society. Parents wept to see their children taken from them and sent to live among a different people in a foreign land. And their worst fears were rapidly realized by the disruption that such education caused to their children and to family life.

Yet the Eskimos were in some measure persuaded that education was the only hope of any solution to the present problems and to the problems the future would surely bring. In recent years, however, the Eskimos have come to regard the school itself as a problem, and have begun to criticize educational institutions and teachers. Many Eskimos now see education as a direct and conscious assault on Eskimo culture. The residential schools have been condemned, but concern has now spread to the whole philosophy of education and even to the operation of local day-schools.

I think the time at which the most real changes came here can be judged by looking at the age of the young men. Look at the ones who were taken away from us when they were young, taken away from our homes and sent to school. Then, at school, they were taught differently, and came home again with their heads full of things they had learned, and things they had been taught away from home. When they were taken away they were taken completely away from their parents' way of life; they were taken to hostels where there was an entirely different way of life.

*

Another thing I always thought of, and with which I disagree very much. And I spoke about it at a meeting in Churchill only last week. We had a meeting there with officials at regional headquarters, and we were asked what we thought of the idea of sending teenagers to those places of education. Mary and I disagreed with the idea. My answer was that it does good for a very few, but not to most. The majority of teenagers are sent for training. Then, if they do not do very well they do not do any good. They are just left. The people training them say: you are not doing any good at this, you are not learning anything, so you have to go home again. Then those young people are lost; they did not get any training; they did not learn; they did not get any job; and they have not learned the Eskimo way. Those teenagers are sent home, but they have got used to comforts and they have learned *something*. But they cannot do anything with that something when they get back to the settlement, and they cannot go to any other settlement to find work. I do not agree with those results. It happens to many of our young people. They take the children away when the children become teenagers; then the parents are told that the children are no good and cannot learn anything. It seems that the job is far from finished; the job is not complete; therefore when they are not complete they are lost completely. They are sort of half White and half Eskimo. I am always trying to think of a solution to the problem of the teenager who is sent back with no job and nothing to do.

*

It is a very good thing for the young to get involved with the Whites. They are going to have to get involved with Whites. But they are going to have to remember their Eskimo ways. They must learn both ways. Those who go to school all the time will never learn anything of the Eskimo way. No doubt those who work full-time will be like Whites. Yes, they will be very like Whites. But there will always be some without jobs, and they will have to hunt. They will have to know what Eskimos do, how Eskimos live. They do not learn that in the school. They are not even taught to write the Eskimo way, or any parts of Eskimo culture, when they are in the school. Just one afternoon each week an old man talks to them. But they are not learning the things that they need to know. There are some Eskimo things and some White things, and there are some things that just do not fit together. And there are some Whites who just do not know how to work [i.e. work on the land, or do physical work]. Sometimes if you do know how to work like that, then you can make money. If you are an Eskimo you can always do that kind of work, and if you can't work the White way, then you can always be a hunter. But if you spend all your time at school you might not learn enough of those ways. And those who go to school, well, it may be that some of them will not complete their education, and some may give up going to school. And then they would not know either hunting or work. Then the government would have to help many of them, and that would be a bad thing.

The Education Division of the Northwest Territories Government is at present trying to modify the curriculum in Eskimo schools by introducing readers that contain material bearing on the local or regional environment and regarding 'cultural inclusion' as a working principle. But the main emphasis of the educational system is still incorporation into national life as a whole, and therefore the Education Division is committed to grade schools and a syllabus that are comparable to Canadian national standards. The Northwest Territories Government has committed itself to more education in the settlements. At present, very few settlements have schools that go beyond Grade Seven, and virtually all special or vocational training is centred in schools far from the small villages. The Government has also promised to expand facilities for adult education and reduce the need for residential education in the south.

As part of this programme, the Government opened a residential school in Frobisher Bay in 1971. Frobisher Bay *is* an Arctic centre, but among the smaller communities of Baffin Island it has a black reputation for drunkenness, violence and prostitution. Older Eskimos think of it as a place of sickness and danger; northern Whites see it as a hotbed of iniquity and the embodiment of all that is wrong in northern development and administration; young Eskimos may find it exciting or unnerving.

In 1971 children from many of the smallest and remotest settlements were sent to the new school. The school was originally proposed by officers of the Federal Government in 1961 but the plan was abandoned on instructions from the highest levels. In 1967 the proposal was revised and architects were engaged. Construction began in the autumn of 1969, and the school was completed by 1971. During that period, from 1967 to 1971, there was a bare minimum of consultation with families whose children would be expected to attend the school. Discussions did take place within the relevant sections of the Federal Civil Service, but criticisms of the scheme were not made known in the north and, in any event, were largely ignored. In the spring of 1969, some teachers in one of the Arctic settlements heard of the proposed school, and they submitted a petition in protest, only to be reprimanded by their superiors for such an activity. There was never any open discussion of the subject with the Eskimos, despite the fact that Eskimo parents had been complaining for years about a residential school in Churchill.

When the school opened in Frobisher Bay parents in the small communities expressed their anxiety about sending their children to such a notorious place. And when, after an unhappy time at Frobisher Bay, the pupils began to trickle home, their parents were often quick to express their relief. I once overheard a mother exhorting her son by telephone to come home (some 800 miles) from the school; she said she was sure everyone was unhappy in the school and there was no reason to endure such unhappiness. The decline in the number of students attending the school since it first opened is striking indeed. Between 1971 and 1973, total enrolment fell from 220 to 100, and the numbers in residence (with a capacity of over 400) fell from 150 to 60.

Those figures represent a revulsion against the institution and against Frobisher Bay by both parents and children of many communities. Despite the Eskimo distaste for residential education, the Frobisher Bay school was established with a complete disregard for what the authorities knew the Eskimo attitudes to be, and there it now stands in the face of widespread opposition from pupils and parents alike – hardly very useful for its purpose.

Pupils at the school have returned home with stories of drunkenness and violence within the residence. Girls have told how they lay awake at night, their doors locked, fearing assault. All the pupils from one settlement went home together.

It is not surprising, therefore, that parents raised a host of questions with local officials and senior civil servants about the school. One theme was recurrent: how could any parents feel easy about their children in a residential school in Frobisher Bay? They discussed discipline and rules, they encouraged those responsible for the school to adopt now one, now another strategy to counteract the evil influences of its location. But, behind these remedial suggestions, the parents are ready to discourage, or to forbid, their children to go to the school.

The case of this school indicates how clearly the parents of today's school-children are conscious of education as another of their communities' problems. Their consciousness includes many elements – their fears of delinquency, alcoholism and demoralization combine to create nervous uncertainty about the future. The settlement, the place of Whites, the place where they must face uninterrupted contact with a different culture and must accommodate to endless pressures for change and adaptation, is inevitably the scene of widespread anxiety that finds many specific expressions. Southern culture has gone beyond merely impinging on the Eskimos' quasi-traditional life; it has now transformed every aspect of Eskimo life. Eskimos in settlements who live in government-built houses with subsidized rents and southern services, who are under the direction of southern political institutions and southern officials, are bound to be worried and indignant. They must try, somehow, to stand against and perhaps to rise above the flood of White influences the settlement brings them, even though the ground they stand on is forever shifting.

10 • Family Life

Innumerable books and articles have described the distinctive features of what is supposed to have been traditional Eskimo family life, and indeed a few of these features, namely those related to sexual practices, have entered Western folklore. Perhaps the intellectual imagination of Western man is captivated by the relation between natural environment and cultural form, and certainly most students of the Eskimos believe that here is a people who live at the very limit of the habitable world, in an environment so extreme that it moulds their whole culture. Few of the students who argue for the existence of causal links between specific natural conditions and a specific cultural response seem to have been aware that the Eskimos are only one of several cultures that have thrived in the Arctic environment. It seems to me unlikely, for example, that the family life of people of the Dorset culture, who preceded Eskimos of the Thule culture, had much in common culturally with the Eskimo of today – although they occupied the same territory.

Whether or not one adopts a materialist and determinist theory of culture, the Eskimos had evolved an unusual and distinctive pattern of family life. Since many elements of that pattern survive in the lives of Eskimos today, some description of its traditional form is necessary background to an account of its recent disruptions and transformations. Family life has, in the present, become a focal problem for Eskimo people.

Jean Briggs, in *Never in Anger*, offers a fascinating survey of relationships within the family, especially between parents and their small children. This book is based on field experience carried out in 1969 and 1970 in a tiny inland camp of the Netsilik Eskimos. There she had occasion to witness some of the dramatic moments of family life as well as its general ambience. She also outlines the metaphysical basis of the consciousness that informs behaviour. Of particular importance is the link she discerns between the parents' non-authoritarian attitude towards small children and their belief in *ihuma*, the capacity for rationality and therefore for adulthood. Since that capacity grows with the child, small children who have no or very little *ihuma* cannot be held accountable for their behaviour. Parents would therefore be foolish to become angry with childish behaviour. Inhibition against the display of anger and the disapproval of interference are complementary behavioural ideals. And since these ideals are integral to contemporary attitudes and values, the qualities of family life that Briggs described are still, to some extent at least, effective today.

The parent–child relationship is, of course, only one element of traditional family life. Many authors have noted that among the Eskimos the nuclear family was firmly determined by economic and environmental conditions: they were therefore small, rarely with more than two or three children and perhaps one or two grandparents. The difficulties that arose from being unmarried were so severe that every young adult had to find a spouse, even if that necessity was met by acceptance of inferior status as a second and lesser husband or wife. Acute interdependence between husbands and wives mitigated patriarchy to give a relation nearer equality. Eskimo family life was based on a clear definition of sexual roles: almost every task was specific to men *or* women. Male authority was often expressed in extramarital sexual relations, for the man determined the special relationships that extended sexual links beyond the husband-and-wife unit. Male superiority was also expressed by the men's taking priority in eating and being served preferred parts of meat. Such privileges were extended even to small boys, who tended in any case to be family favourites. Female infanticide was occasionally practised, usually only when there were no alternative means, such as adoption, of disposing of the child.[1]

Many of the traditional customs and beliefs depended for their coherence on the Eskimos' highly mobile life and subsistence hunting. From what I have described of settlement life, and from the nature of the shifts first to camps and then to settlements, it is evident that some of this coherence has been lost. The material and economic context for traditional social practice has been transformed. The present-day settled pattern of life, combined with economic subsidies, improved medicine and other forms of welfare, have permitted the existence of much larger families. Since the early days of the fur-trade, in the 1920s and 30s, families of ten children have not been uncommon; today it is unusual for an Eskimo household to have fewer than six children. The progressive introduction of federal welfare policies has also altered the nature of husband–wife interdependence: in the settlement, a woman can look to a wider range of kin, all of them close neighbours, and also to administrators for economic help. Indeed, wives frequently cannot depend exclusively upon their husbands, and husbands reciprocally depend less on wives, for they *could* have clothes made by neighbours, or purchase factory-made clothes at the local store. In ordinary settlement life, and even for hunting trips, store clothing is adequate and may be preferred.

Yet customs and beliefs do not change in equal and direct proportion to their change of context. Social life and culture develop in far more complex and far less mechanistic a fashion. Even in the largest and most modern of today's Arctic settlements, social and cultural practices still exist that are distinctively from an earlier and more traditional time. Parents continue to be extremely forbearing and tolerant in their attitude towards children. Even very small children are permitted to play out of doors, and they often roam quite far from the village. They are well clothed before they set out, but there is a minimum of quizzing or reproaching, or other evidence of the

1. Infanticide was regularly practised immediately a child was born, before it was named. Giving a name (*atik*) was equated with providing a soul. That was quite separate from *ihuma* or *isuma*.

anxiety that parents show towards small children in southern Canada. Children eat in whatever house they wish, and since mealtimes or bedtimes are irregular, it is unusual to hear a parent express unease about the whereabouts of a child at any particular time. How the child uses its day is felt to be its own concern. Similarly, the child is generally held to be the best judge of his own needs; whatever food or drink he wants is, if possible, provided. The southern observer will not find evidence of socialization in any careful and self-conscious provision of what parents hold to be the child's real needs. To such an observer, this absence of discipline might be taken as an absence of any socialization at all,[2] but in fact it is the continuation of the traditional avoidance of manipulative or authoritarian treatment of young children.

Another example of a family custom that has its roots in tradition is the division of sexual roles. Eskimo men and women are still very aware of what are and what are not tasks appropriate to their sex. Although it is not unusual to see a man sweeping his house or doing traditionally domestic jobs, such role confusion tends to be an object of pointed jokes. Once I entered a house where a man was making tea and washing dishes, and he immediately pointed out the joke against himself by using an expression reserved exclusively for men who are dominated by their wives. His question was, in an approximate translation: 'Am I not a pathetic little hen-pecked thing?' On another occasion I was using the chance of being alone in a house to repair some tears in my trousers. In the middle of my work I was interrupted by a visit from an elderly neighbour. He was shocked by my sewing and said that I must stop at once and tell one of the women of the house to do it for me. I replied that it was no bother to me, and the work would soon be done. As we continued to discuss the matter, the woman he had re-

---

2. It may be that, in a rapidly changing social setting, the absence of traditional forms of socialization may come close to an absence of any form of socialization, and that such an absence may have a great deal to do with the appearance of delinquent behaviour in children brought up in periods of radical and rapid social change. But hypotheses of this kind can be easily overstated.

commended came in. The old man ordered her to take over my work forthwith, adding that it was not at all good to see a young man sewing. The girl, embarrassed and apologetic, assured the old man that in the past I had insisted upon doing such work myself, despite her repeated offers to do it for me. She also felt that sewing was woman's work.

It must be added that this division of roles is a matter of pride in the home, but when men are on hunting trips unaccompanied by women, it is normal to see them sewing their own clothing. Moreover, many of the older men are proud of such domestic abilities and even insist on showing younger and less experienced hunters how to do them. Such work does not therefore in itself bring any loss of self-esteem; it is the performance of it at home, where, because of the division of labour, it is felt to be inappropriate and an offence to male pride.

Such examples of traditional attitudes and practices, however, are less striking than the evidence of real changes that are taking place in family life. Crucial among these recent changes is the position of women within marriage and within the household. The inevitable shift in the traditional balance between men and women, on which I have already remarked, has in many families been sharp. The wife in many settlement families is now clearly the dominant partner. Such women send their husbands on errands, do not hesitate to serve themselves first with the best pieces of meat, and feel quite entitled to enter extramarital sexual liaisons without regard to their husbands' views on the matter. Most such women today refuse to accompany their husbands on hunting trips except during the fine spring weather, when many women enthusiastically undertake fishing trips.[3] No doubt there have always been a few families in which the wife was atypically powerful (I know one woman, now elderly, who had once set up as a full-time hunter, despite being married), but the proportion of dominant women has certainly changed. There are no figures to indicate the scale of the change, but a number of factors suggest that it is very large indeed.

3. Women traditionally regarded fishing, especially through lake ice, as the one form of hunting in which they could participate with equality.

The traditional division of sexual roles was firmly related to a clear distinction between the home and the hunt,[4] but settlement life has resulted in reduced hunting and an expansion of the home. The charge of a permanent house and large numbers of children has consolidated the position of women; the shift to sporadic hunting and occasional wage-labour has undermined the position of most men. Traditional roles of authority were based on realities; role fulfilment and status were solidly pragmatic. Any weakening of the husband's status would have weakened his right to demand the complete fulfilment of his wife's role. Now that a man can no longer depend on his wife's unquestioning acceptance of her traditionally subservient position, he is apt to feel uneasy and suspicious. This is very apparent on hunting trips away from the settlement, when more men are reluctant to stay away very long. Because the expression of uneasiness and suspiciousness is regarded as a fault of character, most men tend to keep such feelings to themselves and repress them, accepting, to all appearances, their predicament and their wives' activities. It is not surprising, therefore, that a man, when drunk, may attack his wife with considerable ferocity.[5]

The man's uneasy position is further exacerbated by his role in local politics. White officials expect the men to take prominent positions in local government institutions. But since those positions all too often are seen to be devoid of power, the men who occupy them are criticized as ineffective. The problems that bedevil local government in the north, particularly the contradictions between what White officials say may happen and what in fact does happen, reveal the impotence of locally elected and appointed Eskimo men. Some men refuse to accept positions of 'authority' for precisely that reason: to accept is to become a target for criticism and ridicule. Very few Eskimo women have ever had a prominent position in local government; but not many women are made to feel ineffectual and vulnerable by working for southerners. On the other hand, most Eskimo

4. See p. 133n. above for other comments on this distinction, especially with regard to the rise in the price of fox skins.
5. Some of these matters have been discussed in a study of Western Arctic communities. See Lubart (1970), p. 19.

men who work as wage-labourers are under the direct authority of Whites who decide who will work, what precisely they will do, and whether the work is adequate. This totally subordinate position can only diminish a man's self-respect and demonstrate that he is at the mercy of other men.

Emasculation of the Eskimo man is seriously aggravated by the sexism of Whites in their dealings with Eskimo women. Whites, from their earliest visits to the far north, have been delighted by the Eskimos' uninhibited attitude to sex. Eskimos accepted that any man who is travelling without his wife will need sexual liaisons, and Whites have usually gone north alone. Armed with great power, as these Whites were, and supplied with an abundance of goods that Eskimos needed or coveted, they did not need to restrain their sexual appetites. It was prestigious and rewarding to fuck the White man; Eskimo men were early forced to accept that their women were enthusiastic about such liaisons. Perhaps in the early days of this prostitution, the husbands were truly indulgent.[6] No stigma attached to women who bore half-caste children, nor is there any evidence of such children having suffered because their fathers were White. I have, however, heard Eskimos criticize Whites for having left children in whom they apparently took no subsequent interest, and for not having offered any material help to the children's mothers.

Today, Eskimo men are still obliged to watch Whites establish casual and brief sexual attachments with Eskimo women, and to see that the women are often enthusiastic about such attachments. Whites often ply the girls with alcohol and may be able to offer a comfortable refuge from overcrowded homes. In places such as Frobisher Bay, conventional prostitution is well established, and short-term liaisons are very common. It is assumed that Whites will avail themselves of local women, whereas a liaison between a White woman and an Eskimo is rare and the cause of astonished gossip. Young Eskimo men, how-

6. Probably, however, Whites who reported this indulgence were deceived by the Eskimo's reluctance to show anger or to be manipulative or to risk confrontation with such powerful, and therefore dangerous, visitors.

ever, are becoming more hostile and more ready to express hostility towards the women involved. They are also readier to confront White sexual rivals. At a party in Frobisher Bay, a young man whose girlfriend was rather drunkenly flirting with the White men there, turned to me and angrily whispered, 'Go in that bedroom there and fuck her. Go on, go and fuck her. But after you've fucked her, let me fuck her.' He did not speak in any spirit of generosity or friendship. I replied that I was just going to leave the party, and he showed me the door. Because of repression, it may be only rarely that one can see the anger of Eskimo men in this frustration, but it has nonetheless become an integral feature of contemporary settlement life.

Within the family, as within the broader context of community life, men are more obviously disadvantaged than women. In most, if not in all aspects of family life, women have benefited to some extent from modernization, although very few women would indicate unqualified approval for settlement life. They are outwardly more cheerful than the men, who appear, not surprisingly, to be withdrawn – a withdrawal that may be interrupted by sporadic outbursts of anger and indignation. This tension is most conspicuous when there is drink involved. Alcohol associated with family violence – a price women seem to be forced to pay for their relative advantages – is going to become more common as the present situation develops.

But however difficult relationships *within* generations may be, it is relationships *between* generations that the Eskimos themselves regard as most serious. Parents naturally regard dissident or deviant children as a direct threat to their society as well as to their own personal futures. This problem is readily apparent to any observer.

Eskimos under, say, the age of 20 are conscious of a vast gulf between their parents and earlier generations and themselves. In many households there exists an extraordinary silence between teenagers and adults. Because it is considered impolite to be openly curious about another person's activities, the silence is never broken by commonplace queries about comings and goings. And because very few Eskimo adults are authoritarian or verbally critical, the silence is not broken by instruction or complaint. Young Eskimos do not usually know when or where their fathers are going hunting, what game they hope to kill, nor even when they can be expected home again. Although that vagueness is at least partly the consequence of the hunters' necessarily tentative plans, they do have a much clearer idea of the hunting plans of their peers and siblings. On the other hand, parents rarely know of their children's plans. During my stays in northern communities, I was frequently asked by parents if I could tell them where their children would be going, when, and by what means. The gulf that separates Eskimo parents and their children today is an extension of the traditional preference for quiet, unobtrusive, non-manipulative interpersonal contact. A young person who chooses not to communicate is unlikely to be under much pressure to do otherwise.

Despite this gulf, some young Eskimos emphatically insist that their elders are forever interfering in their lives. They feel watched, 'spied on', criticized, and they complain about a general lack of privacy.[7] Much of this feeling is defensive and, as such, indicates a strong sense of obligation to the older generation. Those few who deny any such sense of obligation do so with the excess that indicates the intense emotional difficulty of such a denial.

The use of English is one means that many of the young use to maintain or even to widen the gulf. Most settlement Eskimos between 12 and 16 years of age speak and write a little English, and even those with the most slender knowledge often like to use English among themselves. Most significantly, they frequently choose to speak English to one another within their parents' hearing. By so doing they affirm their possession of a special and modern skill, and can ensure a limited but certain privacy. It is startling to see an elderly couple, perhaps with a visiting neighbour, sitting at the kitchen table, drinking tea and listening attentively to one another's anecdotes and reflections in Eskimo, while in another corner of the same room a group of teenagers more excitedly exchange remarks – their grasp of the

7. This does *not* often result in a wish to leave the north, although a number of young men and women did express to me their hope of moving to some other Eskimo community.

language usually permits nothing more detailed – in English. The two groups have little cause for communication; it is customary for each to help himself to whatever food or drink he wants, and it is not customary to interrupt another's talk. In much the same spirit of defensive privacy young Eskimos like to write notes to one another in English, notes that are often trivial and a simple celebration of knowledge, but most of which are devoted to romance.

Marriage is the issue that arouses young people to their most angry protest and at the same time indicates the degree of ambivalence that the young actually do feel towards the wishes and preferences of the old. In many settlements of the Canadian Eastern Arctic, parents still expect to arrange their children's marriage, even though they may not anticipate uninterrupted marital harmony or sexual fidelity in the marriage. That expectation has been shaken, however, by the circumstances of settlement life, and few parents can now direct their children in marriage with any ease. But in most families parents may still oppose a 'bad' choice or simply forbid it. Most young persons resent and in varying degrees resist such direction, although their resistance may be undermined by strong feelings of obligation to their parents. Here is the history of one marriage that illustrates the discord that can exist and the kind of pressures that are then exerted. It happened in one of the smallest and least developed settlements in the Canadian Eastern Arctic, and it was told to me, partly in retrospect and partly as it happened, by the principal participants.

Joe was 18 when he made Mina pregnant. Both sets of parents received the news with joy: they thought Joe and Mina's marriage to be an ideal arrangement. But Joe was reluctant, and for reasons that his family did not understand he said he was not ready to marry. After the child was born, pressure on Joe was intensified. When it became clear that Mina was again pregnant, a missionary made it his business to persuade Joe to 'do the right thing'. That missionary was, in fact, neither sanctimonious nor authoritarian in his attitude, but he hoped that Joe could be reconciled to the match, and he did not think the marriage would be a disaster. The parents had expected to use the missionary as a strong force in persuading Joe. Although the missionary did not entirely favour heavy-handed tactics, to Joe he represented another argument in support of his parents' wishes. Mina, throughout these events, wanted to marry Joe.

Eventually Joe agreed that he would marry Mina at the next wedding (weddings usually occurred in groups, because the missionary had to travel 100 miles from his own village to the community). This agreement still allowed Joe the possibility of changing his mind, for there would be other marriages on the appointed day, whatever his final decision turned out to be. Joe continued to be troubled and unhappy as the time approached. He was in fact in love with another girl. He remembers that time vividly and in particular recalls one afternoon.

I was thinking I would jump off some hill into the sea. I went out walking from our house. My mother saw me go and came after me. I was walking and she caught up with me. She told me I did not need to lose myself and I did not need to walk out of our home. I came back to our home with her. That way I did not get married.

So Joe successfully resisted all the pressures on that occasion. Then, a year later, pressure was applied again. Neither Mina's nor Joe's parents had abandoned their determination to see their children married, and they once more brought the missionary into the situation. He talked with everyone concerned and concluded that the marriage could and would work well. Joe, he reported, had agreed to end his relationship with the other girl, and was ready to marry Mina. Joe told me, 'Mina was going to have another baby. They said I should marry her. That next time I married her.'

After the marriage, Joe continued to have relations with other girls, including the one he had previously wanted to marry. Then he left home to take a course in another settlement. On return, he did not live with his wife and, at the time I met him, he was determined to find some way of getting a divorce. He knew, he said, that he was on the way to being an outcast in his own home, because the older people in the settlement would not countenance divorce.

Stories of this kind may be heard in every settlement. Each

party feels that vital interests are threatened. There are other stories that reveal the anxiety that now surrounds pre-marital sexual relations in general. It is no longer possible for parents to tolerate easily casual sexual relations among their children if such relations, which are a matter of preference, lead to marriages of which parents must disapprove and which they would have arranged differently. It is, therefore, in the face of strong parental opposition that young people today persist in relationships of their choice. That persistence contributes to the sharply increasing number of Eskimos who are still unmarried in their early twenties. It also contributes to parents' growing suspiciousness of all sexual relations among the unmarried, and so encourages a trend towards more repressive attitudes to sex.

The teenagers in one village tried to establish a canteen – a tiny one–roomed shack, which they repaired and roughly furnished themselves. They installed a kettle for making coffee or tea and stocked a small supply of cigarettes, confectionery and soft drinks to sell at low prices. They also wished to use the canteen for music making and set up an electric guitar and an amplification system. But the adults in the community, hearing of this project, were keenly hostile to it. Eventually they agreed to tolerate its existence under the conditions that it would close at 10.00 p.m. on weekdays and not open at all on Sundays. These rules were necessary, they told me, or the young would be using the canteen for making love.

During my discussions about local political matters, it was also often noted that many young men did not like to go to public meetings. This reluctance worried their parents, who thought that they should attend because otherwise 'they're going to be with the young girls'. Evidently many parents now feel that their children of marrying age must at all times be supervised because of the constant threat of an unsatisfactory marriage. In a comparatively large settlement, where opportunities for secret encounters between conspiratorial lovers are abundant, the anxiety of parents is acute indeed. This anxiety is compounded by their general feeling that their children are already almost beyond parental control.

The children did not cooperate because they have been away to school. They have never really heard of hunting the way we know about hunting. I worry about it, because the young people do not hunt; maybe it is because they do not want to get cold. Some of the young people help their parents and some do not. They think they are living like the White man; they think it is better not to help because they have learned the way Whites live. Now they are teaching children here about Eskimo things; on one day of each week the children learn in school about the way we used to do things, about real Eskimo ways. Are the Whites going to make the children do everything the way we used to do things a very long time ago?

*

These young people listen to music, and they act entirely differently from the way young people used to, when people like me were young. When people of my age [about 55] were young we had a completely different way of enjoying ourselves, and of enjoying our youth, than these present-day young people. They tell us older people to go and enjoy our life, but the old are not used to that kind of thing. When we hear the young say 'share with us, share our enjoyment', we think 'What is the enjoyment in that?'

*

I think at the present time, the young people, the way they are going, they are in the fog, they are lost, the Whites have led them into a foggy place. Not only the Whites are to blame; the young read comic books and go to the movies whenever they can, and those two things are also misleading them. It is not just what they get from the Whites who are living in the settlement, but magazines and comics too. They get many bad ideas from them. If I had someone to talk to, then maybe we could figure out what we should do with the young people. The problem in this community is complicated by another problem; a problem creates a problem. The old would like the young to be involved in the community's affairs, but the young do not want to be involved, so the young and the old fight. Because they will not become involved in the community they have created a problem, but the older people cannot talk to them about the problem.

*

One thing I have been noticing over recent years is that the young men do not seem to be interested in looking after their families.

These days young people often have some money; they can make a lot of money sometimes, and then they want to keep it themselves instead of giving it to their parents. In the old days they could not easily get any money, but they would share what little they did get. Today's youth are not inclined to share the way we used to. Maybe it is in part the fault of the parents, because they do not ask and insist, and do not even find out what reasons there are for not sharing. I myself cannot give any definite reason for this change; it is not easy to explain why the young people do not like to share what they earn. It might be a result of all the education the young people have been receiving. Today's youth are more educated, for they have been brought up in the White man's ways, following all his rules and following his wishes, they might have had to go that way. When I was young like these young men we had to work really hard trying to get food; there were difficulties; often we had no success. But today the young are not helping the way they should. The young do not like to go to public meetings and to church meetings. Part of the blame for that is the kind of teaching there has been here; education and schools are partly at fault. I feel that when teachers first came here they should have asked the Eskimos to give them assistance, to tell them how to teach the young. But when the teacher came here he wanted to be alone, teaching the White way. It was far too late when they did start asking Eskimo parents to become involved in teaching, so the present young people have only learned some White ways. Now they are like lost people. They do not want to be involved with older people; some do not even want to go to church, nor to meetings. That is a very bad thing.

*

I am sad that the young people are no longer enthusiastic about hunting. It could be that they stand around in the settlement waiting for someone to ask them to work, and are afraid of going hunting because if they did they might lose the chance of well-paid work. That could be one of the reasons. They should be interested, also, in going to meetings; they are the future leaders. And if they avoid meetings they will not become involved, and so will not be able to help the people here. Perhaps the young are not encouraged enough to go to meetings; perhaps no one really asks them to go. I am not sure why that should be. But they should be encouraged more, because some day they will have to do many things; they will have to try and lead our people.

*

People sometimes make good money but spend it on themselves. Then parents ask for money and are given only one or two dollars, even by children who have a pocketful of money. I have been trying to tell other people, 'Do not be *afraid* of your children; try to help them.' People to whom I said that agreed that even if they did try to be unafraid of their children, or tried to tell them to be more helpful, the children would never obey. They said that their children would spend money sending for things from outside, through mail-order, because most of them know how to write English and can therefore write out their orders. Even if the things are not useful to themselves, or of no use to their households, or even if they are made simply to look nice, and parents therefore told them not to order such things, the children would not listen. Mostly it is our own fault. Parents agreed when teachers asked to take the children into school; the children were taken and taught to read and write and speak English; the parents thought: 'If they can do those things then they are somebody.' But parents feel that they cannot order their children, that they cannot tell the children what they should do, for the children have come to know things that the parents have never learned. The children got into the way of telling their parents off, and ceased to be afraid of their parents: the parents became afraid of the children. Right now we are preparing a programme for the young people. It is to start this coming autumn. We are asking them all to come to a meeting, and at that meeting we will tell them what we used to do in the old days, how we used to do it, how difficult it was to look after the children when they were very young. In that way we should make a start at getting the children to be more obedient to older people. Right now the young people do not like to go to meetings. That again is the fault of parents. Maybe a parent told a young person to go to a meeting, told him once, and the young person did not go. Well, the parents have been afraid to say it a second time. Even though parents think that the young do not go to meetings because they want to drink and have sex with the young girls, they are still afraid to keep telling them to go.

In the last of these comments, in speaking of the older generation's fear of the young, the old woman used the word *ilira*. It will be remembered that *ilira* may be used to suggest the sort of awe or fear young children are supposed to feel towards a strong father, and it has an extended usage that captures Eskimo feelings about Whites in general. Today it is the young who have become relatively powerful and unpredictable, and inspire the feelings of awe, respect and apprehension to which the term *ilira* relates.

This respect for the young is in part an extension of respect for Whites. Because the young have been to school and have adopted a number of White ways, in their parents' eyes they have begun to participate in the powerful White society. Teachers have sought to convince parents of the usefulness of educating their children, pointing out the social and economic advantages that would arise from such participation. Parents have begun to be cynical about such propaganda, but, as one of the persons quoted said, it is too late to go backwards. Today parents are determined to try to salvage their authority, and therefore to redeem the future; they feel that they are personally and culturally threatened and they are unwilling to resign themselves to material or psychological dependence upon their wayward and frightening children. They are becoming hostile to dependence upon the young as they are to dependence on the Whites.

The young are more readily employed than the old, and wage-labour is now the mainstay of economic life in the settlements. However, if parents feel that their children cannot be relied upon to share the fruits of their labour, then their own future is in doubt, and their present feelings of poverty and deprivation are aggravated. That feeling of poverty in turn aggravates the feeling that hunting and trapping are no longer viable. Insecurity is therefore compounded by a double dependence on children who are so undependable. The older generation is right to be apprehensive.

But, all this having been said, older people tend to exaggerate the extent to which the young are caught up in southern ways; they see each and every difference between the generations as a sign of creeping destruction. In fact young Eskimos find their own predicament uncertain and troubling, and they recognize that they are clearly not equal nor fully acceptable participants in White society and its opportunities, and they certainly do not wish to become part of that society. There is virtually no migration from north to south, and the few Eskimo girls who have married Whites are usually outspoken in their anxious determination to keep their husbands in the north. The most sophisticated and acculturated Eskimos, some of whom have spent years in schools in the south, keep their minds firmly on their northern home and return there whenever they can. The kind of out-migration that has occurred in remote rural communities throughout most of the rest of North America and Europe is most unlikely to occur in the Canadian Arctic. Reluctance to move south is a sure sign that today's youth has not accepted enough southern culture and aspirations to be convinced that their futures lie in southern towns and cities. And in the course of expressing reluctance to move south, or when recalling time spent in the south, they talk without shame or reserve of being Eskimo and belonging in the north. But the north in which they live is not an easy place for them, and signs of personal derangements among contemporary Eskimos are multiplying.

Suicide among the young is the most dramatic expression of their predicament today. Statistical expression of suicide rate is not meaningful in a population group as small as that in the Canadian Eastern Arctic, for one or two isolated cases will push the extrapolated rate per 100,000 of population far above national averages. But the incidence of suicide, especially among the young, is increasing rapidly; during 1972 there were two successful and a number of attempted suicides in one Baffin Island settlement. Each person involved was young. There is good historical evidence to suggest that in traditional times suicide was an accepted way of confronting privation or disaster. In some areas, notably among the Netsilingmiut, the custom appears to have been widespread and to have followed exact procedures.[8] But any attempt to show a causal link between traditional suicide and the suicides among the youth of today would be wrong. The young Eskimos who now try to kill themselves do not see their death as a solution to any problem that faces the community; they do not face starvation, nor do they link their own death with the prospects of their family and neighbours. Their wish for death is the expression of an entirely private unhappiness. Moreover, they have decidedly not been brought up

8. See, for example, Balikci (1961).

within cultural and metaphysical conventions that suggest suicide as a solution to personal discontent.[9] This unhappiness is a measure of social difficulties and social distress that is entirely modern, and therefore bears no relation to any of the traditional reasons.

It is quite possible that the suicide rate among the young will increase: the problems of contemporary settlement life aggravate their uncertainty, confusion and pessimism. They say so themselves. They say they do not know what to do – about jobs, daily life and their relations with parents. They feel under many kinds of pressures. Whites tell them to take courses, to do this or that; in part these suggestions are welcome, because they help to give direction in the void in which they find themselves; in part they are confusing, because they correspond only remotely or indirectly to their own personal desires and abilities.

One young man, who had received further education in the south, and was a favourite with White officials, received jobs and opportunities that Whites and many Eskimos saw as ideal, indeed irresistible. He earned good money and had the prospect of an economically successful future. He once visited me in great despair to say that he felt he was being pushed and directed. His parents wanted him to train for the ministry (a missionary had suggested the idea); the settlement manager wanted him to become a mechanic; he himself wanted to spend the next winter trapping foxes. But he had not spent a winter in his home community for eight years, and he was therefore not sure if he would still be able to trap – he had no confidence in his ability to travel on the land. The next day he visited me again, looking more despondent than ever. For a few minutes we did not speak, but I eventually broke the silence by saying, 'You look pretty gloomy tonight.' He answered, after a moment's hesitation, 'I wish I could *be something*.'

Time weighs heavily on the young. Those who feel unable or disinclined to hunt and trap must spend many hours trying to

9. The old and sick might be exceptions, but they now have medical services and they are not liabilities – indeed their pensions are often of economic advantage to their families. It is the young and healthy who are suicide-prone.

amuse themselves, by meandering here and there in the villages, visiting, gossiping, sitting, dreaming. In such a monotonous round, it is not surprising that they welcome the diversion of drink and the soft drugs that occasionally find their way even into the remotest settlements, and that they sometimes experiment with alcohol-substitutes, such as drinking after-shave lotion and sniffing gasoline. It is still rare to hear of excesses in such entertainment, but as settlement life develops these opportunities will increase. There is a growing interest in being intoxicated or high.

The boredom of inactivity, uncertainties and malaise that nurtures a preoccupation with alcohol and drugs also creates a desire for intensely romantic love affairs. Such intensity provides a kind of emotional security, which can substitute for relationships built on common activities and shared purposes. Since marriage is often problematical in these love affairs, and seldom does either partner expect a lasting relationship built on true interdependence, there is the hollowness to these romances that bedevils relationships between adolescents in Western industrial societies. There is little to share beyond mutual attraction and acute feeling, and there is, therefore, little to sustain the relationship. The pattern is very like that in the south: couples who have been profoundly emotional in their attachment suddenly end it. But in the north, this back-and-forth of shifting affairs takes place in an atmosphere heavily charged with powerful, desperate feelings. In such an atmosphere, the eruption of anger and morbidness is commonplace.

The behaviour of the young is often infected by latent aggression and recurrent despair. They do not see a future like that of their parents, but nor do they see a future in assimilation. They resent the intrusive concerns of their elders, and are hostile towards the Whites. They feel wronged – and they are right so to feel. Silent, remote and resistant as they are, this troubled generation inevitably inspires nervous apprehension in their parents. In any case, parents of teenagers are victims themselves of a colonial situation; the heads of a family have suffered a radical diminution of their influence and powers. No longer able to decide where to live or hunt, unable to make or even buy the equipment on which they depend, periodically dependent on others, parents are continuously aware of how little control they have over their own situations and over the future. Deviant or dissident youth is, in that context, doubly alarming and threatening to them. Growing opposition to the initiatives, independence and privacy of older children must be interpreted in the light of the parents' own weakened and uncertain position.

Thus parents now – and untraditionally – assert themselves in the family because they have such limited possibilities for meaningful assertion outside it. Schools, youth programmes, boy scouts and other colonial institutions have created a youth group that breaks into family groups. Protracted schooling has taken much of the responsibility for the socialization of children out of the parents' hands. And the schools that have assumed this responsibility are now in fact declaring the children to be failures. Parents are conscious of the former circumstance; the children and some of the parents are conscious of the latter. Shift in the responsibility for education away from parents towards an essentially foreign institution has done what it can only do – create nervousness about the future and weakness in the present. The complex of changes which this and earlier chapters have described means that the Canadian Arctic has its share of 'physical pollution, social polarization and psychological impotence: three dimensions in a process of global degradation and modern misery'.[10] So parents – particularly fathers – try to assert themselves against the young in the family. In so doing they resist their own ineffectiveness and seek to reverse trends that are threatening the future. By doing this they indicate some opposition at least to much of what the southern presence represents and has created. Their fear of the future is given urgency by their anxiety over problems in the present, and the two feelings are united in the difficulties that are natural between generations.

Now I would like to tell you a story, about the time the first missionary came here. He used to preach and talk in those old days – that was the time of my mother's generation. Those people of that generation used to be told in church: In the future you are going to have children and some of those children will be good and some

10. See Illich (1971), p. 1.

will be bad. Some day some of your children will be alive when the time comes when Whites start to live in your homeland. If you have bad children, then you will have bad grandchildren; the bad things will remain with you. The missionary also said that in the future the Whites would bring a great number of different things that are not too good for the Eskimos. We learned that there were going to be problems, problems of two cultures getting together, problems like drinking and war. The missionary talked of how things in each generation would get worse and worse. Now we are sort of half way. The generation after this one will be worse again than the present one, when the present young men and women grow up. Then, when I am no longer alive, they'll have more problems. I believe that those things prophesied by the missionary are happening now. I believe that more things will happen, things the missionary talked of. He said, 'One day a government will come to you, your children, and to your grandchildren, and that government will bring all kinds of help. But the help will not last long; one day they will come and give much, and another day they will leave you.' I believe that the government has come, but will soon stop being helpful. I've seen things go that way. It's going downhill now. I believe the next administrator will be worse and the one after him worse again, and finally the end of White help will come.

What defences do the Eskimos have against the difficulties they foresee? What continuity can there be? What are the young going to do? At least within the family there can be some struggle against these trends, and at present they can look beyond the immediate family to southerners for help and for reassurance. But the heads of households are now embattled, surrounded by shifting difficulties which confuse and threaten to engulf them. The older generation struggle with the young, and they urge Whites to be more committed in their support. The younger generation try to find a way of life for themselves, independent of the family, beyond the manipulation of outsiders. The final irony is of course to be discovered in the result: the Eskimo family has begun to experience the family life that is normal to and typical of the dominant society – private, tense and unsatisfying. It is in this newly constituted family that every Eskimo feels most acutely the disadvantage of the changes that the south has brought to the north.

11 • The New Frontier

'The emergence of the Northwest Territories as a
political and economic force promises to be the
twentieth century's greatest saga.

'It will include industrial developments on a scale
suited to the size of the land, giving employment
to thousands of modern pioneers. It will be a
modern re-enactment of old frontier days –
accelerated and magnified by world pressures of
population, increased commercial demands and
heightened by competition for mineral resources.
It will be rocketed ahead by computer-oriented
technology'

– Stewart Hodgson, Commissioner of the
Northwest Territories, 1970

'We very much dislike White people taking our
land for granted. It seems that they feel that they
can destroy our land any time they feel like it
without even asking for permission. We want to
have freedom with the animals. They steal the raw
materials without even consulting us or giving the
Inuit a percentage of what they are taking. We
need to get power to control the land'

– Elijah Takkiapik, Vice-President of the Fort Chimo
Community Council, 1974

Colonialists express colonialism in many different ways. They
like to offer 'solutions' to 'problems': each so-called solution
indicates more or less clearly what they believe to be the problem. The problems that colonialists believe to be central reveal
the kind of colonialism they support and seek to justify. Some
advance the notion of aboriginal poverty: the natives were – and
perhaps still are – savage, heathen, and therefore impoverished.
The solution to that problem is 'civilization'. Some are concerned with giving natives qualifications, and want to train them
for some form of labour. Others focus on the poverty and dis-

tress that contact with outsiders has created and therefore advocate various welfare measures. Others again note a poverty of the spirit and argue that the solution lies in a return to 'traditional' values and practices, and they will, if necessary, teach the natives to be natives.

Canada, like many other industrial and industrializing nations, is experiencing rapid internal colonial expansion on a massive scale. Northern native peoples are implicated in development, and are being subjected to ever more administration. And they have thus become a 'problem' for which contemporary colonialists have their various new 'solutions'.

I have argued that many Whites consider the Eskimos to be in need of many things, from Jesus Christ to knives and forks. Stereotyped views of Eskimo culture, tradition and recent social change have combined to cause confusion in the minds of colonial agents and have led to a series of contradictory programmes. Perhaps the educational system reveals this kind of muddle at its worst. The 'fuzzy objectives' of northern education were pointed out more than ten years ago by a teacher of considerable experience in the Northwest Territories.

Insofar as aims and purposes for education in the north are concerned – and they should be of fundamental importance – the department [of education] has failed to come to any definite conclusions. Whether the object is to preserve the native cultures, to replace them with Canadian culture, or to combine the two in some way has not yet been determined. Members of the department have made official statements that may be interpreted to support each of these; actual practice not infrequently contradicts their statements.[1]

The educational muddle is complicated by federal and industrial interest in Arctic development. The interests of industry throw a bright light on the ambiguous position of the Eskimo who is neither hunter nor skilled worker, neither nomadic nor well-settled into the southern economy and its social habits. The problem has some new aspects: there is a new need for some of the land on which Eskimos once depended, and there is a new need for Eskimo workers who no longer depend on their land. Since neither the land nor the labour is available in the desired

1. See Hepburn (1963), esp. p. 17.

form, a new 'solution' suggests itself: resolve the question of entitlement to land and train Eskimo men to work in the extractive industry. Peoples who prefer a mixed-economic life, who depend on a pre-capitalist mode of production as well as on wage-labour, are a problem for such endeavours.

Yet Eskimos do base their lives on a mixed economy. The aboriginal dweller of the Arctic, uncontaminated by Euro-American technology, invulnerable to the marketplace, undisturbed by money and a need to produce surplus-for-exchange, disappeared long ago. His was probably a good life: evidence from the Eskimos and from other hunting and gathering societies suggests that they enjoyed more efficient and secure ways of life than the societies that almost everywhere overwhelmed or destroyed them.[2] The independence of subsistence Eskimos was quickly lost, and soon gave way to social and ideological disparities as well as an economic order that the Eskimos today regard as their own tradition. The *Inummariit* described in Chapter 7 were men and women involved, albeit indirectly, in a market economy; they were traders; they needed credit or money for trade goods. This new 'traditional' life, the life now regarded as traditional by contemporary Eskimos, was founded on a mixed economy: there was hunting, and there was trading. Those who now work for wages and live in a government-designed settlement continue to maintain a mixed economic system; even full-time, year-round employees hunt when they can. It is quite possible that the distinctive Eskimo culture and personality that tradition-oriented anthropologists so meticulously reconstruct are the products of a mixed economy. The culture and personality of pre-contact Eskimo life may be too far removed from us to be known.

This 'problem', then, has two sides and is deeply rooted. Here is a people who, regarding a mixed economy as part of their tradition, as integral to their cultural identity, need their land, now as they did before. Others want rights to the land, and the problem caused by that desire is compounded by the whole history of the northern frontier.

2. For a more general elaboration of this point, see Sahlins (1974), esp. Ch. 1.

The expropriation of North American Indian lands was eventually secured by the reserve system: Indians were given title to enclaves of land which were for the most part of only marginal use, along with token compensation for the loss of millions of acres of other land. This established a system of occupancy and land use consistent with the colonialists' ideas of and need for land tenure. Subsequent questions about mis-application of, or indifference to, property laws as they arose between Indians and North American settlers could, in theory, be resolved by the courts. The reserve system, however, did not reach far beyond lands the newcomers actually wanted to occupy. Some treaties did involve sub-Arctic forest and trapping areas, but their terms are notoriously vague; signatures seem to have been obtained with a grand indifference to where the sig-natories or their ancestors came from, and referred to lands in-habited by peoples they had scarcely heard of. The treaties made in the sub-Arctic did not create reserves, but were the extension of a southern practice to northern territory where it made no sense. Almost all the lands beyond the tree line were beyond even the incoherent northern treaties: the Eskimos never signed away their land. Alternatively, in colonialists' law, the Eskimos were never confirmed in any title to it. The traders and others, who urged economic and social changes on the Eskimos and whose attitudes I summarized in Chapter 2, could achieve their profitable ends without owning the land themselves. Indeed, traders maximized their profits by urging trappers to make sys-tematic use of more and more land.[3]

But today the Arctic is being rediscovered. The latest rush to the north, the passion for the 'new frontierism' that grips many who wield great influence in the Canadian economy, has raised questions about the principles of land rights that were debated in North America when the last buffalo were dying on the plains

3. The native populations of the far north were therefore vulnerable to attitudes more characteristic of Spanish than of Anglo-American colonialism. Whereas the Spanish wanted to transform Indians 'from heathen barbarians into good Christians', the Anglo-American approach 'was dominated by the idea of pushing the Indians out of their way and keeping them apart from themselves'. (See Castile, 1974, p. 220, where he quotes Spicer's *Cycles of Conquest*.)

and Indians were being urged to become farmers on their reserves. The analogy is instructive, if only because the frenzy of activity in the Arctic evokes the frenzy of colonial advance in the other, earlier era.

Before 1964 fewer than 6,000 claims for non-renewable resources north of latitude 60 were staked annually. Then the surge began. During 1964–9 the Pine Point area, just south of Great Slave Lake, was the target of 51,000 claims, and the Coppermine region of another 39,000. These claims were made principally in anticipation of the development of base metal deposits, and later production figures appear to have justified the enthusiasm of the rushes. In 1970 the total mineral output for the Yukon and Northwest Territories was valued at approximately $200 m. – an increase of 32 per cent over 1967 – and in 1970 the Northern Economic Branch of the Department of Indian Affairs and Northern Development anticipated that 1971 output would be worth at least $230 m. The 1967–70 increase, however, came primarily from a single mine at Pine Point – scarcely 100 miles north of the Albertan–Northwest Territories border. During the period just before 1970, official forecasts for the productive value of the three other mine sites in the Northwest Territories had fallen. Then, in 1970–71, even the Pine Point mine suffered reverses: lead sales fell by 40 per cent and zinc sales by 20 per cent. But, between 1968 and 1970, eager and optimistic attention had shifted to oil and gas in the far north.

The first exploratory oil-well in the Canadian high Arctic was drilled in 1961 on Melville Island, but after 1968, following the discovery of oil at Prudhoe Bay, Alaska, the oil and gas interest really came to life. By 1972, $20 m. had been spent on studying the feasibility of an Arctic pipeline that would cost an anticipated $6,000 m. This scale of expenditure would, it was said, be justified by discoveries in both the Mackenzie River delta and the Canadian Arctic islands. By 1971 the Mackenzie delta gas fields were estimated to contain 15 trillion cubic feet of gas whereas the North Slope of Alaska was estimated to contain 26 trillion cubic feet.[4]

4. Officials of the Canadian Department of Indian and Northern Affairs recall that various visions of a new northern frontier played a part in

In the meantime, between 1968 and 1972 Panarctic Oils in collaboration with other companies discovered gas on Melville, King Christian and Ellef Ringnes Islands, and some oil on Ellesmere Island. By the end of 1972, these discoveries brought the known gas resources of the Canadian Arctic halfway to 25 trillion cubic feet – approaching the viability threshold point. Prospects began to brighten for at least a Mackenzie Valley pipeline, and there was talk of a pipeline reaching from the Eastern Arctic Islands to Montreal. Wild speculations began to receive much coverage in the Canadian press. In August 1972 a professor of geology at a university in the United States was reported to have stated that potential gas and oil reserves inside the Arctic Circle were equal to all known sources – and that a sizable proportion of those reserves lay inside Canada. To get these reserves meant getting the Eskimos' land.

The 1973–4 popular obsession with energy, together with a rapid rise in the prices of base metals as well as hydrocarbons, made the industrialists' haste all the more pressing. This sense of urgency was exaggerated by optimistic assessments of Arctic resource potential. The notes for the speech made by Jean Chrétien, then Minister of the Department of Indian and Northern Affairs, at the opening of the Fifty-First Northwest Territories Council provide an example of the mood which came to dominate official thinking:

What of the future? The potential of the north is surely limitless. At the risk of being mistaken for a Texan, I would like to explore with you some of this potential: I think of the many trillions of cubic feet of natural gas already discovered in the Arctic islands and in the Mackenzie delta after a few short years of exploration activity. This represents only the tip of the iceberg of what lies undiscovered. Half of Canada's conventional oil and gas reserves are estimated to lie north of [latitude] 60. I think of the mountain of rich ore at Mary River with reserves of 128 million tons – uneconomic today but not tomorrow. I think of the lead-zinc deposits at Arvik on Little Cornwallis Island, at Strathcona Sound and the Bathurst-

---

northern policies during 1950–60, but agree that the realities of northern development carried the vision to the stock exchange with real effect only in the late 1960s.

Norsemines deposit at Hack River. I think of the many rivers and lakes of northern Canada which contain nearly 50 per cent of Canada's fresh water supply and very substantial hydro-electric potential. On the Mackenzie River, to give but one example, preliminary studies indicate an installed capacity of approximately 14,000 mW. is possible – this is approximately three times the capacity of Churchill Falls and would represent 45 per cent of current total Canadian hydro capacity.

Senior officers of the Federal Government assumed more confidently than ever that the far north was on the verge of massive development. More specifically, hopes were increasingly pinned on the oil and gas potential as the immediate and compelling resource; Chrétien pointed out in a speech (18 January 1973) that in 1970–73, expenditure on exploration for oil and gas rose from $34 m. to $230 m. The 1973 Annual Report of the Government of the Northwest Territories echoed the excited optimism in Ottawa, and recorded the happy expectation that in the coming year wells would 'be deeper and drilled in remote and frontier areas'. By the end of 1972, leases covered 426,561,084 acres of the Northwest Territories.

To the layman, the arithmetic is too astronomical to grasp; but everyone could see, and begin to feel, that the frontier was alive again. The dreamers were dreaming of new roads, pipelines and towns, and, for the entrepreneurial at least, fortunes were ready for the making. What place was there, in all these schemes, for the Eskimo? Dramatic illustrations of the new north began to appear in magazines, newspapers and reports, and these pictures rarely failed to include the smiling native, a distinctly Eskimo face, taking his place alongside the southern hard-hat, sharing the work, participating in the great national endeavour. Unfortunate precedents were forgotten; not much mention was made of the failure of the mine at Pine Point to improve the social and economic lives of its neighbouring Indians. No, if the exploitation of mineral resources brought 'problems', it also brought the final 'solution'; Eskimos would now take their rightful place in the national economy and, newly re-trained, would become key operators in these ventures. Suddenly (once more) the north – the whole north – was believed to have a great future.

The early 1970s consequently saw the highest-minded, most confident statements about the prospects of northern native people. The first three of the Federal Government's priorities for the 1970s were plainly stated.

They are comprehensive in scope and closely related to Canada's national goals and interests. These objectives are:

1. To provide for a higher standard of living, quality of life and equality of opportunity for northern residents by methods that are compatible with their own preferences and aspirations.

2. To maintain and enhance the northern environment with due consideration to economic and social development.

3. To encourage viable economic development within regions of the northern territories so as to realize their potential contribution to the national economy and the material well-being of Canadians.[5]

Today there is a new requirement for shifting emphasis toward people programmes, but by a smooth adjustment of all programmes rather than an abrupt change.[6]

And the Minister made reference to the iniquities of earlier northern adventurers who, he noted, had shown little regard for the well-being of the real northerners. They had been interested in 'getting in, getting rich and getting out'. 'Development of that kind is the antithesis of the steady-balanced and humanistic expansion which is the Government's main concern in this statement.'[7]

The Commissioner of the Northwest Territories, Stewart Hodgson, in the 1973 Report already quoted, echoes federal affirmations of 1972. The report refers to 'the Commissioner's expressed philosophy that the Territorial Government intends to see to it that native people have a choice to follow either the traditional ways or the ways of the southern wage economy'.[8]

5. Introductory remarks by the Honourable Jean Chrétien, Minister of Indian Affairs and Northern Development: *Northern Canada in the Seventies*, a report to the Standing Committee on Indian Affairs and Northern Development on the Government's northern objectives, priorities and strategies for the seventies, 28 March 1972, p. 4.

6. ibid., p. 5.   7. ibid., p. 7.   8. op. cit., p. 20.

Both Federal and Territorial Government officials showed their unbounded enthusiasm for industrial development, and expressed bland confidence that native people only stood to gain from such development. Notably, development was supposed to give Eskimos and northern Indians real alternatives. Belief in the economic system that was to bring industry to the Arctic established – at least in the minds of those who expected to gain from it – the conviction that maximum investment in non-renewable resources would somehow give the Eskimos their freedom.

In fact, the far north is to a certain extent invulnerable to the excesses of uncontrolled free enterprise. The capital needed for exploration, and the capital needed to cover transportation and overcome problems of climate, are prohibitive for individual entrepreneurs. Moreover, such costly undertakings have to be on a scale that will, in the long run, offset the high costs: ore deposits, for example, must be exceptionally large, of high grades and have secure long-term markets.[9] The capitalism that can meet these requirements is an alliance of international corporations and the State: numbers of companies unite, with federal subvention, to minimize individual risk. In early 1972, the exploration manager of Imperial Oil Ltd (Toronto) voiced his view of the problems of Arctic oil developments. After explaining the land tenure difficulty, the high cost problems, and countering pessimistic estimates of undiscovered hydrocarbons in Canada, he summarized:

What all this means is that when companies risk their capital in exploration in new basins such as exist in Canada's frontiers, a few may make substantial profits, a greater number may make marginal profits, and an even greater number may make no profit at all.[10]

But the exploration manager did not here anticipate the possible scale of federal involvement, or the effect of that involvement in minimizing risk to companies. Another consequence of federal involvement is the Government's possible role as moderator of the impact of large-scale development on native

9. See Brody (1973), for elaboration of this theme and its implications for Eskimo politics.
10. See McIvor (1972).

people. The fine talk of the period could, after all, become fine, working policies: if Eskimos wished to have a real alternative to labouring for the frontier corporation, that could perhaps be guaranteed. As a major stockholder in the companies concerned, the Canadian Government has in many cases been in a position to influence such things as hiring policy and the location and speed of development; as subventor of development and owner of all mineral rights in the regions, the Government has been in a position to demand conditions on which development could take place. As it happened, the Government's record in this was, in the 1970–73 period, abysmal.

Peter Usher's study of the Eskimos of Banks Island shows that when this prosperous trapping community felt that its interests were menaced by oil companies' seismic exploration, officers of the federal department concerned colluded with the industrial interests in order to overwhelm local opposition.[11] The publication of the third volume of Usher's report caused a furore in government circles, but, if failure to answer his charges is a basis for judgement, his charges are unanswerable. In November 1973 the International Work Group for Indigenous Affairs (IWGIA) published a résumé of the legal aspects of six cases, including that of the Bank Islanders, which illustrate the range of ways in which Central Government has at times failed to protect the rights and local economic integrity of native peoples.

The IWGIA report also raises the employment 'problem'. Since the northern frontier is not agricultural, there is no possibility of turning hunters into farmers. Jean Chrétien is quoted as having said:

The only alternative to more welfare or forced southern migration is to create additional job opportunities. Since 1961 the population north of [latitude] 60 has grown by 50 per cent. This increase, largely indigenous, is almost three times the national average – the highest rate in North America.[12]

So the trap is set. Northern development is good because, among other advantages, it gives native people a greater range of choice: they will, with education and industrial advance at

11. See Usher (1971), esp. Vol. 3.   12. See Sanders (1973), p. 30.

the frontier, be able to choose between a life on the land and wage employment. But, we are also told, a life on the land is no longer possible – the population is too large and the renewable resources are insufficient. So federal policy must be directed at creating jobs. Therefore economic development is urgently needed – in order to solve, of course, the Eskimos' problems. With this circular and self-justifying argument policy-makers effectively narrow down the alternatives: Eskimos must become wage-labourers.[13] And as long as federal investment in or support of the hunting and trapping alternative is minimal, Eskimos are under direct and heavy pressure to accept the wage-labour option. They need money, and must go where money can be earned.

The most important employment-for-Eskimos scheme since the beginning of the 1970s rush to develop the north is that of Panarctic Oils Ltd. The story is instructive.

Panarctic, a combination of many companies, was granted exploration and development rights to oil and gas in large areas of the Eastern Arctic. The Canadian Federal Government, in return for a subvention, received a holding of a little under 50 per cent in the venture. The early stages of Panarctic's operation involved exploratory drillings. Workers were hired in southern Canada by hiring agents based in Edmonton. A shift system was devised to meet the needs of a southern work-force, based on a twenty-days-on and ten-days-off rota. Employees were flown out to Edmonton for their ten-day breaks.

After the hiring scheme had been established, the Federal Government discovered that Panarctic drew none of its labour-force from Eskimo settlements. Federal Government officials therefore proceeded to pressure Panarctic (and, later, its employment division, Peben) into extending the twenty-days-on, ten-days-off scheme to Eskimos of Pond Inlet and Arctic Bay.

13. It is also often said that Eskimos and northern Indians do not want to live on the land any more, and that a trend towards wage labour is perfectly in accord with local aspirations. In Chapter 7, I have, I hope, shown the absurdity of that view. But, when such a view is held by policy-makers it is dangerously self-fulfilling. (Usher, 1971, has discussed this in relation to the Western Arctic.)

When those responsible for adult education services in these two communities heard that local men were to be hired to work on Panarctic sites, they asked to discuss the question with the company or its agents. They hoped to ensure that the company's requirement for high-paid southern labour should be extended to Arctic villagers in the best possible way, and were especially eager to ensure that Eskimo workers were properly trained for skilled work, and would not only do the most menial jobs. They also wanted time to discuss the whole matter with the communities concerned. But apparently Panarctic's agents refused to negotiate with them and – the adult education officials say – insisted that the only thing the agents would discuss was the names of the new employees. As a result, a hiring scheme devised for Edmonton miners was extended directly and abruptly to Eskimos of north Baffin Island.

By early 1973, sixteen men from Pond Inlet and eight from Arctic Bay were taking home between $700 and $900 per month. The impact of these earnings on the settlements was predictably very great, but no serious effort was made to monitor, still less to ameliorate, the consequences for the communities concerned. In July 1973 Eric Gourdeau of the Arctic Institute of North America prepared a paper entitled 'The social impact of Panarctic's employment policy in Arctic Bay and Pond Inlet'. He was paid to do so by Panarctic.

Gourdeau's paper is among the silliest documents ever to deal with the Canadian north. He spent a total of three days in Pond Inlet and two days in Arctic Bay; he does not speak Eskimo; and he had virtually no background information. Thus equipped, he assessed the changes caused by employment. Although ignorant of the communities before the arrival of Panarctic, Gourdeau insists that both communities were still 'unspoilt', and had 'high morale'. He leaves his readers with the impression that an addition of $400,000 over thirteen months to the economies of two small Eskimo communities had only good effects. Panarctic's directors were, one hopes, delighted to hear such good news. Gourdeau is particularly reassuring on the troubled question of alcohol. He tells us that the employees wished to avoid a reputation for drunkenness, and there is therefore no real alcohol problem in either community. Four months after his paper was written, however, the Oblate missionary in one of the communities reported that in one month fifteen cases of hard liquor had been delivered by air. Two years earlier, the delivery of two cases in a month was unusual. Then, in January 1974, the Commissioner of the Northwest Territories reported that there were so many complaints from Pond Inlet about drunkenness that he had decided to 'cut off' the supplies.[14] Response to his action was angry, and the decision was soon overturned. In April 1974, thirty cases of hard liquor arrived in Pond Inlet. Perhaps the newly prosperous workers had not read their Gourdeau.

Despite this and other problems that income from Panarctic had aggravated, if not caused, many men in the settlements continue to be eager to work on the oil and gas sites. They and their relations need money. If one hears but little protest against the wage-labour option, it is because there is no viable alternative. Men who live by hunting and trapping, or by a mixed economy, tend to be regarded as unemployed, and are listed as potential workers. So long as the lists of unemployed are long, industrial development can be said to be solving a local problem, as well as creating wider opportunities. The ideological commitment of developers provides its own justifications. Unfortunately the Federal Government has in practice and from the beginning allied itself with the corporations and their purposes.

Despite the bonanza mood on the northern frontier, and loud echoings down the corridors of power in Ottawa and Calgary, there are less sanguine views of northern development to be heard. Many theorists of underdevelopment have revised the orthodoxies and now urge the view that development of the poor by the rich, of the colonized by the colonizer, tends to increase the differences between them – making the rich richer at the expense of the poor. Confident assumptions that any economic development helps those whose land is being developed should by now have been overthrown. More specifically, capital-intensive extractive industries require large inputs of

14. See *Ottawa Journal*, 26 January 1974.

labour only in their initial stages. In the short to medium term they can generate local dependence on high levels of wage-earning that will not, by the very nature of the development, be long maintained. When the plant (or pipeline) is built and the construction-force discharged, the local economy may be seriously deranged.

Some doubt has also been expressed about the real value of the northern frontier's still-hidden treasures. These remarks, for example, strike a note that is very different from that of many official publications:

> Nobody suggests that there will be no interesting discoveries made in the High Arctic. There have already been some made. But finds of anything up there would have to be of huge magnitude to be of any use to anybody. To be of any use to the present generation of Canadians, or to the next one, the finds would also have to be of something Canadians genuinely need – crude oil, bauxite, gold, silver, mercury, chrome – and that the High Arctic is likely to be well-endowed with any of these materials is unsupported by any worthwhile evidence.
>
> It is time some of the scientists in government or industry joined the handful of people openly expressing the fear that this second side of the Arctic coin will turn out to be the one we actually have to stare at. Many thoughtful Canadians already acknowledge privately their fear that the Arctic has been seriously oversold.[15]

It would appear to be more than merely conceivable that northern development will not take place in the degree or forms that are at present anticipated so widely and enthusiastically.[16]

But there is a momentum to ideas of economic development that makes them unresponsive to discouraging facts. The frontier is strongly ideological; it is a belief necessary to politicians and public, whilst businessmen may make some profit from

15. North (1973), pp. 306–8.
16. The bias in developers' opinions can play a very large part in the 'difficult, inexact science' of resource assessment. In this connection the Canadian press picked up a remarkable passage in a brief to the Commons Standing Committee on National Resources: 'In making decisions in face of this uncertainty, we must choose the probability level that is appropriate for decisions at hand' – Charles Lynch reporting in *Ottawa Citizen*, 26 January 1974.

enthusiasm for it alone – at least so long as enthusiasm encourages the flow of government subsidies. Cost what it may, 'progress' will not be halted. The costs, of course, are social as well as economic: the Eskimos will pay the former, and the Canadian taxpayer the latter.

The Nanisivik mine is the latest, and at the time of this writing, the plainest example of rationalized frontierism. During the 1950s deposits of lead and zinc were discovered near to the shores of Strathcona Sound, on the north-west tip of Baffin Island. In 1962 samples of ore were examined. In 1972–3, Mineral Resources International (MRI), a company with addresses in Calgary and Toronto, began to urge the Canadian Federal Government to subsidize exploitation of this ore. During the winter of 1973–4 senior officials in the Department of Indian and Northern Affairs and Treasury Board considered applications for more than $15 m. MRI argued that the mine would prove profitable if initial subsidies were on such a scale. In the course of reviewing MRI's proposal, economists pointed out that, from Canada's point of view, the mine could not be economic. Canadian processing and manufacturing facilities were too small; the ore would be exported in crude form to West Germany and Holland; and the advantages to shipbuilding would not be Canada's. There was no pressing need within Canada for the mine's exploitation; it could not be justified by reference to larger national interests.

Although the economic rationale for going ahead was in disarray, the mine's proponents insisted on its social merits. It would, they claimed, provide employment for Eskimos in nearby settlements. What these enthusiasts did not take time to find out, however, was whether or not there was much unemployment in the neighbourhood. Father Guy Mary-Rousselière, editor of *Eskimo*, could have helped them with their homework. His editorial in the issue of *Eskimo* for summer 1974, expressed doubts about the mine's social worth, recorded his surprise 'that the decision has been taken prior to any solid economic survey', and mentioned the employment argument:

It is claimed, it seems, that this enormous expense is justified by the need to provide local employment. Now, precisely, since Panarctic uses Eskimo labour, there is no unemployment in this area. We were told recently that meat had to be brought in by plane from the south to a small settlement because there were no longer enough hunters to supply local game: a bewildering situation!

Interested social scientists also expressed concern about the proposed mine. The impact on the communities of north Baffin Island would, they pointed out, be massive, and could be drastic, especially on Arctic Bay, only fifteen miles from the site. Some urged the Federal Government to delay the opening of the mine until the local social and economic background work could be done, and ways of minimizing its impact could be devised. Since the economic and employment justifications were not at issue, they argued, there was nothing to be gained – and there was much to lose – by rushing ahead.

Despite these and other doubts, the Government and MRI signed an agreement in June 1974. Work on the site had been under way for some months: approval in principle had been given earlier in the year. Production would be under way by 1977, and by 1980 at least 100 Eskimos are expected to be working there – helping private industry to ship approximately $820 m. of Canadian ore to Europe.[17]

The mine was hurried into existence by persons determined to have development at any price. These same persons who had, at other times, insisted on the importance of alternatives to wage-labour failed to suggest that the national economy devote some of its surplus to subsidizing those alternatives. The Nansivik mine illustrates how development can take place for development's sake.

When looked at alongside the cost to the nation of subsidizing industrial advance at the frontier, the sums spent on maintaining Eskimo hunting and trapping – 'the traditional options' – have been negligible. Fur prices have never been guaranteed, nor has welfare been used in any systematic way to ensure a minimum income to those who choose to live by harvesting renewable resources. In January 1974, the superintendent for game of the Northwest Territories announced 'incentive grants'

17. See Clare Balfour, 'Ottawa aided mine to process outside Canada', *Edmonton Journal*, 5 July 1974.

for licensed trappers. The incentives amounted to a $60 grant for a trapper who made $400 from sale of furs in one season, and $150 for a trapper who made $1,000.[18] At the same time as that scheme was being formulated, the Federal Government was proposing to develop a multi-million dollar, non-economic, ill-considered mine site. It is hard to believe that the fine talk about guaranteeing the 'traditional' option has amounted to very much at all.[19]

Developers have found a ready acceptance in Eskimo communities for whatever employment scheme they have to offer. People who feel themselves to be utterly dependent on provision of foods and services from the south are slow to bargain over or complain about terms and conditions. Chapter 8 dealt with the kind of fear that many Eskimos feel towards Whites in general; in Chapters 9 and 10, I dealt with the economic and familial strains that settlement life has brought. The combination of all these circumstances means that most Eskimos – especially the older generations – acquiesce in what representatives of Government seem to think should be done. An elderly man once explained his silence to me: 'I feel that if we say things that the southerners do not like, then they will send in soldiers. We would quickly be beaten in such a fight.' A reporter covering the Nanisivik mine quoted the words of an Arctic Bay resident who had been urging his people there to welcome the development:

Fox furs were being sold for a very small amount. We were not able to get enough money from hunting. Our cost of living was rising; the cost of food was rising and we were not able to raise enough money to meet the cost of living. We decided that if there was an alternative we were willing to work towards it so that the cost of living won't be so hard on us.[20]

18. See *Tukisiviksat*, Vol. 4, No. 1, Feb. 1974.
19. Most recently (1974–5) the Territorial and Federal Governments have begun to float ideas for revitalizing camps or outposts. Such plans, if properly expanded and offered as an acceptable option, may not be too late to help those who have managed to maintain confidence and determination against being recruited as labour for the extractive industries.
20. Tremayne (1974), p. 4.

When negotiations over the mine were under way, the Arctic Bay community council sent a letter to government agencies interested in the project to say that they 'have agreed to let the companies in. The people in Arctic Bay do not want to live the old way of life, without a gun, boat, or even a stick.' The letter ended with a remarkable passage:

... in the present plan *Inuit* have nothing. Since we have nothing the Government could start going against us. If we tried to stop them or they can just forget about us. The Government may even start thinking about death or they might split us up. But if our land is going to be worked on, we should like to know the plans before the activity starts so we can help each other. Also, so the companies will have enough workers on their staff.

So we can understand more fully, we would like a letter from the mining company stating the number of workers they want so we can look around for the men.

Despite their statement of generous intent, it is indeed hard to see what alternatives the Government and industry have given to the people of the Canadian Eastern Arctic; they can work as labourers, or live in continuing poverty, dependent on others for a meagre livelihood.

Eskimos of the Eastern Arctic will be able to live in ways that reflect their own preferences only if the dominant society's intrusion can be minimized. Since the nineteenth century, when British and American whalers first used Eskimos for labour and trade, southern agencies – equipped with wealth and powers that the Eskimos could scarcely imagine – have instigated and directed change. In more recent years, successive government policies have all had in common an idea about how Eskimos or northern Indians ought to live. The most recent trends are pushing native people increasingly towards the lowest and least certain rung on the national class ladder: if separated from his own means of production and unable to have a sure relationship to the intruders' means of production, the Eskimo – like many Canadian and American Indians before him – will be turned into a migrant worker, a casual labourer, and – as this lumpenproletarian condition develops – prostitute, petty thief and beggar. Abundant signs of this course of events are already visible. The problem will not be cleared away by promises of high pay at the golden frontier: short-term booms that are so characteristic of frontier development only worsen the problems that will follow.

In these ways, the Eskimos and Indians of the Canadian far north share a predicament with many other peoples who are being made to 'settle down'. In many regions their economies have been and are being disrupted by neighbours' incursions into vital lands: pastoralists by farmers and ranchers, hunters and gatherers by farmers and developers, virtually all by ideologies that equate settlement with progress. Since Canada's Eskimos never made treaties with the Federal Government, they have no clear legal grounds for opposing the invasion of industry. Indeed, as I have pointed out, many Eskimos are deeply apprehensive about their present predicament and cannot forget their dependence on Whites, and so feel they have no alternative but to welcome whatever development takes place among them.

Since 1971, however, a growing number of northern peoples have become interested in the question of their legal rights to the land they occupy. They now recognize that a clear title to land, and some rights to control what takes place on their land, are the only available ways to minimize the destructive power of southern society. A land settlement is the 1970s way of signing a treaty, and reflects the pressures on 1970s' Indian and Eskimo societies. But there are also dangers.

Many treaties with North American Indians are notorious for the way in which they gave Indians title only to poor land, and, in any event, to less land than had been found necessary for maintenance of a hunting economy. The treaties also gave some small financial and welfare benefits in return for the alienation of vast tracts of land to settlers. They also were the basis for a continued domination through local bureaucracies and administration set up on reserves and run by Whites. Treaties and the reserve system did not mean that Indians were left to direct their own affairs – even within their enclaves. Indeed, the non-viability of the reserve ensured that continued dependence was built in.

In the United States Indian policies have shifted, in recent years, away from ideas of assimilation and directed change. Congress has now accepted the idea of 'a potentially more viable alternative' which has been referred to as a 'sustained enclave'.[21]

Similar notions have influenced some Ottawa-based policy-makers – hence the fine talk I quoted earlier. But direct administration of affairs in Eskimo communities has become a habit of mind; and it is a habit too deeply embedded in the concept and design of northern administration to be easily shifted towards even such a notion as 'sustained enclaves'. Some gestures have been made in that direction, but it is hard to avoid the feeling that, from the civil service point of view, Eskimos do not yet fully subscribe to the kinds of ideas and objectives designed for them in Yellowknife and Ottawa. Until they ask for things and behave in ways that fit in with the ways of the civil service, more time and money will be invested in modernizing Eskimos than in finding out what sort of change they might want for themselves.

This persistent erosion of the Eskimos' Eskimo alternative, and the parallel imposition of administrative notions and purposes, could be mitigated by a land settlement that focused on the Eskimos' right to create a political enclave as well as to have control of territory. Given contemporary views of native rights, as reflected in the stated policies of both Canada and the US, today's treaties may avoid some of the pitfalls that bedevilled those of the nineteenth century. There are reasons for both optimism and pessimism about a land settlement affecting the Eastern Arctic Eskimo. The Alaskan land settlement of 1971 included large amounts of land and money that could be used by villagers for their own purposes, and the Canadian Government has shown itself willing to subsidize native organizations to help them prepare their claims. On the other hand, there has been a strong tendency for negotiators to think that large sums of money can buy well-being and represent justice. The deal in Alaska is memorable for the sums involved, not for any new provision for Alaskan natives to determine their own affairs.

21. See Castile (1974), p. 20.

More alarmingly, the James Bay settlement of early 1975 involves money rather than land, and makes little mention of Cree communities' right to their own bureaucracy, police force, schools, and – in each of these – the right to hire and fire personnel.

If a settlement between Eskimos and the Canadian Government does make a 'sustained enclave' a real possibility, then social and personal adjustment to rapid change may also be a possibility. No doubt some Eskimos, whatever the local conditions may be, will choose to be full-time workers, and some will probably play a part in the extractive industries. But a settlement may be able to provide what government policy has so far failed to achieve: a real, viable alternative to wage-labour, especially for those men and women who much prefer to live in close contact with their land. If the settlement concentrates on money, and Eskimos are paid – no matter how vast a sum – to give up their land, then they will be in appalling difficulties.

No Eskimo in the Canadian Eastern Arctic wants to return to the old days, neither to the subsistence hunting of his ancestors nor to the life of hunting and trapping at the mercy of traders, missionaries and policemen. But the Eskimos do want a mixed economy in which it will still be possible to be an Eskimo, an *Inummarik*. The Whites working in the settlements, although themselves the agents of colonialism, are aware of the difficulties in which many Eskimos now find themselves. But the interface between Whites and Eskimos is one of those difficulties, aggravating the others. As the industrial frontier pushes deeper and deeper into the Eskimos' world, so the difficulties are compounded: the possibility of a mixed economy decreases, while the knowledge, skills, and ways of life most eastern Eskimos prefer, are directly threatened.

Whatever form a land settlement takes, and whatever happens to the Canadian national conscience, individuals who call themselves Eskimos will not disappear. And Eskimo society – whatever mixture of fur trade, subsistence and wage economy on which it comes to rest – may not disappear. But the future of Eskimos, Eskimo society, and Canada's role in the north will be determined by agreements and relationships between a powerful government and a tiny minority of the nation's population.

It could happen that *Inuit Nunangat*, the people's land, will continue to be a place for *Inummariit*, the real people. If it does not, and a land settlement fails to secure the wishes and protect the interests of a majority of Eskimos, colonialism will once again have separated people from land they have always thought was theirs.

Bibliography

This bibliography is neither comprehensive nor a reader's guide to Arctic literature. It is merely a list of books and articles to which the text refers, on which data are based (e.g. maps and tables), from which quotations have been selected, or which, though not explicitly mentioned in the text, directly contributed to the process of writing this book.

ADAMSON, J. D., et al. (1949), 'Poliomyelitis in the Arctic', *Canadian Medical Association Journal*, Vol. 61, No. 4, pp. 339–48.

ARBESS, S. E. (1966), *Social Change and the Eskimo Co-operative at George River, Quebec*, Ottawa, Department of Northern Affairs and National Resources (NCRC 66–1).

ARMSTRONG, TERENCE E. (1965), *Russian Settlement in the North*, Cambridge University Press.

BALIKCI, ASEN (1961), 'Suicidal behaviour among the Netsilik Eskimos', *North*, Vol. 8, No. 4, pp. 12–19.

—— (1970), *The Netsilik Eskimo*, Garden City, New York, Natural History Press for the American Museum of Natural History.

BARAN, PAUL A. (1970), 'On the political economy of backwardness', in Rhodes, R.I. (ed.), *Imperialism and Underdevelopment*, New York, Monthly Review Press.

Beaver (A Journal of Progress), Winnipeg, Hudson's Bay Company, 1920–   (in progress).

BERG, GÖSTA (ed.) (1973), *Circumpolar Problems: Habitat, Economy, and Social Relations in the Arctic*, a symposium for Anthropological Research in the North, September 1969. Pergamon Press. (Wenner-Gren Center. International Symposium Series, Vol. 21.)

BINNEY, GEORGE, et al. (1931), *The Eskimo Book of Knowledge*, London, Hudson's Bay Company.

BIRKET-SMITH, KAJ (1930), see: Rasmussen, 1929–32.
—— (1959), *The Eskimos*, Methuen. [Revised edition; first published in English in 1936.]
BORN, DAVID OMAR (1970), *Eskimo Education and the Trauma of Social Change*, Ottawa, Department of Indian Affairs and Northern Development (Social Science Notes, 1).
BRIGGS, JEAN (1968), *Utkuhikhalingmiut Eskimo Emotional Expressions*, Ottawa Department of Indian Affairs and Northern Development.
—— (1970), *Never in Anger: Portrait of an Eskimo Family*, Cambridge, Mass., Harvard University Press.
BRODY, HUGH (1971), *Indians on Skid Row*, Ottawa, Department of Indian Affairs and Northern Development (NSRG 70–2).
—— (1973), 'Eskimo politics: The threat from the South', *New Left Review*, Vol. 79, pp. 60–70.
—— (1974), 'But what is anthropology for?', *Polar Record*, Vol. 17, No. 107, pp. 177–80.
BULIARD, ROGER (1953), *Inuk*, London, Macmillan.
CASTILE, GEORGE P. (1974), 'Federal Indian policy and the sustained enclave: An anthropological perspective', *Human Organization*, Vol. 33, No. 3.
COCCOLA, RAYMOND DE, and PAUL KING (1955), *Ayorama*, Toronto, Oxford University Press.
COPELAND, DONALDA M., and EUGENIE LOUISE MYLES (1960), *Nurse among the Eskimos*, Toronto, Ryesson Press.
CRANTZ, DAVID (1820), *The History of Greenland: Including an Account of the Mission Carried on by the United Brethren in that Country*, London, Longman, Hurst, Rees, Orme & Brown. 2 vols.
DEPARTMENT OF INDIAN AFFAIRS AND NORTHERN DEVELOPMENT (1970), *Mines and Minerals North of 60*, Ottawa, Northern Economic and Development Branch.
DESGOFFE, C. (1955), 'Contact culturel: Le Cas des esquimaux des Iles Belcher', *Anthropologica*, No. 1, pp. 45–61.
DUNNING, R. W. (1959), 'Ethnic relations and the marginal man in Canada', *Human Organization*, Vol. 18, No. 3, p. 117.
ELLIS, HENRY (1946), 'Eskimo of 1746', *Beaver*, Outfit 277, June, pp. 30–33. (Reprinted from Ellis's *Voyage to Hudson Bay*, London, 1748.)
Eskimo: Country, Customs, Catholic Missionaries, Churchill, Manitoba, published by the Oblate Fathers of the Hudson Bay Vicariate, 1945–   (in progress).

FEDERAL FIELD COMMITTEE FOR DEVELOPMENT PLANNING IN ALASKA (1968), *Alaska Natives and the Land*, Achorage, Federal Field Committee for Development Planning in Alaska.

FINNIE, RICHARD (1936), 'Lost in the Arctic', *Beaver*, Outfit 267, No. 1, pp. 28–32, 66.

—— (1942), *Canada Moves North*, New York, Macmillan.

FLEMING, A. L. (1931), *The Hunter – Home, or Joseph Pudlo, a life obedient to a commanding purpose*, Toronto, Missionary Society of the Church of England in Canada.

FREEMAN, M. M. R. (1971), 'Tolerance and rejection of patron sales in an Eskimo settlement', in Paine, R. (ed.), *Patrons and Brokers in the East Arctic*, St John's, Memorial University, pp. 34–54.

FRENCH, STEWART (1972), *Alaska Native Claims Settlement Act*, Montreal, Arctic Institute of North America.

FRIED, JACOB (1963), 'White dominant settlements in the Canadian Northwest Territories', *Anthropologica*, N.S. Vol. 5, No. 1, pp. 57–67.

GAGNÉ, R. C. (1961), *Tentative Standard Orthography for Canadian Eskimos*, Ottawa, Department of Northern Affairs and National Resources. [2nd revised ed., 1962.]

GOULD, S. (1917), *Inasmuch: Sketches of the Beginnings of the Church of England in Canada in relation to the Indian and Eskimo Races*, Toronto, Missionary Society of the Church of England in Canada.

HAGEN, EVERETT E. (1962), *On the Theory of Social Change*, Homewood, Dorsey Press.

HALPERN, J. M. (1967), *The Changing Village Economy*, New York, Prentice-Hall.

HAWTHORN, H. B., A. LAFORET and S. M. JAMIESON (1973), 'Northern people', in *Science and the North: A seminar on guidelines for scientific activities in northern Canada, 1972*, Ottawa, Information Canada.

HEPBURN, D. W. (1963), 'Northern education: Façade for failure', *Variables* (University of Alberta, Edmonton), Vol. 2, No. 1.

HODGSON, STEWART M. (1970), Introduction to *Explore Canada's Arctic*, Yellowknife, NWT, Government of the North West Territories.

HONIGMANN, JOHN J. and IRMA HONIGMANN (1965), *Eskimo Townsmen*, Ottawa, Canadian Research Center for Anthropology.

—— (1970), *Arctic Townsmen, Ethnic Backgrounds and Modernisation*, Ottawa, Canadian Research Center for Anthropology.

HORNAL, R. W. and D. B. CRAIG (1970), *Mineral Exploration North of 60: Trends and Achievements*, Ottawa, Oil and Mineral Division, Department of Indian Affairs and Northern Development.

HUGHES, C. C. (1960), *An Eskimo Village in the Modern World*, Ithaca, Cornell University Press.

IGLAUER, EDITH (1966), *The New People: The Eskimo's Journey into our Time*, Garden City, N Y, Doubleday.

ILLICH, IVAN (1971), *Deschooling Society*, Calder & Boyars.

JENNESS, DIAMOND (1928), *The People of the Twilight*, New York, Macmillan.

—— (1957), *Dawn in Arctic Alaska*, Minneapolis, University of Minnesota.

—— (1962–7), *Eskimo Administration*, Montreal, Arctic Institute of North America, 4 vols.

KLEIVAN, HELGE (1966), *The Eskimos of Northeast Labrador: A History of Eskimo–White Relations 1771–1955*, Norsk Polarinstitutt Skrifter, No. 139.

—— (1969–70), 'Culture and ethnic identity, *Folk*, Vol. 11–12, pp. 209–34.

KLUCKHOHN, CLYDE (1943), 'Covert culture and administrative problems', *American Anthropologist*, N.S. Vol. 45, p. 255.

KOSTER, D. (1972), *Ambiguity and Gossip in a Colonial Situation*, St John's, Memorial University (M A thesis).

KUPFERER, HARRIET (1963), 'Cherokee change: A departure from linear models', *Anthropologica*, N.S. Vol. 5, No. 2, pp. 187–98.

LANTIS, MARGARET (ed.) (1960), *Eskimo Childhood and Interpersonal Relationship; Nunamiut Biographies and Genealogies*, Seattle, University of Washington Press.

LEDYARD, GLEASON H. (1958), *And to the Eskimos*, Chicago, Moody Bible Institute.

LEIGHTON, A. H. and C. C. HUGHES (1955), 'Notes on Eskimo patterns of suicide', *Southwest Journal of Anthropology*, Vol. 11, pp. 327–38.

LOTZ, JIM (1970), *Northern Realities: The future of Northern Development in Canada*, Toronto, New Press.

LUBART, J. M. (1970), *Psychodynamic Problems of Adaptation: Mackenzie Delta Eskimos*, Ottawa, Department of Indian Affairs and Northern Development (M D R P 7).

LYON, G. F. (1824), *The Private Journal*, London, J. Murray.

MCCONNELL, JOHN (1965), *An Historical Geography of the Fort Smith Region*, Toronto, University of Toronto (M A thesis).

MCIVER, DONALD K. (1972), 'The hydrocarbon potential of the Canadian Arctic', a presentation to the second annual meeting of

238 Bibliography

the Division of Production of the American Petroleum Institute in Houston, Texas.

MANNONI, O. (1956), *Prospero and Caliban: The psychology of colonization*, Methuen.

MARRYAT, FLORENCE (1892), 'What is the School Board doing?', *Winter's Magazine*, London, p. 214.

MOORE, PERCY E. (1954), 'Health for Indians and Eskimos', *Canadian Geographical Journal*, Vol. 48, pp. 216–21.

—— (1964), 'An epidemic of tuberculosis at Eskimo Point, NWT', *The Canadian Medical Association Journal*, Vol. 90, No. 21.

MOWAT, FARLEY (1951), *The People of the Deer*, Boston, Little, Brown.

—— (1959), *The Desperate People*, Boston, Little, Brown.

NANSEN, FRIDTJOF (1893), *Eskimo Life*, Longmans, Green.

NORTH, F. K. (1973), article in *Science in the North*, Ottawa.

NORTHERN QUEBEC INUIT ASSOCIATION (1974), *The Northerners*, La Macaza, Quebec, Manitou Community College.

OSWALT, W. H., and J. W. VANSTONE (1960), 'The future of the Caribou Eskimo', *Anthropologica*, N.S. Vol. 23, pp. 154–76.

PAINE, ROBERT (ed.) (1971), *Patrons and Brokers in the East Arctic*, St John's, Memorial University, Institute of Social and Economic Research (Newfoundland Social and Economic Papers, No. 2).

PARSONS, G. F. (1970), *Arctic Suburbs: A look at the North's Newcomers*, Ottawa, Department of Indian Affairs and Northern Development (MDRP 8).

PEARSE, ANDREW (1971), 'Metropolis and peasant: the expansion of the urban–industrial complex and the changing rural structure', in *Peasants and Peasant Society*, Teodor Shanin (ed.), Penguin.

PEART, A. F. W., and F. P. NAGLER (1952), *Measles in the Canadian Arctic, 1952*, pamphlet distributed by the Canadian Department of National Health and Welfare.

PITSEOLAK (1972), *Pictures out of my Life*, Toronto, Design Collaborative Books and Oxford University Press.

PONCINS, GONTRAN DE (1941), *Kabloona*, New York, Reynal & Hitchcock.

PRICE, RAY (1970), *The Howling Arctic*, Toronto, Peter Martin.

PRYDE, DUNCAN (1971), *Nunaga: My Land, My People*, MacGibbon & Kee.

RASMUSSEN, KNUD (1927), *Across Arctic America*, New York, Putnam.

RASMUSSEN, KNUD, and KAJ BIRKET-SMITH (1929–32), *Report*

of the Fifth Thule Expedition (Volumes 4, 6, 7, 8, 9), Nordisk Forlag, Copenhagen.

REDFIELD, ROBERT (1965), *The Little Community*, Chicago, University of Chicago Press.

RICH, E. E. (1960), 'Trade habits and economic motivation among the Indian of North America', *Canadian Journal of Economics and Political Science*, Vol. 26, No. 1, pp. 35–53.

ROGERS, GEORGE W. (1962), *The Future of Alaska. Economic Consequences of Statehood*, Baltimore, John Hopkins Press.

ROWLEY, GRAHAM (1972), 'The Contemporary Canadian Eskimo', *Polar Record*, Vol. 16, No. 101, pp. 201–5.

SAHLINS, MARSHALL (1974), *Primitive Economics*, Tavistock.

SANDERS, DOUGLAS ESMOND (1973), *Native People in Areas of Internal National Expansion: Indians and Inuit in Canada*, Copenhagen.

SIMPSON, R. N. (1953), 'Epidemics in the Eastern Arctic during 1953', *Arctic Circular*, Vol. 6, No. 5, pp. 53–5.

SMITH, BERNARD (1960), *European Vision and the South Pacific 1768–1850*, Oxford University Press.

SMITH, D. G. (1971), 'Natives and outsiders: Pluralism in the Mackenzie River Delta, Northwest Territories, Canada', unpublished PhD. thesis, Harvard University.

SPECK, FRANK G. (1935), *Naskapi, the Savage Hunters of the Labrador Peninsula*, Norman, University of Oklahoma Press.

STEENHOVEN, G. VAN DEN (1962), *Leadership and Law among the Eskimos of the Keewatin District, Northwest Territories*. Rijswijk, Uitgeverj Excelsior (PhD. thesis).

STEFANSSON, VILHJALMUR (1913), *My Life with the Eskimo*, New York, Macmillan.

STEVENSON, A. (1973), 'The changing Canadian Eskimo', in *The Eskimo People Today and Tomorrow*, 4th International Congress for Nordic Studies, ed. Jean Malaurie, Paris, The Hague, Mouton.

THOMAS, D. K., and C. T. THOMPSON (1972), *Eskimo Housing as Planned Culture Change*, Social Science Notes 4, Department of Indian Affairs and Northern Development, Ottawa.

TREMAYNE, TERRY (1974), 'Nanisivik, Canada's first Arctic mine', *North*, July–August.

TWOMEY, ARTHUR C. (in collaboration with Nigel Herrick) (1942), *Needle to the North: The Story of an expedition to Ungava and the Belcher Islands*, London, Jenkins.

USHER, PETER (1970–71), *The Bankslanders: Economy and Ecology of a Frontier Trapping Community*, Ottawa, Department of Indian Affairs and Northern Development, 3 vols. (NSRG 71-1, 71-2, 71-3).

—— (1971a), *Fur Trade Posts of the Northwest Territories 1870–1970*, Ottawa, Department of Indian Affairs and Northern Development (NSRG 71-4).

VALLEE, FRANK (1967), *Kabloona and Eskimo in the Central Keewatin*, Ottawa, Canadian Research Centre for Anthropology.

WEYER, E. M. (1932), *The Eskimos: Their Environment and Folkways*, New Haven, Yale University Press (reprinted 1962, Hampden, Conn., Archon Books).

WILLIAMSON, ROBERT G. (1974), *Eskimos Underground: Sociocultural Change in the Canadian Central Arctic*, Uppsala, Institution for Allmän och Jamfurande Etnografi Vid Uppsala Universitet (Occasional Papers, 11), (PhD. thesis – Uppsala University).

YOUNG, ARMINIUS (1931), *One Hundred Years of Mission Work in the Wilds of Labrador*, London, Stockwell.

ZASLOW, MORRIS (1971), *The Opening of the Canadian North, 1870–1914*, Toronto, McClelland & Stewart (Canadian Centenary Series, No. 17).

Maps

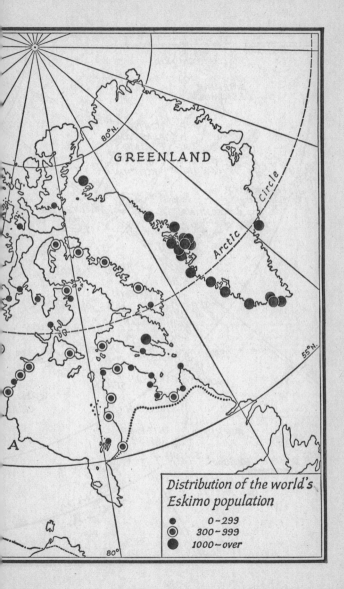

GREENLAND

80°N.

Arctic Circle

55°N.

A

80°

Distribution of the world's
Eskimo population

●   0 – 299
◉   300 – 999
⬤   1000 – over

The principal original inhabitants of northern North America and adjacent Arctic lands

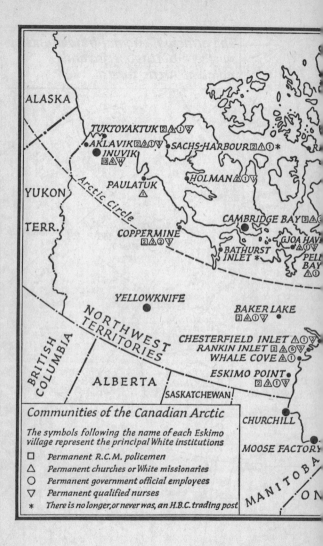

Communities of the Canadian Arctic

*The symbols following the name of each Eskimo
village represent the principal White institutions*

□   *Permanent R.C.M. policemen*
△   *Permanent churches or White missionaries*
○   *Permanent government official employees*
▽   *Permanent qualified nurses*
*   *There is no longer, or never was, an H.B.C. trading post*

GREENLAND

SE FIORD ②△◐▽*

TE BAY ②△③▽

CTIC BAY △②▽
POND INLET ③△③▽
CLYDE RIVER ①△①▽

Arctic Circle

BROUGHTON ISLAND △△▽

IGLOOLIK ②△◐▽
HALL BEACH △◐▽

PANGNIRTUNG ②△⑦▽

PULSE BAY △①▽

CAPE DORSET
③④▽
CORAL HARBOUR
△①▽

FROBISHER BAY ④△▽

LAKE HARBOUR ②△◐▽

SUGLUK △③▽   PORT BURWELL △②

IVUJIVIK ②▽*   WAKEHAM BAY △③▽
KORATUK ①▽*

OVUNGNITUK
△③▽

PAYNE BAY
②▽
LEAF BAY
①*

GEORGE RIVER △②▽

FORT CHIMO ②△⑦▽

PORT HARRISON △③▽

SANIKILUAQ △①▽

NEWFOUNDLAND

GREAT WHALE RIVER ④△④▽

RIO   James
Bay   QUEBEC

77
35
INUVIK
318
210
417
966
CAMBRIDGE E
1601
371
679
YELLOWKNIFE
392
CANADA
160
234
265
CHURCHILL
MOOS
FACTO

Distance (air miles) of Canadian Eskimo
villages in the Northwest Territories from
hospitals to which patients are usually referred

- An Eskimo village
- A village or town with hospital facilities

Arctic Circle

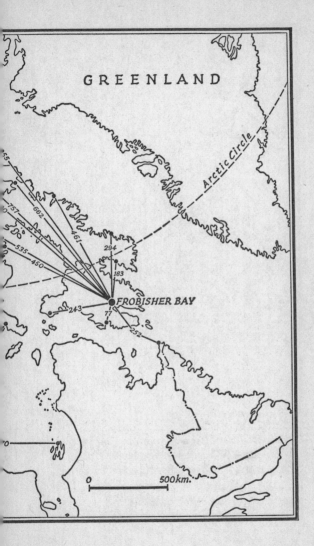

GREENLAND

Arctic Circle

655
757
662
461
535 450
294
183
243 77
FROBISHER BAY
252

0   500km.

More about Penguins and Pelicans

Penguinews, which appears every month, contains details of all the new books issued by Penguins as they are published. From time to time it is supplemented by *Penguins in Print*, which is a complete list of all titles available. (There are some five thousand of these.)

A specimen copy of *Penguinews* will be sent to you free on request. For a year's issues (including the complete lists) please send 50p if you live in the British Isles, or 75p if you live elsewhere. Just write to Dept EP, Penguin Books Ltd, Harmondsworth, Middlesex, enclosing a cheque or postal order, and your name will be added to the mailing list.

In the U.S.A.: For a complete list of books available from Penguin in the United States write to Dept CS, Penguin Books Inc., 7110 Ambassador Road, Baltimore, Maryland 21207.

In Canada: For a complete list of books available from Penguin in Canada write to Penguin Books Canada Ltd, 41 Steelcase Road West, Markham, Ontario.